P9-CEV-738

A Beauty Refined

Books by Tracie Peterson

www.traciepeterson.com

SAPPHIRE BRIDES
A Treasure Concealed
A Beauty Refined

BRIDES OF SEATTLE
Steadfast Heart
Refining Fire • Love Everlasting

LONE STAR BRIDES
A Sensible Arrangement
A Moment in Time • A Matter of Heart
Lone Star Brides (3 in 1)

LAND OF SHINING WATER
The Icecutter's Daughter
The Quarryman's Bride
The Miner's Lady

LAND OF THE LONE STAR
Chasing the Sun
Touching the Sky • Taming the Wind

BRIDAL VEIL ISLAND*
To Have and To Hold
To Love and Cherish
To Honor and Trust

STRIKING A MATCH
Embers of Love
Hearts Aglow • Hope Rekindled

SONG OF ALASKA
Dawn's Prelude
Morning's Refrain • Twilight's Serenade

ALASKAN QUEST
Summer of the Midnight Sun
Under the Northern Lights
Whispers of Winter
Alaskan Quest (3 in 1)

BRIDES OF GALLATIN COUNTY
A Promise to Believe In
A Love to Last Forever
A Dream to Call My Own

THE BROADMOOR LEGACY*
A Daughter's Inheritance
An Unexpected Love
A Surrendered Heart

BELLS OF LOWELL*
Daughter of the Loom
A Fragile Design
These Tangled Threads

LIGHTS OF LOWELL*
A Tapestry of Hope
A Love Woven True
The Pattern of Her Heart

DESERT ROSES
Shadows of the Canyon
Across the Years
Beneath a Harvest Sky

HEIRS OF MONTANA
Land of My Heart • The Coming Storm
To Dream Anew • The Hope Within

LADIES OF LIBERTY
A Lady of High Regard
A Lady of Hidden Intent
A Lady of Secret Devotion

RIBBONS OF STEEL**
Distant Dreams • A Hope Beyond
A Promise for Tomorrow

RIBBONS WEST**
Westward the Dream
Separate Roads • Ties That Bind

WESTWARD CHRONICLES
A Shelter of Hope
Hidden in a Whisper
A Veiled Reflection

YUKON QUEST
Treasures of the North
Ashes and Ice • Rivers of Gold

༺ঞৎৡৡৎঞ༻

*All Things Hidden****
*Beyond the Silence****
House of Secrets
A Slender Thread
What She Left for Me
Where My Heart Belongs

*with Judith Miller **with Judith Pella ***with Kimberley Woodhouse

SAPPHIRE  2 BRIDES

A Beauty Refined

TRACIE PETERSON

BETHANYHOUSE

a division of Baker Publishing Group
Minneapolis, Minnesota

© 2016 by Peterson Ink, Inc.

Published by Bethany House Publishers
11400 Hampshire Avenue South
Bloomington, Minnesota 55438
www.bethanyhouse.com

Bethany House Publishers is a division of
Baker Publishing Group, Grand Rapids, Michigan

Printed in the United States of America

All rights reserved. No part of this publication may be reproduced, stored in a retrieval system, or transmitted in any form or by any means—for example, electronic, photocopy, recording—without the prior written permission of the publisher. The only exception is brief quotations in printed reviews.

Library of Congress Cataloging-in-Publication Data
Names: Peterson, Tracie.
Title: A beauty refined / Tracie Peterson.
Description: Minneapolis, Minnesota : Bethany House, a division of Baker
    Publishing Group, [2016] | Series: Sapphire brides ; 2
Identifiers: LCCN 2016001805| ISBN 9780764213366 (cloth : alk. paper) | ISBN
    9780764213250 (pbk.) | ISBN 9780764213373 (large-print pbk.)
Subjects: | GSAFD: Love stories. | Christian fiction.
Classification: LCC PS3566.E7717 B43 2016 | DDC 813/.54—dc23
LC record available at http://lccn.loc.gov/2016001805

Scripture quotations are from the King James Version of the Bible.

This is a work of historical reconstruction; the appearances of certain historical figures are therefore inevitable. All other characters, however, are products of the author's imagination, and any resemblance to actual persons, living or dead, is coincidental.

Cover design by LOOK Design Studio
Cover photography by Aimee Christensen

16 17 18 19 20 21 22   7 6 5 4 3 2 1

Dedicated to Helen Motter with thanks for being such an incredible editor. You have made the stories so much better with your input and eagle eye. May God richly bless you in all that you do for Him.

1

I'm quite certain you will find these rooms to be to your
liking, Count Von Bergen," a young bellman declared as
he ushered the Von Bergen party into a suite of rooms. "The
Broadwater Hotel has only recently been reopened, and we've
worked hard to make it an appealing and welcoming retreat."

Phoebe Von Bergen glanced around the large sitting area. The
wood floors had been polished to perfection. Colorful carpets,
mostly Turkish or Wilton velvet, were placed in strategic order
to offer beauty and comfort while complementing the dark
wood beneath them. Gold and blue silk velvet draperies framed
wood-trimmed windows of beveled glass, and cascaded to brush
the floor. The room was decorated with expensive pieces of
cherry, mahogany, and walnut furniture, as well as statuettes
and other bric-a-brac to enrich the surroundings. The fireplace
mantel held several books, which Phoebe promised herself she'd
investigate at a later time.

"This door opens to your bedchamber," the young man announced as he opened one of the doors in the room. "I believe

you'll find everything in order. Your luggage has already been delivered. There is a complete bathroom with facilities designed to give you whatever comfort you desire. There is hot and cold running water." He paused and pointed to the far side of the room. "Behind that door is another room for your valet. Your daughter's room will be across the hall and her maid's room will adjoin. These are the keys." He placed two keys atop a nearby table. "We can bring wood for the fireplace, but each room has a radiator for heat as well. The nights are quite chilly, even cold to some."

Phoebe watched her father take in the surroundings. "It isn't nearly as opulent as I was led to believe," the stocky older man declared in his usual detached manner. The younger man opened his mouth to reply, but Count Frederick Von Bergen, or Graf Von Bergen, as he was titled in his homeland of Germany, wasn't one to be interrupted. "I suppose it will have to suffice. We will have our meals served here, *ja?*"

"If you like," the young man said, glancing at Phoebe and then to their two servants. "We have three beautiful dining rooms, however, and our chef is French. It is said that our meals are as good as any served in the finest hotels and restaurants in America . . . and Europe."

"I suppose," Phoebe's father said, dabbing a handkerchief to his mouth, "that shall remain to be seen. However, I believe *frühstück*—breakfast—should be enjoyed at leisure in the privacy of one's own rooms. I would like to see it delivered at precisely eight o'clock each morning."

"For you alone, sir?"

Phoebe felt sorry for the younger man, who seemed completely intimidated by Graf Von Bergen. Despite her father's short stature and stocky frame, he had a look about him that put people on edge. Phoebe put herself between the two men as she came to her father's side. "I should enjoy trying the dining rooms, if you don't mind, *Vater*."

Her father glanced at her momentarily and nodded. "Very well. Bring food for me alone. You will, of course, inform my manservant where he and my daughter's maid might dine."

"Yes, sir." The young man looked hesitant. "Ah . . . I . . . that is, you should also know that the natatorium is open for your enjoyment. The pool is one hundred by three hundred feet and fed by nearby hot springs. There are swimming outfits available in all sizes in the men's and women's dressing rooms. Also we have a billiards club complete with a private bar for . . ." He glanced at Phoebe and gave her a hesitant smile before adding, "gentlemen only. There are also a variety of diversions on the grounds that might appeal to the ladies. The gardens are beautiful."

Von Bergen gave a grunt. "Thank you."

Phoebe could tell by her father's dismissive tone that he'd heard more than enough. As if to prove this, he signaled his man, Hubert, who led the hotel bellman away. As her father's valet and bodyguard, Hubert was used to handling unwanted people. Phoebe saw Hubert tip the man, then all but shove him from the room.

"Gerda, please see to our rooms." Phoebe took up the key and handed it to her maid. "Also prepare a bath, and I should like the burgundy silk for dinner."

"Ja, I'll do it right now." The dark-haired maid curtsied and took the key.

Phoebe waited until she had gone and Hubert had taken himself off to arrange her father's bedchamber before she spoke. "I am quite spent after the train trip here. I do hope you won't expect me to keep late hours tonight." She used their native German, hoping it would soothe her father's tense nature.

"Not at all," her father said, pulling out his watch. "I have meetings tomorrow with the sapphire mining representatives and do not intend to make it a late evening for myself. It's nearly four. You should have time for a rest before dinner."

Phoebe nodded. "That was my hope. Just come for me when you desire to go down to dinner. I promise to be ready."

Her father sank into a wing chair. "Very well."

Again that dismissive tone signaled Phoebe to leave without pressing any other issue. Her father's limited patience could be particularly tried when people failed to realize his mood. After twenty-two years of life, Phoebe could read him quite well.

Making her way to the room across the hall, Phoebe suppressed a yawn with one gloved hand while opening the door with the other. This room was not nearly as large as her father's, and the sitting area was combined with the bedroom.

Gerda bustled about the room, rambling on in German. "The bathing room is just over there." She pointed. "My room is at the far end." Again she pointed. "I have the water running for the bath and have just put in some lavender salts. Your bath soaps are laid out, as well as a fresh nightgown."

Phoebe pulled off her gloves and placed them on a lovely oval table of walnut. Next she removed her hatpins and then the hat. She placed these beside the gloves and stretched her arms overhead in a most unladylike fashion. Gerda didn't say a word as she hurried to assist Phoebe with her clothes.

Phoebe switched back to English. "I hope I don't fall asleep in the tub."

Gerda smiled and spoke English for the most part. "It has been a long day, ja?" She put aside Phoebe's traveling jacket and then began to unbutton the high-necked lacy blouse.

"Well, Vater assures me it won't be a late evening for us. In fact, while I'm down to dinner, feel free to enjoy the bathing facilities here. I know there was mention of a shared bathroom for servants, but I cannot see you having to go out among strangers."

"*Danke, gnädige Fräulein.*"

Phoebe smiled at her maid's words. *Gnädige Fräulein,* or *gracious miss,* was the common way servants addressed her, but it seemed much too formal for America.

"Use English, Gerda, and just call me miss or Miss Phoebe."

"Ja—yes, miss." Gerda bobbed her head and began to remove Phoebe's blouse. "I will arrange for your traveling clothes to be cleaned."

"It's hard to believe we've been away from home for over a month now." Her home along the Rhine in Baden seemed a million miles away, but Phoebe had enjoyed the travel. She had seen a good portion of Europe with her father and mother, but that was years ago. Never until now had Phoebe been to America, and she found it all very fascinating. It was truly nothing like her homeland.

"Ja, I think we will not see it again for months to come." Gerda helped Phoebe from her skirt. "But America is beautiful, ja?"

"Ja, *es ist schön,*" Phoebe said, slipping into her native tongue again, despite having admonished Gerda to refrain. Phoebe had been trained to speak English, German, and French, but since her mother's death ten years earlier, English was seldom spoken at home.

Gerda finished helping Phoebe from her corset. "I can manage the rest." Phoebe yawned. Her eyelids suddenly felt like lead weights. "Danke, Gerda."

The woman, who was not quite twice Phoebe's age, gave a bobbed cursty. "I'll shut off the water and then turn down the bed." She hurried ahead of Phoebe and took care of the water. Next she arranged a thick towel and washcloth in close proximity. "If you need anything, I will be in the next room."

"I'll be fine, Gerda. Thank you."

Phoebe closed the bathroom door and sighed. She felt an overwhelming sense of emptiness. There was really no good reason for it, but thoughts of her mother always seemed to make her sad.

Sinking into the deep porcelain tub, Phoebe closed her eyes and eased back, letting the water soothe her tired muscles. They were in America on behalf of the Sapphire Duchess, an eccentric old Prussian noblewoman who demanded all of her jewelry be designed with sapphires. Phoebe's father had fallen into the job of assisting the old woman with her purchase of gemstones via a family friend who had introduced them a score of years earlier. For as long as Phoebe could remember, her father had traveled to various parts of the world for the duchess, and now his travels had brought him to America. Of course, this was only a portion of their travel, and Phoebe presumed it to be personal. The duchess demanded her stones be purchased in Ceylon, where she believed only the best-quality gems could be had. They were only in America because her father had heard all about Montana's Yogo sapphires from his gemstone connection in London. Phoebe wasn't sure what he hoped to gain by coming here. Her father never allowed her to question him about his business affairs, and as a result she had learned to keep quiet regarding such dealings. Besides, Father's interest in America had afforded her an opportunity to accompany him and see new lands.

The hot water intensified her exhaustion, so Phoebe reluctantly opened her eyes. To her right were two arched stained-glass windows. Their design in colors of lavender, gold, blue, and rose reflected muted light against the white-and-gray marble fixtures. Phoebe thought it all quite perfect. She took up a bar of rose-scented soap and smiled. So far she had really enjoyed America. They had docked in New York City and experienced all sorts of wonderful entertainments and delightful meals. The hotel there had been beautiful, easily meeting her father's standards. He had grumbled throughout their journey by ship that America was a very savage and unrefined country. New York had given him a pleasant surprise.

Since then they had traveled by private rail car, and as the stops had become fewer and less opulent, her father's foul mood had become more and more prominent. The Broadwater Hotel and Natatorium had been advertised and praised as a European resort in the wilderness. One advertisement stated it was "the true Carlsbad of America." Phoebe had gone to the Karlsbad resort in Bohemia with her parents and remembered it as quite beautiful. Several people had recommended this respite in Montana, and while lovely, it seemed completely different from the spa in Karlsbad. Apparently her father thought so too, despite its being highly recommended to him by the mining representatives he was to meet. He was also quite disappointed with the small town nearby. Since Helena was the capital city of the state, her father had been certain the town would be large and offer the best choices. Perhaps in Montana this was one of the largest towns, but that wasn't saying a whole lot.

Phoebe thought the hotel decor was finer than any she'd seen since leaving New York City. However, it didn't seem to hold the grandeur that her father had come to require in life. Their own palatial home in Germany was proof of her father's demands. The entire house was designed with the finest of woods, crystal chandeliers, marble, and gilded trimmings. They dined on the finest china, walked on the richest of rugs, and enjoyed enough fine art pieces to fill a museum. To Phoebe it didn't matter, but perhaps that was only because she'd never known anything but the finer things of life. Nevertheless, the American West fascinated her. She had seen vast open lands of crops and herds of cattle. She had seen her first cowboys on the train out of Chicago. These ruffian men with their broad-brimmed hats were quite a lively bunch. They spoke in boisterous voices about branding and roping and something called *rodeos*. She didn't dare voice her fascination about it. Her father believed, as did many in her class, that those of noble birth were to never offer any overt display of emotions.

With her bath finally complete, Phoebe managed to dry off before donning her nightgown. Her last chore was to pull out all of the pins that held her blond tresses in neat order. When this was done, she didn't even bother to brush her hair, but instead hurried to climb into bed. The soft mattress seemed to wrap itself around her, and Phoebe closed her eyes with a sigh.

She awoke some time later when Gerda called her name. "Miss Phoebe, I'm so sorry. It's nearly six. Your vater said to tell you that he'll escort you to dinner at exactly six thirty."

"You should have awakened me earlier," Phoebe said, springing from the bed. "Goodness, but now we shall be in a rush."

"I am sorry. I'm afraid I stretched out to rest for just a moment and fell asleep."

"It's all right, Gerda. I'm sure you were as tired as I. We shall simply have to do our best to make me presentable." Her father would never have tolerated such behavior from a servant, but Phoebe treated her maid with greater patience.

Phoebe allowed Gerda to hurry her into her undergarments, stockings, and shoes. After Gerda cinched Phoebe into her corset, the maid went to retrieve the gown.

"I pressed out the wrinkles," she said, opening the skirt of the gown to slip it over Phoebe's head. The silk splayed out around her. Gerda adjusted the rounded bodice, then saw to the narrow cap of black lace that constituted sleeves. As soon as Gerda finished up the buttons, she directed Phoebe to sit.

"Don't make my hair too elaborate, Gerda. We simply haven't time." Phoebe rubbed her bare arms. Perhaps this gown had been a poor choice. "It's cold in here. Didn't that bellman say that each of the rooms had a radiator?"

"Ja. I'll see to it that it's running and warm by the time you return. I put out long gloves and a shawl for you. I heard one of the workers say it gets quite cold at night." Gerda brushed out Phoebe's waist-length blond hair and then fashioned the mass into a simple upswept style.

With this accomplished, Gerda hurried to bring Phoebe the gloves and shawl. The clock atop the dresser chimed the half hour just as a knock sounded on the hotel door.

"That will be Vater, likely upset because I wasn't ready and waiting in his suite." Phoebe motioned Gerda aside and opened the door. "Hello, Vater." She pulled on her elbow-length gloves.

Her father eyed her with a frown. "I've been waiting."

Phoebe wrapped the black lace shawl around her shoulders and smiled. "Well, you needn't wait any longer."

Her father grunted a reply, then offered his arm. They made their way downstairs, and only when they'd reached the dining room did Phoebe comment.

"It's quite lovely, don't you think, Vater?" Across the room were artistically arranged tables draped in damask tablecloths and set with beautiful crystal and silver.

"I suppose." Her father surveyed the room as a waiter approached.

"Good evening, sir. I will show you to your table."

The waiter seated them near one of the bay windows. Phoebe

smiled at the scene. "I'm glad it's still light enough to see the grounds. Aren't they beautifully kept?"

Vater barely murmured an acknowledgment and instead focused on the menu. "It would seem that if the menu choices are any indication, we might fare well enough this evening. They are offering eight courses, including *consommé châtelaine*."

"There, see? You love that, as well as the *mousse de faisan chasseur*." She knew the buttery demi-glace of mushrooms and shallots atop the pheasant mousse would please her father as long as it was executed properly. "And it looks as though they are offering some very fine wines to accompany the dishes."

"I'll no doubt need them to settle my stomach."

Phoebe put the menu aside. "I look at all of this as a great adventure, Vater. We can certainly allow that the food will be different from what we have at home. However, that needn't keep us from enjoying ourselves."

The waiter approached, and Phoebe allowed her father to order for them both. Meanwhile, Phoebe glanced around the room at the sparse collection of diners. Perhaps others had dined earlier. Americans seemed to be well-known for that. Nevertheless, she wouldn't fault the establishment, nor Americans as a whole. She pulled off her gloves and set them aside.

"I do hope you'll find something to enjoy about this place."

"I'll enjoy getting my business tended to," her father snapped. "As I remind myself, I will often be gone from this . . . place."

Phoebe decided to leave off with the small talk. It was apparent her father's thoughts were consumed with other issues, and nothing she said would change his mood.

When their first course of varied *hors d'oeuvres* appeared, Phoebe selected several that looked promising. She sampled the deviled kidney but found it rather bitter. Next she had a bit of the pickled lamb's tongue, but this was too tart for her taste. Last of all she took a bite of the *carciofini*. The artichoke was savory with just the right amount of garlic butter. When the consommé arrived, Phoebe realized she was famished. She sampled the soup, finding it delicious, although fearing the flavor of chestnuts to be a bit strong for her father's taste. The courses continued with Vater saying very little. Halfway through the meal, however, he let his thoughts be known.

"I credit them for palatable food." He finished off the last of his beef. "The mustard-and-red-wine sauce on this beef is quite acceptable."

Phoebe nodded. "Indeed, Vater." When the dessert finally arrived, Phoebe found herself too full to partake. She was just about to say as much when two gentlemen approached the table and introduced themselves to Phoebe's father.

"Graf Von Bergen, or should we call you Count Von Bergen?" one of the men asked.

"Either will suffice."

Phoebe knew the title was important to her father. A graf was equal to a count or earl, and that entitled her father to a nobleman's respect. And her father definitely demanded such.

Not wishing to appear rude, Phoebe tolerated the introductions. The men were apparently connected to the mining interests of her father. She didn't recognize their names, nor did she have any desire to partake of their conversation.

She pulled on her long gloves. "I can see that you gentlemen would like to talk. If you'll excuse me, I should enjoy a short walk before it grows too dark." One of the men assisted her as Phoebe rose.

Her father waved her away while the two gentlemen took chairs at the table. Phoebe made her way to the hotel lobby, noticing the enticing pattern of colorful squares and triangles on the floor. She thought it a fine contrast to the rich woodwork everywhere else in the hotel.

"How are you this evening, Miss Von Bergen?" a man asked.

Startled, Phoebe looked up and recognized the hotel manager. "I am quite well, thank you."

"It's a beautiful evening."

She nodded graciously as she'd been taught all of her life. "Indeed. I believe I will enjoy a walk before turning in for the evening."

"Oh, you should definitely do that. You might want to walk down to the natatorium—just to get a look. It's inspiring."

"Thank you. Perhaps I will."

Outside she strolled along the porch for a time, breathing in deeply of the crisp dry air. The skies held a glorious display of orange-gold and pink against a fading blue as the sun slipped behind the mountains. Phoebe found she liked this rustic location. Its isolation gave Phoebe a momentary sensation of being one of the last people on earth, a feeling she quite liked. Cities had always been much too crowded and noisy for her taste.

Finally Phoebe followed the path along the well-manicured lawns and cottonwood trees to the natatorium. She had been fascinated by the idea of an indoor public pool here in the middle of the Wild West. Especially one fed by hot springs. It conjured up all sorts of thoughts about Roman baths, a seeming anachronism for this western retreat.

The natatorium, unlike the American cottage style of the hotel, was done in elaborate Moorish architectural designs. Phoebe paused for a moment to marvel at the exterior, where a line of no fewer than nine circular stained-glass windows flanked each side of the triple-arched entryway. Beside the entry, two large towers rose, topped by tiered, onion-shaped domes. The intricate tile work and Moorish details gave the building an exotic and altogether foreign appearance in its present location.

Phoebe made her way inside and was immediately aware of the warmth and the heavier, damp air. She marveled at the interior of the building just as she had the exterior. At one end of the massive pool was a waterfall she guessed to be nearly forty feet high. Water cascaded over large granite boulders and into the pool.

"You're pretty like my mama."

Phoebe startled. To her right a young boy in wet swimming togs smiled up at her. "My name is Kenneth, but people call me Kenny." His blue eyes seemed to twinkle. "I'm learning to swim."

She smiled at the blond-haired boy. "That's an admirable goal . . . Kenny."

"What's your name?"

"Phoebe."

"You can come swim with us, Phoebe."

She shook her head. "I can't swim, but thank you for the invitation."

"Ian can teach you. He's teaching me." The boy surprised her by taking hold of her hand and pulling her in the direction of a rather handsome stranger who was using a towel to dry himself.

"This is Ian. He told me everybody ought to learn to swim."

The man he'd called Ian stopped what he was doing and looked up with a smile. The smile faded, however, as he stared at her in what Phoebe could only describe as a dumbstruck manner. Perhaps he was just as startled by her appearance as she had been by Kenny's. On the other hand, Phoebe knew she was considered quite beautiful. She'd had numerous suitors vying for her hand since she'd turned fourteen. Maybe this Ian was simply taken aback by her looks.

Phoebe tried her best to dispel the tension that seemed to mount by the second. "I am sorry for the interruption. We only just arrived this afternoon, and I thought to see what the natatorium was all about."

"It's about swimming," Kenny said in a matter-of-fact manner. He looked up at Phoebe and beamed her a smile. "I like the way you talk. You must be from someplace far away."

Phoebe's training gave way and she found herself laughing. "I must say that I like the way you talk as well, and yes, I am from far away."

"Well, now you're here and you should learn to swim. I'm almost ten and Ian says I've wasted way too much time."

She glanced again at Ian and then back to the boy. "You are quite charming, young Kenny." She looked again to the man. "I do apologize. I will take my leave now so you can return to your instructions."

The boy shook his head. "Don't go." He turned to Ian. "She doesn't know how to swim and I told her you could teach her."

The man cleared his throat. "I . . . uh . . . I should be the one to apologize." His gaze never left her face. "I . . . well, you remind me of someone."

"You can teach her to swim, can't you, Ian?"

Phoebe felt her face grow hot with embarrassment. She couldn't think of how to explain to Kenny the inappropriateness of having Ian teach her to swim, but then the handsome man spoke first.

"I'd be happy to teach her," Ian replied, fixing Phoebe with a lopsided grin. "Anytime."

2

After changing into their dry clothes, Ian rubbed Kenny's wet head with a towel. "What say we go find my mother? She should be just about ready to head home. Your mama is probably done for the day as well."

"Do you think Grandma Harper will have some cookies for us?"

Ian smiled and nodded. He and his mother, Georgia Harper, had been friends with the boy and his mother, Elizabeth, for the last few years. They had grown so close, in fact, that Georgia had insisted Kenny call her Grandma, especially since he had no other grandmother. Elizabeth thought this quite acceptable, which pleased Ian's mother to no end.

They headed around the back side of the hotel and entered through the doors to the kitchen. Ian found his mother looking over some recipes while others of the kitchen staff were still busy at their tasks. Ian knew she had been there since before dawn and must be exhausted.

"Are you ready to head home, Mother?"

The gray-haired woman smiled. "Indeed I am." She looked

at Kenny. "But I'm going to need some help. You see, I have this bundle of cookies and no one to give them to." She picked up a cloth bundle that had been tied at the top with a small piece of twine.

Kenny grinned and extended his arms. "You can give them to me, Grandma Harper."

"I'm sure he'll find them a good home," Ian added, tousling the youngster's damp hair.

The boy looked up to Ian with hope in his expression. "Swimming always makes me hungry."

The older woman smiled and handed Kenny the cloth bundle. "You can have one now, but the rest will have to wait until you get back to your cottage. They are even better with a glass of milk."

"Okay, Grandma," Kenny agreed, setting the bundle down on the table. "I made a new friend today," he went on as he untied the string and took a cookie. "She's real pretty."

With a raised brow and a teasing twinkle in her eyes, Ian's mother fixed her son with a smile. "I don't suppose *you* think she's real pretty too?" She retied the cloth covering the cookies.

"I thought her quite beautiful," Ian replied. "In fact, she looks like Elizabeth."

His mother chuckled. "You've always thought Elizabeth comely, so it seems only natural that you would look for those features in a younger woman."

Ian shook his head. "You don't understand. This woman is the spitting image of Kenny's mother."

Kenny nodded enthusiastically. "She looks just like Mama."

"Who looks like me?" came the question in a soft British accent. The trio glanced up to find that Kenny's mother had come in through the back door to join them. "I thought I'd find you here," she added. "It seems you're always hungry." She gave Kenny a hug as he crammed the last of the cookie in his mouth.

Ian looked at the boy's mother. The resemblance was uncanny. The same piercing blue eyes and blond hair. The same high cheekbones and narrow nose. Elizabeth was still a beautiful woman despite her age and hard life.

"We met this lady at the pool," Kenny said, pulling away from his mother. "She looks just like you, Mama."

Elizabeth laughed. "Perhaps the light was playing tricks on you."

Ian shook his head. "Kenny's right, Elizabeth."

She met his gaze and seemed to lose her amusement. "I'm sure we all have a twin somewhere."

"Her name is Phoebe," Kenny added. "And she doesn't know how to swim, but I told her Ian could teach her."

Elizabeth's face lost all color. "What did you say, Kenny?"

He shrugged. "She can't swim."

"No." Elizabeth's voice quivered. "You said her name."

The boy nodded. "It's Phoebe."

Ian barely caught Elizabeth as she fainted.

"What's wrong with my mama?" Kenny asked. He moved closer to Ian as he lifted Elizabeth in his arms.

"She's just real tired," Ian's mother declared, exchanging a look of concern with Ian. "And it's plenty hot in here. Ian, take her outside. The cool air will help."

He nodded. "Come on, Kenny. You get the door."

CRELLE

The next morning, Phoebe dressed in a comfortable walking-out suit. She was most grateful that the S-shape silhouette that women had favored at the turn of the century was being given over to a sleek, straighter line. She had never enjoyed the way those corsets manipulated the body, and she hated the pigeon-breasted bodices. When newly designed corsets had debuted in Paris, Phoebe had been one of the first to try them. She found them far less restrictive, although longer in length.

She looked at her image in the mirror to make certain nothing was amiss. This was one of the very latest fashions, which her father had purchased for her in New York. The cream-colored gown fell in a shapeless manner, but it was brought in to show a more tailored look by a snug brown plaid vest that barely reached her waist. Over this a brown cutaway coat gave the entire fashion a look of no nonsense. The calf-length coat was collared, but not designed to button, and was trimmed in piping the same color as the gown. Phoebe adjusted the lace cravat and turned to Gerda.

"I believe that should do it. Now I'm ready to explore Helena."

Gerda nodded and helped Phoebe with her large matching hat. Phoebe fussed with the piece for a moment, then sighed. "I do wish hats would go back to being smaller. I feel like I'm trying to balance a potted plant atop my head."

Her maid smiled and handed her kid gloves. "You look beautiful as always. The ladies of Helena, Montana, will be green with envy, and the men will fall instantly in love." She pulled on a large-brimmed straw hat of her own.

"Well, I certainly hope not. I would just as soon pass unnoticed."

"That would never be possible, miss. You are far too beautiful. The men will be vying for your attention and offering you proposals of marriage."

"They've been offering them since I was much too young to marry, and as far as I'm concerned they can keep their offers to themselves. I have no desire to wed anytime soon."

Gerda frowned. "But your vater said you were soon to become engaged."

"I know that's his desire, but it isn't mine." Phoebe's tone was dismissive. "Vater will give way to my thinking when he considers how lonely he'll be without me."

"But a truly great beauty like you should marry and have beautiful children," Gerda countered. "Perhaps you might marry an archduke."

Phoebe ignored the woman's comment and headed out of the room. Gerda had only been her maid for the trip to America, and Phoebe was still rather uncertain of her. Phoebe found it difficult to trust people, and at times Gerda seemed to be prying. She waited as the maid locked the room behind them, then led the way to the polished mahogany stairway. Her outfit, designed for walking, was not quite so easily managed on the stairs. Phoebe found it necessary to take the steps very slowly and to raise her narrow skirt a bit more than she thought appropriate.

She repeated the procedure for the outside porch steps and then again for the climb onto the trolley that ran throughout the day from Helena to the hotel resort and back again. The conductor handed her up and smiled.

"You may have a seat anywhere you like, seeing as how you two ladies are my only passengers."

Phoebe led Gerda to a wooden bench seat near the front. "This looks nice. We should be able to see quite well."

"Do you suppose there will be cowboys and Indians walking the streets?" Gerda whispered as the conductor took his place.

Phoebe shook her head. "I hadn't given it any thought, but I suppose there might be." The car began to move.

"It's quite exciting, ja?" Gerda said.

Phoebe nodded. She had to admit there was a sense of excitement in the unknown. They had only seen a small part of the town when they'd first arrived by train, and she was anxious to see more of what Helena had to offer. Gerda seemed just as eager to explore as she gazed out the trolley window at the passing scenery.

The sun overhead appeared almost painfully brilliant. Phoebe had to shield her eyes with her gloved hand, despite the wide brim of her hat. The landscape was one of hills, mountains, and rocks that gave way to a great many buildings as they approached the downtown area of the capital.

"There's plenty to see," the conductor told Phoebe as he helped her from the trolley. "And we have some very fine clothing stores. You ladies might enjoy some shopping."

Phoebe thanked the man, then turned to make her way down the sidewalk. Gerda positioned herself in a protective manner on the left of Phoebe so that none of the men could accidentally brush up against her mistress. The town hummed with the noise of people bustling to and fro. Carriages, wagons, and motorcars were vying for position on the crowded streets. Ladies and gentlemen hurried along the walkways, seeming most intent on their destinations, and because it was summer and school was no longer in session, there were quite a few children running around, not to mention a variety of animals.

"It's much busier than I expected."

"Ja, very busy," Gerda agreed. "Oh, here's a store that sells clocks and music boxes."

Phoebe paused to look in the window of the small shop. "Those cuckoo clocks look like they might have come from Heidelberg." Gerda nodded in agreement.

They continued their walk, noting various stores, including a candy shop that Phoebe decided to visit in order to purchase a treat for her father. She knew with his sweet tooth he would appreciate the caramels and chocolates.

For the most part people were friendly and in some cases too friendly. Phoebe found the attention of several cowboys toward herself and Gerda to be annoying, but she said nothing. She often found that silently ignoring offenders was much more effective than making a scene.

By noon Phoebe was quite famished, and Gerda agreed it was time to stop for something to eat. They located a respectable restaurant and were seated at a table near a gathering of ladies, who appeared to be arguing about an upcoming church function. Gerda rolled her eyes, and Phoebe smiled at her maid's annoyance. They ordered from the menu and waited for their food, all while the ladies next to them continued to take umbrage with one another.

Phoebe drew off her gloves and glanced around. The restaurant appeared to be doing quite well, filled mostly with businessmen and a lady or two in addition to the noisy bunch to her right.

When their roast beef and Yorkshire pudding arrived, Phoebe wasted no time in sampling the fare. Finding it very tasty, she dug in wholeheartedly. Gerda ate in silence, but Phoebe could see that she was just as curious to watch the people around them.

"They all seem to be in such a hurry," Phoebe commented in hushed German as several groups of men exited. The staff barely had time to clean the tables before a new group arrived.

"Ja. It makes me breathless," Gerda agreed in her native tongue.

Phoebe nodded. Americans definitely seemed always in a hurry. In New York City, they had rushed from one event to another. And yet Phoebe found this American style of life most exhilarating.

"It's almost contagious," she marveled. "I feel myself hurrying to eat my meal."

Gerda nodded. "Americans must suffer terrible indigestion."

Phoebe laughed lightly, but it was enough to draw the attention of the arguing women. They looked over as if to ascertain who dared laugh when matters of such grave disagreement were at hand. It took but a moment, however, for them to turn back to their own interests.

Phoebe and Gerda drank their tea in a leisurely manner, despite the waitress coming over constantly to see if they had finished. Apparently she was in a hurry to bring in another customer. When Phoebe could take the pestering no longer, she signaled the young woman and paid the bill.

Outside once again, she and Gerda found the same constant flow of people. They considered a few more shops where Phoebe made several purchases. She couldn't resist buying an American-designed ladies riding outfit. The split skirt would allow her to ride astride if she so chose. Gerda carried the packages as they made their way back to catch the trolley. The maid seemed unimpressed by the town, but Phoebe had to admit that she rather liked Helena. The people seemed friendly, even if they were in a rush.

When they reached the hotel grounds, Phoebe dismissed Gerda so she could enjoy the beauty of the day alone. "Please see to these packages. Find Vater if he's around and see what he plans for the evening."

Gerda nodded and headed toward the hotel while Phoebe took a seat on one of the garden benches. She breathed in deeply and lifted her face toward the sun. Even as she did this, Phoebe was reminded of her mother. Mutter had always loved the out-doors and had insisted they maintain acres of beautiful gardens on their grounds. Often she and Phoebe had strolled among the well-tended flower beds, enjoying the shade of towering trees and the musical twittering of the birds that had taken up residence there. Sometimes they would sit together, and Mutter would raise her face to the sun, marveling at its warmth and brilliance.

"God has made His earth so beautiful," she would say. "I can scarcely imagine what heaven will be like."

Phoebe felt a deep aching in her heart. She missed her mother very nearly as much today as she had that horrible moment ten years earlier when Vater had called her into his study to announce her mother's death. Phoebe hadn't even known her mother had taken a trip, but Vater declared that although he had advised against it, the trip had been a last-minute arrangement. An ill-fated one, just as he had feared. The ship she'd taken to America had sunk, and all had been lost at sea.

Phoebe was only twelve, and the loss had been almost insurmountable. Her older brother, Dieter, seemed to take it all in stride, but Phoebe spent hours each day sobbing, praying that it was all a mistake and her mother would come home. Her father soon tired of her brooding, tears, and questions and whisked Phoebe off to a boarding school in Switzerland. He assured her the change in scenery would help her with her grief. It didn't. Instead it seemed like she had been abandoned by all who had once loved her.

Not only that, but the girls at the school were cruel and teased her mercilessly for her tears. Even the teachers admonished her to comport herself in a more staid and ladylike manner befitting a nobleman's daughter. Once again, the lesson was to refrain from showing one's feelings. Phoebe thought them all heartless and buried herself in her studies, as well as art and music. By the time she completed school and returned home, she had learned quite well what was expected of her as the proper daughter of a graf. It didn't stop her, however, from asking her father for more details about her mother's death and why there wasn't at least a memorial stone erected in the cemetery. Her father thought it foolish to erect a stone when there wasn't a body buried beneath it. Not only that, but he did not want to think about her mother. In Phoebe's absence he had taken down the large oil painting of her mother and had moved it to the attic. Phoebe found it there and secreted it away in her room, where she could look at the portrait daily and remember a happier time. Losing Mutter had created an emptiness in her that could not be filled, no matter how hard Phoebe tried.

The loss remained acute even now. Phoebe looked out across the lawn and sighed. It all seemed so unfair. She knew that she favored her mother in appearance and perhaps even in her inquisitive spirit. Her mother was not one to let a matter lie if she found it of interest. Vater said this stemmed from the American side of the family. Apparently her mother's mother had been an American who had married into English nobility. However, Phoebe knew nothing of her mother's English or American relatives, and when she asked her father about them, he insisted they had all passed away. It seemed strange to imagine there was no one left.

❧❧❧

Two days later, after hiding in her cottage on the hotel grounds with Kenny, Elizabeth found herself having to face her best friend.

"You're going to have to talk about this sooner or later," Georgia told Elizabeth. "You might have fooled Kenny with that excuse that you were overly tired, but you and I both know that something is wrong. Even Ian knows, which is why he took Kenny to town with him just now."

"I'm grateful for that. My poor little boy. He was practically beside himself when I made him stay inside with me these last two days."

Elizabeth wasn't even able to look her good friend in the eye and kept her face lowered. Georgia deserved the truth. But the truth could put an end to the happy life Elizabeth had finally managed to eke out for herself managing the cleaning staff at the Broadwater Hotel. She had thought herself perfectly isolated from her past in this far western retreat in the Montana mountains.

"I promise you, Elizabeth, I will help you no matter what you tell me."

Elizabeth finally lifted her head, but she still didn't know what to say. She had maintained the lie about her life in America for so long, she had actually convinced herself that her former life and connections no longer existed. How could she possibly explain any of this to her dearest friend in all the world?

She got up and went to the stove for the pot of coffee she'd made earlier. Her mind was made up. She had to be truthful and hoped that Georgia would keep her secret. "I'm not who you think I am."

Georgia waited as Elizabeth filled their cups and then nodded. "Go on."

Elizabeth sighed. "My name isn't Elizabeth Bergen. It's actually Von Bergen." She looked at her friend and shook her head. "I hardly know where to start." She sank into her chair opposite Georgia at the tiny kitchen table.

"I find the beginning is always best," Georgia said with a sympathetic smile. She reached out to pat Elizabeth's hand.

Elizabeth nodded, took a big breath, and began. "I was raised in England, as my accent attests. My father was a wealthy Englishman of noble birth, and my mother was an American. I was an only child, and when my father grew ill it was decided I would marry a German graf—that's the equivalent of an English count. You see, my English family members were intermingled with German relatives, and we spoke German fluently. It was all a very natural process. My father arranged for me to marry Graf Frederick Von Bergen. I was only nineteen, and he was . . . *is* fifteen years my senior. There was no thought that I might do anything but obey. Arranged marriages in titled families are quite expected, and I had been brought up with the understanding that my parents would choose my husband."

She drew another deep breath. "In the beginning things didn't seem too bad. I was lonely at times, but I had a household to run and that took a great deal of my time. Not only that, but Frederick liked to entertain and did so often. Our parties were lavish and extensive. The year following our wedding, I bore a son, and Frederick was the happiest man in the world. At least for a short time."

"So what happened to change that?"

Elizabeth shrugged. "I suppose I changed. I had been raised to be most obedient, and as long as I did nothing to question Frederick's choices, our marriage was quite amiable. Unfortunately, I started to confront him about concerns I had. He was often gone on business, but no one seemed to know where he had gone. Our son was rather sickly as a baby, and I worried constantly. Frederick, however, refused to even acknowledge there were problems. He dismissed it as something all babies endured and assured me our son would outgrow his problems. When Dieter was three I gave birth again—this time a daughter."

"Phoebe?"

Elizabeth nodded. "Yes." Tears came to her eyes. "Phoebe was a delightful baby and never sick. Dieter did eventually outgrow his sickliness, just as Frederick had assured, but it was very difficult for him in those early years. It was difficult for all of us. I learned that my husband was gambling, and quite heavily. He had gone through most of his inheritance yet had a public image to uphold. To be known as a gambler and someone who held debts, Frederick would have suffered great humiliation. By this time my parents had died, and a portion of the fortune was settled on me. My husband began to go through it quickly. When he started selling off some of my mother's jewelry, I protested, and . . . he . . . beat me."

"Oh my," Georgia said, shaking her head. She added a spoonful of sugar to her coffee and stirred it in silence.

"It became a routine after that. If I questioned him about his spending or approached the subject of his gambling, he became violent. After a time, he seemed to need no excuse and would hit me whenever the notion took him. He beat me so badly on several occasions that I . . . I . . . miscarried. I lost three unborn children that way." Tears streamed down her face, but Elizabeth didn't even attempt to wipe them away.

"Was he only harsh with you?"

Elizabeth shook her head. "He was most demanding of the servants and often resorted to striking them. I once saw him beat a groomsman who had been unable to control my husband's horse. When Frederick attempted to mount, the horse reared and the groomsman lost control. My husband beat him and then had the horse brought to him. He killed the animal on the spot, and even after it lay dead, Frederick kicked the poor beast over and over." She paused a moment to regain her thoughts. "It was horrifying, and even the other servants were alarmed at his abuse.

"He was also quite hard on our son, Dieter. I believe this came in part from Dieter being small and sickly. I tried more than once to intercede, but Frederick only turned more violent. He seemed to get pleasure out of hurting people. The only person he held any kindness for was our daughter, Phoebe. But then, she was always a most compliant child and gave him no reason to be severe. He actually went out of his way to shield her from his violent temper."

"So what happened to make you flee to America?"

"I learned I was expecting Kenny. I wanted nothing more than to protect my unborn child, so I tried my best to stay out of Frederick's way and be always in agreement with whatever he wanted. But one night he flew into a rage when a neighboring landowner dammed up one of the streams. Phoebe was twelve and Dieter fifteen. Dieter was hard like his father by this time. My son could act quite ugly; in fact, he suggested that he and his father simply have the neighbor beaten. Without thinking, I protested. Frederick gave me a look that left me little doubt I would pay for my interference. To his credit, however, he never struck me in front of the children."

"How very considerate," Georgia said, her tone full of sarcasm.

Elizabeth remembered the night as if it were yesterday. "I knew Frederick would confront me later when we were alone. I had no doubt that he would beat me unmercifully, and I knew I would have to leave before that happened or risk losing my baby. So while Dieter and his father were sequestered away in the library trying to figure out how to make our neighbor pay, I slipped upstairs and gathered my things. I couldn't take much, obviously. To do so would alert the entire staff. I had managed to save back money from the household expenses, and I still had some of my jewelry, so I knew I could get as far as England. I had planned to take Phoebe with me, but when I was ready to leave, I couldn't find her. My time was running out and I knew that if I didn't hurry, someone would figure out what I was doing and report to Frederick. So I decided I would send for her later."

"It must have been very hard to leave her behind," Georgia sympathized. "I couldn't imagine having to leave any of my children."

"I had hoped it wouldn't be forever. I thought, prayed really, that Frederick would realize the harm he'd caused and change. I even left him a letter saying as much. Of course, it didn't matter to him. He lied to the children and told them I was dead."

"Dead?"

Elizabeth nodded. "I didn't know this at first. I went to stay with an elderly aunt in London. She was the last of my family still living. Once established there, I sent a friend of the family to speak with Frederick on my behalf and to bring Phoebe back to England when he returned. But Frederick had already sent Phoebe off to a boarding school and told the children that I had died. He told them I had been determined to take an emergency trip to America and that, despite his protests, I insisted and went anyway. He told them my ship sank and I was dead. He told our friend that if I knew what was good for me, I'd disappear and never try to see any of them again . . . or . . . he would ruin my reputation, perhaps even divorce me. He told our friend he wished I would have died."

"How ghastly! The horrible little man." Georgia shook her head. "I've never known anyone to be so heartless."

"I wasn't all that concerned; after all, I was out of that house and Frederick would have had a difficult time getting to me on my aunt's estate. When I learned where Phoebe was I sent her numerous letters. All of them were returned to me without her ever seeing them. I thought to threaten Frederick with some information I knew about his less-than-honorable business dealings. But before I could, I received a letter from Frederick telling me all the horrible things he would do if I ever tried to reach either of the children again. He threatened to have me killed and said he would rather see Phoebe dead than living with me.

"I feared for my children, and my aunt and I decided I would leave England for America. She gave me money and booked me passage on the next ship available. I was then four months along in my pregnancy. I gave up any hope of ever seeing my older children and decided it would be best for my baby if I simply focused on a new life here in America. I was determined to put the past behind me."

"But now the past has come to you. Phoebe is here."

"Yes. And I don't know for certain, but I would imagine that means her father is here as well. Possibly her brother too."

"Oh dear," Georgia said, seeming to fully understand the situation. "We must find out for certain that this Phoebe is your daughter and learn whether or not your . . . husband is in residence at the hotel."

"If he is, I cannot go back there. Even if he realizes I'm here . . . and Phoebe learns the truth, I can't risk Frederick learning about Kenny."

"I will find out for you." Georgia got to her feet. "I need to get up to the kitchen anyway. It's obvious you aren't feeling well, so when I go to work, I'll simply tell them as much. That way, you can remain here. Then I'll check with the manager and see if Phoebe is indeed Phoebe Von Bergen and who else is in her party. After that, we will know better how to approach this matter."

Elizabeth felt certain that, given Kenny and Ian's description, Phoebe was no doubt her daughter, and while it was always possible she was here with someone else, even a husband, Elizabeth feared otherwise.

"I suppose all I can do is wait until we know for certain. No matter what, Georgia, we must say nothing of this to anyone—especially Kenny."

3

*I*t was late afternoon before Georgia had a chance to return to the cottage. Elizabeth could tell by the look on her friend's face that the news wasn't good.

"Your husband is here with Phoebe and at least two servants. He has some sort of business going on and will be here for an indefinite stay."

Elizabeth felt her knees buckle and grabbed hold of the rocking chair. She swallowed, but her throat was dry and the action sent her into a coughing fit. Georgia guided her to sit in the rocker, then fetched her a glass of water. Elizabeth took it and drank as if she'd been without fluids for days. It did nothing to settle her nerves.

"I'm sorry that the news is as you feared. Still, I think it would be wonderful for you to reunite with your daughter and tell her the truth of what happened."

Elizabeth shook her head. "I don't know whether Phoebe would immediately run to her father with the news."

"Even if she did, Kenny is in town with Ian. I can certainly see that he stays with us a few days while you figure this out.

Perhaps this is God's way of working out the past for you, Elizabeth. You have to see that there is the possibility for good to come out of this."

"There's an even greater probability for harm." Elizabeth took another drink.

"Well, I've been praying a great deal about this. All day since learning the truth, I've known that we would need to seek the Lord on what direction you should take."

"I'll have to quit my job and leave."

"That seems rather rash, don't you think?"

"Georgia, I'm not like you. I don't work for the purpose of keeping myself busy at something I love. You took on the job of baking because you wanted something more to do. I'm here because you were gracious enough to get me a job. I have to work to support myself and my son. Now I can't remain here and work without fear of my husband causing us great harm."

"You could resign and reapply for the job you had in town. The hotel would surely take you back. I know you were highly thought of. You could stay with us just like you used to."

Elizabeth shook her head. "But if Frederick is here for an extended time on business, I don't imagine I would be safe in town. He will no doubt be there as much as he is here. No, I must take Kenny and leave altogether."

"But you've been so happy here."

It was true. Elizabeth couldn't deny it. When she and Kenny arrived some years earlier, the city of Helena had welcomed her with open arms. She had found a little church that just happened to be the same one Georgia attended. She and Georgia became fast friends when the woman opened her home to Elizabeth and her son. They offered the safe housing that Elizabeth feared might never be found, and the church they attended made certain that she and Kenny were not left in need. With Georgia's help, Elizabeth had managed to get a job with one of the hotels in town and immediately offered her earnings to Georgia. But Georgia and her son Ian were fixed quite well financially and instead encouraged Elizabeth to save her wages. Together they had a comfortable life, but Elizabeth couldn't help feeling as though she and Kenny were an imposition. Then when it was announced that the Broadwater was being remodeled to open once again, Georgia encouraged Elizabeth to apply for the position of supervising housekeeper. She received not only the job but also this tiny cottage in which she and Kenny could live. Now it appeared she would lose it all.

"Elizabeth, your husband and daughter won't remain here permanently," Georgia said in a manner that suggested she had a plan. She cocked her head slightly to the right and smiled. "So perhaps you need only leave Helena for a short time."

"But where am I to go for such a short time?" Elizabeth knew wherever she went she would have to immediately find work, and a good position would most likely require her to assure her employer of her desire to remain long-term. She could hardly take up a job with the intention of leaving as soon as her husband and daughter returned to Europe.

"What if we were able to arrange a place where you and Kenny could stay for several weeks, even months? We could explain the situation to the manager. He likes you, and I feel certain if he knew the truth, he would help us."

"But I would still have to find a place for us to go."

"I already have a place in mind," Georgia said with a smile. "My sister and her husband have a ranch near Townsend. It's about thirty-five miles from here. This is always a very busy time of year for them. You could go and work for them through the summer. I'm thinking they would give you room and board in return. Your husband should be gone by fall, and then you and Kenny could return in time for school."

"Do you really suppose it could work?" Elizabeth finally felt the tiniest bit of hope.

"I'm sure it could. I'll send my sister a letter and explain the situation. I could even have Ian ride down and deliver it. That way there would be no delay."

"All right." Elizabeth could see no other way. "I will need to speak to the manager. Do you suppose we could get a message for him to come here?"

"I don't imagine he would be very willing to leave. A large party is due in this evening. However, I know from the staff that Graf Von Bergen was said to have gone into Helena for the day. Phoebe left sometime after that with her maid and took the trolley into town. I would imagine you are safe to go see the manager yourself. Just take the back way."

"But what if Frederick has returned?"

"Well, he'll hardly be using the workers' entrance. You'll be able to slip right through to the manager's office, and no one will be the wiser."

Elizabeth nodded. "Very well. I'll do that. Meanwhile, would you keep Kenny in town?"

"Of course. Ian will be happy for the company."

⌘

"Ian, do you think Mama is sick?" Kenny asked. His expression betrayed his worry.

"I think sometimes we all work too hard and need a rest. Your mama is a hard worker. I'm sure she'll be just fine."

Ian wasn't at all sure what was going on, but he knew something wasn't right. He had a feeling that the young woman he'd met at the natatorium was somehow related to Elizabeth, but precisely how remained to be seen. Not only that, but apparently the matter was of grave concern for Elizabeth. Concern enough that she had sent for him and his mother to come and fetch Kenny.

"Mama does work really hard. She said that the Lord loves a hard worker." Kenny looked up with a smile. "That's why I want to work hard like you do. I want to be a lap . . . lap . . . i . . ." He frowned.

"Lapidary," Ian offered.

"Yup. That's what I want to be. I want to learn to do what you do and be really good at it."

Ian put another grinding lap in place and prepared to facet the lower portion of a sapphire. He had already secured the stone on the dop stick. Now Kenny was hovering over his shoulder. Ian was glad for the excuse to get the boy's mind off of his mother's condition.

Ian held up the six-inch-long wooden stick. "Do you remember what this is called?"

Kenny nodded. "A dop."

Ian smiled. "And what is it for?"

"It holds the gemstone on one end. You cement it there so you can grind it."

"Right. We do that to make it more beautiful. By cutting it a certain way it allows light to reflect." Kenny nodded again and Ian continued. "Now what do we do with the dop stick?"

Kenny pointed to a cone-shaped device that was fixed in place to the right. "You put the other end, without the stone, in one of the holes on the jamb peg."

Ian took the dop stick and secured the pointed end into one of the many holes in the jamb peg cone and angled the other end toward the lap, letting the gemstone barely touch. "We have to figure out just the right angle that we need to facet the stone properly. Each of these holes represents a little different angle. Understand? Remember when I told you about degrees of an angle?"

"Sure, but how do you know which hole to use?"

"I study the stone first and see what would make it the best it can be. I look for the flaws. See, I want to facet the stone in such a way that we eliminate as many flaws as possible. I use the jamb peg so that the facets will be consistent. Once I choose a specific angle, the peg holds it in place so that I don't make a mistake."

The door of the shop opened just then, and Ian rose from the table. "I'll be back in a bit. You stay here."

Ian went to the front counter. "How can I help you?" he asked the gentleman.

"I was told you could cut this stone for me." The man held up a red stone. "It's a ruby."

Ian took the stone and looked it over. "I'm sorry, but it's not. It's a garnet."

The man frowned. "But the man who sold it to me swore it was a ruby. He said he got it on the banks of the Missouri."

Ian smiled. "He may very well have thought it was a ruby. Unfortunately, a lot of untrained eyes mistake garnet for ruby. Montana garnets are quite plentiful and often much larger than rubies. Like your stone here."

"Well, I was going to have it made into a brooch for my wife."

"You can still do that. I would be happy to facet it for you. Why don't you tell me what you have in mind?"

Ian worked for nearly an hour with the man. Once they had figured out what he wanted and expected from the stone, the man left the shop and Ian returned to his worktable. Kenny, however, was no longer there.

"Kenny?"

Ian looked around the shop and found Kenny asleep on a stack of canvas tarps in the back room. Poor boy. No doubt worrying about his mother hadn't allowed him to sleep well. Ian wondered again what it was all about. His mother had assured him she planned to get to the bottom of things. Elizabeth and Kenny hadn't been at church on Sunday, and his mother feared the worst. She'd insisted Ian accompany her to the hotel earlier that morning, and once there, they'd learned that Elizabeth and Kenny had been sequestered away since Elizabeth's fainting spell. Without any ado, Ian's mother had insisted he take Kenny to town with him and keep him there overnight.

Knowing his mother, Ian figured she had no doubt gotten to the bottom of things, but he also knew it may not have been easy. Elizabeth had always been closemouthed about her past. Even when people asked her direct questions about her deceased husband, she said very little. Ian preferred that to telling lies. He'd seen women lie for the silliest reasons, as well as some life-changing ones. That thought brought back memories of Nora.

Such memories were always bittersweet. Nora had been his first and only love. She had come into his life without warning, and he had lost his heart to her immediately. Untested in the ways of love, he'd fallen hard. At her insistence, they had eloped, and only then did Ian learn about Nora's deceptions. She had told him that her parents were perfectly fine with the young couple running away to marry. He soon found out that had been a lie—not the first, but perhaps one of the most damaging.

For all of his youth, Ian had heard his younger sisters lie about one thing or another. His older brother assured him that women did that all the time. Several times Ian had caught his mother stretching or remaking the truth, and while he excused it, he hated it all the same. When people lied, even if it was just a slight deviation from the truth, he couldn't trust them. That lack of trust divided Ian's heart.

He walked back to the worktable and sat down with a sigh.

Shortly after five o'clock Kenny awoke and came to find Ian working. "I'm hungry," the boy announced.

Ian laughed. "Me too. I think we should call it a day and head over to the house. Grandma Harper will be back by six, and we'll have supper. Until then, however, I think she left some pastries with jelly filling. You and I could probably share one and have a glass of milk. How about that?"

Kenny smiled. "I could probably eat one by myself . . . and have the milk too."

Ian rubbed his head. "I'll bet you could at that, but then if it ruined your supper, I'd never hear the end of it."

"I'm really hungry," the boy insisted. "It won't ruin my supper. I promise."

◦≫§§≪◦

Phoebe knew her father was still working with his business associates. It was all very hushed, and she was to leave them alone no matter how long the meeting took. Her father had promised to try to meet her at six for dinner, but he told Phoebe she might have to dine alone. A quick glance at the clock showed that six o'clock was still an hour away. Perhaps a walk might best fill the time.

Phoebe first checked the mirror to make certain her appearance was in order. Her father was quite firm about dressing formally for dinner. Looking at the reflection of the ivory-chiffon-over-peach-satin creation, Phoebe knew her father would be pleased. He'd chosen the gown for her in New York, commenting that it was as if the seamstress had created it with

Phoebe in mind. At first she had feared it might make her look too pale, but instead it made her skin seem a warmer shade. Then again, she had spent quite a bit of time out in the sun, so perhaps her glow should be credited to that.

The gown was cut in a simpler straight-line Empire fashion with sleeves that were fitted to just above the elbow and banded with peach satin and ivory lace. The neckline was fashionably cut, but not too low, and trimmed in ivory lace that matched the sleeves. A beaded band of peach satin was fitted just below her breast, and the same beading was intricately woven throughout the ivory chiffon.

To this Phoebe added gloves, and she allowed Gerda to use some ornate combs in her hair. They were strategically placed amid the Gibson-girl styling, and Phoebe thought them far lovelier than one of her ostentatious hats.

Feeling there was nothing else she could do to make herself presentable, she left her room and headed downstairs. She noted the looks of approval she received from the many gentlemen in the lobby. She did not acknowledge them, knowing it was expected of her class to be viewable but untouchable. Her finishing school headmistress had often said that a smile or even a glance would leave some men with the feeling that she might desire their company. Which she certainly did not. There was only one man who interested her at the moment—Ian Harper. She couldn't seem to get him out of her thoughts, but for the life of her she couldn't imagine why she kept thinking about the swimming instructor.

Outside Phoebe walked leisurely along the path and admired the gardens. She'd been told that because the hotel had been closed for over ten years, the grounds had gone untended. The job of bringing them back to life had been quite laborious but worth the effort. Phoebe paused to study some roses. The delicate scent filled the air and made her smile. Mother had always loved roses. She walked a little farther and saw one of the bellmen approaching.

"Excuse me," she said.

The young man paused and gave her a smile. "Yes, miss?"

"I would like to take the path down to the lake. Can you point me in the right direction?"

"Of course, miss." He was young and gave his collar a nervous tug. "You just go around the hotel to the left." He pointed. "If you go this way, it's shorter and you can avoid having to walk too close to the billiards hall. You will need to cross the trolley and train tracks. The path is clear after that. You can even walk all the way around the lake, if you like."

"Danke. Thank you," she corrected to English.

Phoebe wasted no further time in conversation. She knew that if she was to be at supper by six, she didn't have time to dally.

She made a general survey of the landscape, noting that much of the area had been allowed to grow wild. Perhaps the new owner had no time to groom areas outside the immediate perimeters of the hotel and natatorium.

The lake was small, but she supposed it to be sufficient. She had read in a brochure that the lake was man-made just for the spa. The hotel had canoe rentals if one was of a mind to enjoy such things. Phoebe had come with no interest in boating, but now that she was here, she had to admit that a boat ride might be quite enjoyable. Perhaps Ian Harper could show her how. . . .

Pushing away that thought, she turned back toward the hotel, knowing that time was getting away from her. The fresh mountain air was cool and invigorating. It was as if the very nature around her had somehow embraced her spirit. Perhaps one day she would return to Montana. The thought made her smile.

Deep in her reflections, Phoebe suddenly found herself at

the back of the hotel near the laundry. Workers were carrying large white canvas bags, undoubtedly filled with towels and soiled bedding. The huge smokestack puffed heavy quantities of smoke overhead. No doubt laundry was something that had to be tended to round the clock.

Several men were working to load ice from the icehouse, but otherwise, there wasn't another soul to be seen. Perhaps the other guests were already at dinner. Phoebe took her skirt in hand and raised it just enough to speed up her walk. Father would be most unhappy to find her in the workers' area of the hotel. But he'd be even angrier if she kept him waiting, and this was the shortest route back to the dining room. Being punctual was far more important to attend to than her modesty.

"Besides, there's no one of importance here to see me." She hadn't meant to speak the words aloud. A quick glance around, however, confirmed her statement.

Just ahead were the kitchens, and not seeing any staff outside, Phoebe picked up her pace. She was just rounding the building, however, when she walked headlong into another woman.

"I do apologize." Phoebe straightened and dropped hold of her skirt. She smiled at the woman, then froze. The woman wore the same look of shock that Phoebe knew was on her own face.

She felt an icy tingle go down her spine. "*Mutter?*"

*I*t looks as though you've won the lion's share this afternoon, Graf Von Bergen."

Frederick nodded at the man who'd spoken. "Ja. I do enjoy a game now and then, Mr. Cooper. Gaming has long been a sport that I find worthwhile." He left his man, Hubert, to collect his winnings. "And I must say this was a delightful way to spend the afternoon."

"I find it also allows a man to get to know his business associates in a better way," one of the men replied.

Von Bergen eyed the speaker with a shade of contempt. Mr. Thompson was neither a very good card player nor a man of interest. Thompson's dealings with the American Sapphire Mining Company had caused one of his English associates to include him in this their first meeting, but Frederick had no desire for him to return.

"My man will show you out. The hour is much later than I had planned. I'm afraid I've kept you all from your dinner."

Mr. Thompson pulled on his coat. "Nonsense. One can always get a meal anywhere. But a good card game is an entirely different matter." He moved to the door of Frederick's private hotel suite with the other men. "I hope we can repeat this very soon."

Frederick said nothing. He waited until all but the final man had gone. "Lord Putnam, I wonder if we might have a word in private?"

The tall, skinny man turned and smiled. "But of course." He smoothed his mustache with his index finger. "I had rather hoped we might."

Von Bergen motioned to the more comfortable chairs in his sitting room. "I didn't wish to speak in front of the others. It has been most fascinating to study each of the men. They are much as you related to me in your posts."

Lord Putnam nodded and took a seat. "Each would rob you blind—if given the chance."

Frederick had no doubt of that. He had known Putnam for nearly a score of years, and but for some very damaging information he could use as blackmail against Putnam, Von Bergen knew this man would be no more trustworthy than the others.

"Have you made arrangements for me to visit the English mines?"

"Indeed, I have," Putnam replied. "It's quite some distance from here, you understand. And will have only the most primitive of accommodations, I'm afraid."

"Bah! That's unimportant. What matters is that I get my hands on sapphires that can pass for those from Ceylon, but at considerably less cost."

"We will have no difficulty with that. Generally speaking, the sapphires go straightaway to London to be cut, and of course there are high taxes to be paid. However, I have arranged for you to take possession here, and as we discussed, the gems can be hidden and taxes avoided. I can even point you to a lapidary here in Helena who has world-class skills should you want to get them faceted here rather than in Germany. The man is quite exceptional, and he is a lifelong citizen of Helena, so he will not be a threat to you. Generally I wouldn't recommend Americans to cut stones, as they seem to lack a real artist's touch, but this man is very good."

"I believe it's also possible to have them faceted in Ceylon. We do plan to go there before arriving in Germany. I might even pick up a few stones there just so I can truly proclaim to have purchased sapphires in Ceylon." The graf smiled. "Not that telling a lie or two here or there is unthinkable. We both know how that has benefited us in the past."

"Hmmm, yes." The other man looked most uncomfortable.

Frederick moved to where several carafes of liquor awaited. "Would you care for a bit of Scotch? I find it quite satisfying after a rousing game of cards. Especially after winning." He poured the liquor into his glass.

"Thank you, no," Putnam said, stretching out his long legs. "However, I'm famished. I thought you might accompany me to the dining room. We can talk there."

Frederick shook his head. "What say we have dinner brought here to my room? We can continue to make our plans uninterrupted that way."

"I say, that is a capital idea."

Frederick motioned for Hubert. "See to it that dinner is brought to us, and make certain it is a full meal and not just something à la carte. And see to it that they bring us a decent wine."

"Ja, I will oversee it personally," Hubert assured. He quickly exited the room, leaving Frederick and Putnam alone.

"I am most eager to see to this business quickly," Frederick began. "I have no desire to remain in this wretched country any longer than I have to."

"I quite agree. I don't care at all for it—never have. Everything is so . . . dirty and unrefined. This hotel is advertised as the finest Montana has to offer with its great mineral waters and European décor. However, I find the entire place to be a disaster."

"As do I, but that is beside the point." He brought his drink and sat opposite the man. "You and I have been associates for a very long time. We have been good for each other, have we not?"

The man frowned. "We have."

"I find that arrangements such as we have are to be respected and treated with . . . well, how shall I put it . . . a sort of reverence."

"I agree."

"We both stand to make a great deal of money if we can accomplish this arrangement. I would hate for anything to come between us and success."

The man shook his head. "I'm not at all sure why you feel the need to address such a matter. I thought when I wrote you from London that you understood the matter was all but settled. I have the authority to see to it that you get exactly what you need and can avoid paying taxes on the stones."

Frederick took a drink and considered the man's words. "I don't trust those other men, and I do not wish for them to be involved in our business dealings. I am happy to take their money at the card table, but otherwise I feel our association should be limited."

His friend sat up rather quickly, his expression betraying alarm. "Did you suppose I meant to bring them in on our private arrangement? I assure you, I had no such thought. All of these men are involved in various aspects of the sapphire mining trade, and I thought only to expose you to them . . . in part . . ."—he paused, and the tension in his face eased—"in part because you need to understand that doing business here in America can seem most advantageous and yet turn sour quickly. I know for a fact that Mr. Thompson would love nothing more than to entice you to purchase your stones from his organization, but I can assure you their stones are not of the same quality as those offered by the English mines. Often they even mix in stones that are not Yogos and try to pass them off."

A smile touched Frederick's lips. "And you thought to safeguard me from such devious practices."

"Exactly."

Von Bergen knew it was more about Lord Putnam protecting himself, but he allowed him the lie. "Very good of you." He tossed back the last of his drink and nodded. "Very good indeed. I appreciate that my partner would keep such a careful watch over my welfare."

"It's to the benefit of us both, don't you agree?"

"Ja, I do." Frederick studied the man for a moment. "I also know that you would never consider double-crossing me . . . given our understanding."

Putnam stiffened. "You may rest assured, my dear man, that you have my utmost cooperation. I must say, however, I'm moved to despair that you should even bring up such a subject."

"It never hurts for associates to revisit the foundation of their business arrangements." Frederick smiled, knowing full well he had the upper hand. He'd seen Lord Putnam attempt to work outside of their agreement once or twice, but Von Bergen had applied just the right amount of pressure to rein him in.

"I don't need to tell you how harmful it could be for the truth about either of us to get out. Although I can hardly see the wrong in supplying the duchess with choice stones, even if they aren't from Ceylon." He shrugged. "From my understanding, these Yogo sapphires are soon to surpass the Ceylon and Burmese sapphires in value."

Lord Putnam nodded with great enthusiasm. "Indeed. I can tell you they have been widely received with great praise since their debut at the Universal Exposition in Paris. The quality is unlike anything expected out of America. I believe you are quite right to purchase these for her."

"Well, I shall at least consider their purchase. The right price will convince me one way or the other."

Hubert returned and stood just inside the door until Frederick acknowledged him with a nod. "Your dinner will arrive shortly, *gnädiger Herr*."

"Very good. You may go now and partake of your own nourishment." Frederick looked to his cohort and smiled. "I believe we should now put aside any concerns and enjoy our evening. You were, in fact, going to tell me all about King Edward's trip to Paris."

Putnam smiled. "Old Bertie has had a busy year already, and it looks to only get busier. He took the queen to Paris. Wanted to cheer her up. You know her deafness is most debilitating, and it causes her great bouts of melancholia. She's quite good at reading lips, but it does take its toll. Not only that, but she lost her father last year, you remember?"

"I do indeed."

"Her sister Minnie came to stay for a time after that and that proved to be a good tonic. Minnie even tried her best to encourage her son Nicky to join her, but I suppose his duties to Russia were much too important. Besides, that wife of his is bent on putting up a wall between the tsar and his mother."

"And all of them are putting up walls against Germany," Frederick said in an offhanded manner. "It would seem that given every one of them are related to each other via the royal bloodlines, they would be more considerate of their cousin the kaiser."

"Ah, but Willy does himself great discredit," Putnam continued. "He has such a suspicious mind."

Frederick frowned at the nickname Putnam had assigned the kaiser, but such was the nature of the nobility and upper crust these days. "I hardly think it a discredit to wonder why the king of England met with the king of Spain in secret this past April."

"It was purely innocent. Bertie took the queen"—he lowered his voice— "and his mistress, to sail the Mediterranean Sea. It was only proper that when the king of Spain invited him to visit him in Cartagena that he graciously did so."

"And I suppose it was purely innocent that they worked with French officials and decided on a plan to assure ownership of their Mediterranean holdings without any consideration of including Germany in on the discussion."

Putnam raised his arms and shrugged. "Whoever understands the workings of kingly minds?" He smiled. "Things would go much easier were we in charge, would they not?"

A knock at the door proved to be the delivery of their supper, and all conversation was put aside. Nevertheless, Frederick tucked away all the information his friend had shared. He was determined to return home with any information beneficial to the kaiser. It never hurt to ingratiate oneself with the king.

⁂

"Oh, my precious daughter."

Phoebe stood stock-still and looked into the face of the woman she had thought forever lost to her. "You're alive."

The woman nodded and tears streamed down her face. "Yes."

Phoebe shook her head. "That can't be. Vater said you were dead." Her mind whirled with confusion. Was it possible her father simply didn't know? But none of it made sense. If her mother hadn't died when her ship sank, why hadn't she come home to them?

"Phoebe, I know you're confused. I've always known you were alive, but your father told you that I was dead."

"Your ship sank." Phoebe's voice sounded almost childlike.

"No. It didn't."

Her mother reached out to touch her, but Phoebe shrank back. The look of sorrow on her mother's face did nothing to assuage her fears. This wasn't possible. It made no sense. Either her mother had led them to believe she was dead or her father had lied. Neither conclusion offered any comfort at all.

I know you're quite wounded by all of this," Phoebe's mother said, "but I beg you to hear me out. I've wanted you to know the truth from the beginning."

"But you didn't let any of us know the truth. We thought you were dead." Anger began to replace confusion. "What kind of heartless person allows her children to think her dead?"

"The kind who feared their father and what he might do."

"*Ich verstehe nicht*—I don't understand." Phoebe crossed her arms as if to block out the painful words. "Why should you have been afraid of Vater?"

Her mother glanced around; then her eyes settled back on Phoebe. "Would you please allow me to explain? I only want a chance to tell you the truth of what happened."

Phoebe wanted to throw back an angry refusal but didn't. She knew she'd never have any peace over this startling discovery if she didn't at least attempt to get the truth. "Very well. Explain." Just then a couple of women in hotel maid uniforms passed by.

"Evenin', Mrs. Bergen. Heard you were under the weather," one of the women said. "Hope you feel better soon."

"Thank you, Emily," Phoebe's mother answered.

"Mrs. Bergen? Not Von Bergen?" Phoebe fought to hold back an angry comment at this revelation.

"We can't talk here. Please come with me to my cottage. It's just beyond the main grounds."

"You aren't staying in the hotel?" Suddenly it dawned on Phoebe that her mother might be employed by the resort. "Do you work here?"

Her mother nodded. "I do."

Phoebe drew a deep breath, then lowered her arms. She wanted to refuse her mother, but at the same time she wanted more than anything to hear what she had to say. "Very well. I will come with you."

They didn't share another word until Phoebe's mother opened the door to the small house and turned on the electric lights. "Please come in and make yourself comfortable," she said in German. Perhaps she hoped it would ease Phoebe's discomfort. It didn't.

Phoebe entered the cottage and glanced around. The living room was quite small, but tidy and welcoming. A fireplace graced one wall, and Phoebe noted that logs had been neatly laid for a fire. A small couch faced the fireplace with a rocker positioned on the left and a stuffed chair on the right as if to box in the hearth.

"Please have a seat."

Phoebe nodded and took the chair. She watched as her mother lit the fire. Her last memories of her were of a refined woman directing servants to do such menial tasks. Mutter had been called one of the most beautiful women in all of Germany, even finding admirers in the highest circle. This woman in her simple serge skirt and plain white blouse hardly resembled the elegant wife of Graf Von Bergen, yet there was still an undeniable beauty in the way she looked and carried herself.

Finally, with the fire blazing strong, Mutter took a seat in the rocker. "Have you had your supper?"

Phoebe shook her head. "I'm not hungry." She thought momentarily of her father and how he would be concerned when she didn't show up for dinner. However, he would be even more upset when he learned the reason why.

She felt uncomfortable as she realized her mother had paused to study her. "You are beautiful, Phoebe. I always knew you would be."

"Like you," Phoebe murmured.

Her mother smiled. "We do bear a strong resemblance to each other, but you are a far greater beauty." She folded her hands together. "I know this is very hard for you. I learned only a short time ago that you and your father were staying here at the Broadwater Hotel."

"Does Vater know you're alive?" The question just tumbled out before Phoebe could stop it. "Does he know you're here?"

"Yes, he knows I'm alive, but he doesn't know I'm here."

Her mother's reply cut Phoebe to the heart. Her father knew and said nothing? How could he have been so callous? He knew how devastated Phoebe had been when Mutter went away. She drew a deep breath.

"How long has he known?"

"Since the night I left."

Phoebe gasped. Her stomach clenched. She swallowed back bile and lifted her chin. It had to be a lie. Vater would never have allowed her to believe her mother was dead if he knew she wasn't. But even as the thought came, Phoebe had to admit her fears that he had done just that. She didn't want to believe her mother, but she could see in the older woman's eyes that she was most sincere. "Go on. I want to hear it all."

Mutter nodded. "I've long wanted you to know it . . . all. I have always regretted how I managed things. You must understand first what drove me to leave. Then you must understand what forced me to stay away and remain silent."

Her mother's words sounded ominous. A part of her wanted to run away, but Phoebe knew she would have to remain strong and listen to the accounting.

"As you know, my marriage to your father was arranged by your grandfather—my father. I had no say in the matter, and although I was quite terrified at the prospect of leaving family and England to make a new life in Germany, I obeyed and married the man chosen for me."

Phoebe nodded, and her mother continued. "I was determined to love my husband and make a good life. It was my duty, and I took that responsibility quite seriously. Besides that, I wanted children and a home of my own, and your father provided both. At first, I think he was happy. I don't believe he ever loved me, but I do believe he found the arrangement satisfactory.

"Unfortunately, when you and Dieter were very young, I learned your father was gambling . . . and quite heavily. I tried not to be concerned. After all, men have their vices, and your father had inherited a title and fortune from his family. What he did with his money was entirely his decision. However, I noticed that he grew more and more impatient and always seemed angry. I saw him beat servants and animals. I listened to his ranting over dinner and at parties. When you were born he seemed to calm for a time. He was pleased to have a daughter and he doted on you, to my surprise."

Her mother paused and looked beyond Phoebe as if seeing the past. "He said that sons were to be disciplined and brought up with an understanding of their enormous responsibilities, but daughters were to be spoiled and pampered." She smiled sadly and returned her gaze to Phoebe. "And he certainly did that.

I could not fault him for the love he bore you. I couldn't even bring myself to be jealous. To see him love you so completely was a blessing. I knew he would do most anything for you."

Phoebe knew that what her mother said was true. Her father had doted on her. The only time he'd ever truly refused her was in sending her away after her mother's death . . . or rather, disappearance.

"Go on."

Mutter's smile faded. "The gambling became more of a problem, and your father was often gone from home for long periods of time. When he returned he was often violent. He became more physical with the servants, and one day when I questioned him about the money, he slapped me. Hard."

Phoebe gasped. "Vater would never hit you."

"I never thought he would either, but he did. You must be able to remember some of our heated arguments. I know you were quickly sent to the nursery anytime we had words and definitely before he began hitting me. But it's true. His violence toward me increased to the point that on many occasions I was unable to get out of bed."

"I remember you were sick on many occasions. But our governess told me you were simply having female issues."

"In a way she was right, at least three times. Your father had beaten me so badly that I miscarried. I had wanted more children, but given the increasing danger our home presented, I also feared it."

Phoebe shook her head. "No. You must be exaggerating. Vater couldn't have been so cruel."

"I know it's hard to hear, but I hope you'll let me finish before you judge the matter in full." Her mother lowered her gaze.

"How could we not have known? You want me to believe you, but I can't. Vater was good and kind to us."

"Ask your brother how kind he was. Dieter often faced his wrath."

"Well, Vater said Dieter often defied him and that it was important for a boy to know who was master of the house. Dieter never complained to me about it."

"No, I don't imagine he did." Mutter leaned back in the rocker. "Phoebe, I know you don't wish to hear these things, but I promise you they are true. When you were twelve I found I could no longer bear your father's violence. I had been putting aside some of the household money, and I still had a few pieces of jewelry from my mother. I decided I would take you and flee to England to stay with a relative. Unfortunately, the opportunity to get you didn't present itself, and I decided I would send for you."

"Send for me? You meant to have me join you?"

"Yes." Her mother fixed her with a pleading expression. "I never wanted to leave you behind. It was never my intention. You must understand this if nothing else. I knew Dieter was devoted to his father, despite the occasions of harsh treatment. Frederick had great plans for him and had already arranged for his education. I knew Dieter would be leaving shortly for the school your father had chosen. Then it would be just you and me. I asked your father if I might take you and visit England, but he refused. After that, I knew if I wanted to escape the madness, I would have to leave in secret, but I always planned for you to go with me."

Phoebe tried to make sense of it all. She knew her father could be a hard man. She'd seen him lose his temper with the staff and even with Dieter, but she'd never witnessed the physical violence her mother insisted had taken place.

"But if Vater knew you were alive . . . that you had only gone away, then he would have wanted you to come home. He would have sought to find you and bring you home."

"Your father would have wanted to find me, but not to bring me home."

"Then what?" Phoebe asked.

"To kill me."

Phoebe jumped to her feet. "That's preposterous. You cannot sit here and expect me to believe such lies."

"Please, Phoebe. Let me finish, and then you can decide whatever you like."

"But I see no sense in it." Phoebe glanced at the door. "Besides, Vater will wonder where I am. We were to have dinner together."

"I won't take much more of your time. But I want you to know that I did try to get you back. I paid someone to discover your whereabouts, and once I knew where you were, I sent you a letter at your boarding school. The letter was returned. I sent many more, but all were returned. I decided I would go to Switzerland and see you, but just as I arranged this, a letter came from your father. He told me if I tried to get in contact with you again or ever let either you or your brother know that I was alive—he would see to it that I wasn't. He also threatened your life, telling me he would sooner see you dead than with me."

"No. I don't believe you." Phoebe shook her head. None of this could possibly be true.

Mutter got to her feet and went to the small corner desk. "When I learned you were here, I dug these out. I had them stored away in my trunks for years." She produced a stack of letters tied together with a blue ribbon. "I had hoped one day we would meet again, just as we are now, and I could give you these letters and let you see for yourself the truth of our past."

Phoebe began to tremble as her mother came forward with the letters. A sickening feeling washed over her. What if it all was true? How could she ever face her father again if he was truly the monster Mutter professed him to be?

"Phoebe, please give me just a bit more time. Sit and read these and then . . . well . . . if you still don't believe me, I won't bother you with any of this ever again."

For a moment all Phoebe could do was stare at the letters in her mother's hands. The envelopes were marked from posting, and the paper was yellowed with age. They seemed authentic enough, but Phoebe couldn't quite bring herself to reach for them. If she took them and read them and learned that all her mother had said was true—what then? To know her father had betrayed her by insisting her mother was dead was hard enough. But to imagine he had threatened not only Mutter's life but her own was difficult to stomach. How could there ever be any explanation for such ugly declarations?

"Please, Phoebe. I know you're hurt. I know you don't owe me a thing, but my love for you has never died. These letters will show that . . . and more."

"Very well." Phoebe took the letters and reclaimed her seat. "I will read them."

She noted that the envelopes hadn't been opened. They had clearly printed demands that they be returned to the sender, and the postmarks bore proof that they had originated ten years earlier. Phoebe opened the first envelope as her mother added a log to the fire. The evening temperatures were growing cooler, but Phoebe found her mother's news had already chilled her to the bone.

My dearest daughter,

I have missed you so very much. By now you know that I am in England. I pray your father has not grieved you overmuch in my absence. No matter what, you need to know that I love you and I want you with me. I never planned to leave you behind, but your father made it impossible for me to take you. I plan to rectify that as soon as I can make arrangements to have you brought to England.

The letter went on to tell Phoebe an abbreviated version of what her mother had just explained. She said nothing about the beatings but hinted at the unbearable pain and sorrow Phoebe's father had been responsible for causing.

Phoebe opened the second letter and read much the same. By the third letter, her mother mentioned wanting to come see her, but since the letters were being returned unopened, she wasn't at all certain Phoebe even knew she was alive.

I have learned that your father is telling you and your brother that I am dead—that my ship sank while crossing to America. Obviously this is untrue, but your father fears that if you know the truth, you will want to come live with me.

The fourth letter sounded more desperate. Her mother spoke of letters sent to the headmistress of the school and of her plans to come to the school and insist on seeing Phoebe.

And then Phoebe noticed that the last letter wasn't in her mother's script, nor had it been a letter returned from the school. This one was from her father, written in German.

Elizabeth,

No doubt you felt that in order to assert your independence you would embarrass me by leaving our home. And no doubt you have relayed to your aunt all of the marital miseries you endured. However, as we both know, a wife is subject to her husband's discipline and approval. The first of which you were in constant need of, and the latter of which you rarely were capable of winning. You have caused no small amount of trouble with your childish action of running away. Should the truth of your departure be learned among my peers, I would suffer great embarrassment and ridicule. Therefore you will not return, nor will you make it known that you are even alive.

I have told the children you are dead, that your ship sank as you made an emergency trip to America. What you need to understand now is that if you do not cease in sending letters and trying to see our daughter . . . I will see that my story comes true. Of course, there would be no sinking ship, but the end result would be just the same. I will see to it personally or have it done, but you will no longer be a problem to me. If you ever try to contact our children or return to this estate, I will have you dealt with before either of them has a chance to see you.

Furthermore, if you attempt to visit our daughter at school, I will arrange it so that you will never see Phoebe again. I would rather she be dead than with you. If you love her as you claim, you will not challenge me in this, for you cannot doubt that I would see this through to the obvious conclusion. Your life . . . her life . . . both are quite uncertain unless you cooperate.

Phoebe's eyes widened at this final declaration. Her father's signature was affixed to the bottom as if to pound home the truth. Tears clouded her vision. How could this be? How could her father have been so cruel?

Mutter seemed to understand. She came and took the letters from Phoebe's trembling hands. "Now you know the truth."

Phoebe fought back her emotions. "Yes, but I don't know what to do with it."

6

*Y*ou'd best put that book away for now, Kenny. I need to get you back to your mama." They'd eaten supper and now lounged in the living room reading. Ian had taken the time to scan the newspaper and was now reading the Bible, surprised that his mother hadn't yet returned. She had told him to keep Kenny there until she came for him, but it was already growing dark and there was no sign of her.

"But Tom Sawyer just saw Injun Joe kill Dr. Robinson," Kenny said, clearly excited as he jumped up from his chair. "Can't I read just a little while longer?"

Ian smiled. "Your mama will be wondering where you are. The book will still be here when you visit next time."

The sound of someone coming in the back door drew Ian's attention. His mother entered the living room shortly thereafter, and the look on her face was one of grave concern.

"What's wrong?"

She smiled, but it was forced. "Kenny, I need to talk in private with Ian. Your mama said it would be all right for you to spend the night with us, so why don't you go on upstairs and get ready for bed. You can read until I'm able to come tuck you in. Would that be all right with you?"

"Sure, Grandma!" He jumped up with his book. "This is the best book ever." He headed for the stairs, his nose already back between the pages.

Ian's mother motioned him to follow her into the kitchen and close the door. "There's trouble brewing."

"Elizabeth?"

Again she nodded. Her voice lowered to a whisper. "There are all sorts of complications. The woman you saw at the pool is Elizabeth's daughter."

"I figured such a resemblance was no coincidence."

"Not only that, but Elizabeth is no widow. Her husband is there at the hotel with their daughter."

"What?"

"Shhh. We mustn't let Kenny hear us." His mother pulled on his sleeve and led him out of the house and into the back garden. "Elizabeth is terrified of her husband finding out about her being at the hotel. She's even more terrified that he'll learn about Kenny."

"He doesn't know he has a son?"

"Elizabeth escaped before he learned she was expecting." She filled Ian in on all the details that Elizabeth had given her. After several minutes of explanation, Ian's mother paused. "So that's why the situation is so grave."

"I see." Ian let out a heavy breath. "And what is she going to do now?"

"Well, she wants us to keep Kenny here in town so that her husband can't find him. She hopes he won't know that she's here either, but if he does happen to spot her, at least he won't know about the boy."

"She wants us to lie?" Ian shook his head. Such things didn't sit well with him, especially given the past.

"She hopes to take Kenny and leave the area until her husband and daughter return to Germany. He knows she's alive, but not where she lives. And she certainly doesn't want him to know about Kenny."

"Mother, it's hardly right for us to come between a husband and wife whom God has joined together. You know how I feel about such things."

His mother reached out and patted his hand. "Ian, I know how badly Nora's parents hurt you by trying to tear the two of you apart. I know that Nora's lies destroyed your happiness, but this is different."

"How? How is it any different for us to put a barrier between Elizabeth and her husband? To keep a man from his son?"

"The man is horribly violent. He's a monster who used to beat Elizabeth whenever the notion took him. Would you want to see that happen to her again? Or to Kenny?"

"Of course not, but neither do I want to dishonor God, nor the covenant they made before Him. Mother, have you prayed or sought counsel from Pastor Clearwater?"

"I haven't had time, but the thought did come to mind. My immediate concern was Elizabeth. She was so upset. She was going to just take Kenny and flee, but I convinced her to wait. I thought perhaps I would have you take a letter to your aunt and uncle near Townsend. I thought with all that's going on this time of year they could use Elizabeth's help to cook and help in other ways. That way she and Kenny could be well out of harm's way."

"You mean they could hide there until her husband is gone."

"Yes." His mother frowned. "I know this is a delicate matter. I can't say that I'm completely comfortable with such a solution, but, Ian, I am worried for them both."

"And so am I," Ian agreed. "Even so, there has to be a better solution. What if Elizabeth were to meet with her husband so that they could talk things out? Surely if there were witnesses, no harm could come to her."

"I don't know, Ian. I just know that she's terribly afraid and fears for Kenny. She might lose him if her husband finds out about him."

Ian shook his head. "I need time to think and pray. Why don't you go be with Kenny while I take a walk."

"Of course." His mother put her hand on his arm. "I know Elizabeth and I have responded to this with our hearts. It's our nature, I suppose. However, I also know you are right in saying we must seek the Lord. I'm glad for the reminder."

Ian kissed her atop the head. "You are both good women who love the Lord. I know God will make the way clear."

He walked around to the front of the three-story brick house where he'd spent a good portion of his life and paused for a moment. His father had built this house for his mother in 1888. It had been the height of fashion in an Italianate style that many envied. It wasn't a mansion, nor really all that opulent, but Ian had grown up knowing they had more than most. When he had determined to marry Nora, he had talked his father into helping him build a little house beside the family home, where the couple could live. Having more than enough acreage, his father had eagerly agreed. Then within a span of seven years Nora died, then Ian's brother, and finally his father. It was then that Ian had moved the gem shop from its cramped quarters on Main to the small house he'd built for Nora next door—a house they'd scarcely had a chance to share. And it was there that Ian quietly shaped gemstones and carried on his father's business.

If anyone were to look at it, however, they might never know it was anything other than a small two-story home. A neighborhood had grown up around them as the city spread, and there were dozens of beautiful homes along the treelined street. Ian and his mother had sold off all of their land, save that upon which the two houses stood. That money, along with insurance and savings, had set Ian's mother up for life. He'd even tried to convince her to hire a housekeeper so she could relax and enjoy doing nothing. He smiled. His mother had never been one to sit idle. She loved being busy and being with other people, which made her job at the hotel ideal.

Ian stuffed his hands in his pockets and began to walk. His mother was precious to him, but he wouldn't lie for her or anyone else. It would never bode well for either party. But how could he just cast Elizabeth and Kenny aside and leave them to whatever fate they might have with Von Bergen?

He sighed. It was nearly dark, but that only made it better. The quiet of the evening comforted Ian as he prayed.

This is quite a mess, Lord. I don't honestly know what part we are to play in it, but you know that we care greatly for Elizabeth and young Kenny. Father, I had no idea Elizabeth was bearing such a heavy load. I want to help, but I don't want to do anything wrong. I pray you'll give us all wisdom in dealing with this situation.

He paused for a moment and let his mother's earlier comments really sink in. Elizabeth had suffered much at the hands of this violent man—her husband. Kenny didn't deserve to be thrown into such danger, but neither did he deserve to be robbed of his father. Ian knew that under the law, women had very few rights. Perhaps in Europe it was even worse. Still, might there not have been a better way? Or was leaving her husband the only choice Elizabeth had in order to protect the life of her unborn son? She had suffered the pain of losing three other children because of her husband's abuse. Surely God would not want for another such precious life to be taken in the raging fit of one man's actions.

Ian started walking again, and this time Nora came to mind. Her parents had hated him for taking their daughter away from them. Hated him further because in their minds it was his fault she had died.

She'd been gone for ten years. Ten years, and still Ian felt guarded when he thought of ever allowing himself to love again. Lies and manipulation from the woman he loved had tainted his heart. He had no desire to love again if it meant having to live with that again.

"How can I be a part of encouraging Elizabeth to continue her lie?" he said to himself. But then again, how could he not?

❧

Elizabeth expected to see her daughter that morning. Phoebe had left the evening before in such a state of confusion that Elizabeth had made her promise to return the next morning for at least one more discussion. She had said nothing to Phoebe about Kenny, nor would she unless she felt certain the boy would be safe. Phoebe had agreed to say nothing to her father for the time, and Elizabeth could only pray that her daughter would be true to her word.

When a knock sounded on her door, Elizabeth hurried to open it and found Georgia instead of Phoebe.

"I thought you were Phoebe."

"Phoebe? You've seen her? She came here?"

"Yes." Elizabeth ushered Georgia into the house. "I'm expecting her back this morning. We ran into each other as I was returning from visiting with the manager. She was coming around the back corner of the kitchen area and we collided."

"I would imagine that was quite a shock."

Elizabeth nodded. "More than I can say, but it seemed God had it ordained that we should meet. She agreed to come here, and I told her everything. Well, except for Kenny. I even let her read the letters I'd sent to her and the one her father had sent to me."

"That must have been quite an eye-opener for the girl." Georgia could see that Elizabeth was more than a little nervous. "I hope, however, that it also brought you some joy."

Elizabeth began to pace. "It did, although perhaps joy isn't the right word. I thought I would never see her again, and there she was. It was like an answered prayer. But at the same time I am just as confused as to what to do next."

"I spoke with Ian last night. He's rather uncomfortable with the entire matter. I've told you before that he had a rough marriage. Prior to the wedding, Nora arranged with a friend to set everything in place so that she could sneak off with Ian and get married without anyone the wiser. She lied to her parents and told them she'd been invited to go with her friend's family on a trip to Yellowstone and would be gone for two, possibly three, weeks. Then she lied to Ian and told him that her parents were planning this grandiose wedding, which she didn't want, and that she preferred to elope. She lied again, telling Ian her folks were perfectly happy for them to elope, so Ian didn't see a problem. The truth was, however, they didn't want her to marry Ian at all, or anyone else for that matter."

Elizabeth stopped. "But why? It's only natural that children should marry, and Ian's a wonderful young man. I would think any mother would be proud to have him marry her daughter."

"Well, there were complications. Nora had been a sickly child. Sometime we shall chat about it over a cup of coffee, but only if Ian agrees that I might share his story. Right now, I wanted to come and say that Ian would like for you to come to the house tonight. I thought you might as well pack an overnight bag and stay the night. Maybe even a few days. That way you can explain things to Kenny. I'm sure he'll be worried. He was already concerned that you might be sick."

"I knew he would be. I would be happy to come to the house. Phoebe said something about helping her father host a dinner party for this evening, so I know Frederick will be busy with his friends. I should be able to catch the trolley without being seen."

Georgia nodded, then noted the time. "I must get back to work. I only wanted to stop long enough to check in and invite you to the house. Elizabeth"—she paused and smiled—"I'm praying for you—for all of us."

She departed and was gone only a matter of minutes before Phoebe arrived. Elizabeth smiled at the fashionable white-and-tan dress. It was perfect for a summer's day, and although summer had not truly arrived in Montana, it looked most fitting.

"I hope I'm not interrupting. I saw a woman leave your cottage. If this is a bad time . . ."

"Not at all. That was a dear friend of mine." Elizabeth stepped back. "Please come in."

Phoebe entered the house with the same caution she had shown the evening before. Elizabeth held herself in check. She longed to rush to Phoebe and pull her into her arms for a long embrace, but she knew her daughter wasn't ready for that.

"I've thought a great deal about what you said," Phoebe began. "I can't help but wonder, however, if perhaps Vater is different now. Maybe he felt remorse for his actions and worked to change. You said yourself that you've kept your whereabouts hidden. Perhaps he has changed and would want to find you and make things right."

Elizabeth smiled. "I'd like to think that was possible."

Phoebe nodded and twisted her gloved hands together. "I don't suppose there is any way to be sure." She looked at the floor and gave the tiniest of shrugs. "I am still very confused."

"I know you are, and for that I am sorry. But I'm not sorry that God has brought us together."

Her daughter's head snapped up. "God? What has He to do with any of this?"

A sigh escaped Elizabeth. "Don't you remember how I used to pray with you at bedtime and how I read Scriptures to you and we discussed their meaning?"

"Of course, but I hardly see what that has to do with this."

"I believe God ordains our steps, Phoebe. I believe He controls everything. He is all-knowing and all-present. You are here because God knew it was time for us to be together once again. If only for you to know the truth of what happened and why I left. If only so you would know that I never stopped loving you."

Phoebe's confused expression only deepened. "If God truly controls everything, then why did He not keep you with me? Why didn't He keep Vater from . . . hurting you?"

"I don't know, Phoebe. This life is full of woes and pain. I don't understand it, and I may never know the whys and hows. God will have His mysteries, but I know He loves me even so."

"Well, I don't. He seems most unloving to allow events that would rob a child of her mother."

Elizabeth couldn't help but move toward her daughter. "Oh, Phoebe, He isn't that way at all. Man is sinful and will do sinful things."

Phoebe held up her hand. "I don't want to hear any more religious nonsense. I only came because I promised I would. There is still much I don't understand, but I want to. I have decided I will say nothing to Vater for the time. He is planning to leave tomorrow for several weeks."

"Truly?"

Phoebe nodded. "He's visiting a sapphire mine somewhere east of here."

"Sapphires, eh? Don't tell me he's on a buying trip for the duchess?"

Her daughter seemed surprised. "Ja. But how did . . ."

Elizabeth could see she wanted to ask about it. "He's been helping the duchess for decades, Phoebe." What she wouldn't tell her daughter was how her father had been cheating the woman for nearly as long.

"Well, he will be gone in the morning and won't return until the middle of July. I would like to take that time to know you better, and perhaps you would like to know me."

A smile broke across Elizabeth's face. "Of course I would. I would like that very much."

"But I won't lie for you," Phoebe added, and Elizabeth sobered. "If Vater asks me directly if I have seen you, I will admit I have. I don't imagine he will. I don't anticipate that he has any notion of your being here, but I won't lie."

"I understand, and I don't want you to lie. I couldn't bear it if your father took his anger out on you."

Phoebe's eyes narrowed. "What do you mean?"

Elizabeth wasn't exactly sure how to convey her thoughts. "I . . . well . . . I know your father has always doted on you, but you never gave him cause to do otherwise. You were always a most obedient child. However . . . if you go against him, he might be inclined to treat you as he did me."

7

This is the menu forwarded to you prior to our arrival. I'd like to go over it with you, if you don't mind."

The small man looked down his nose at Phoebe. "I am a chef for over thirty years, and I do not need for you to go over it with me."

"Nevertheless, I must," Phoebe told the irritated man. "I trust you received the ingredients and wines we sent to the hotel." He might be chef of the kitchen, but Phoebe knew what her father expected, and she was his envoy to make certain that nothing went wrong.

The man murmured curses in French.

She gave the chef a pleasant smile. She knew how to deal with difficult servants, especially men. "I have heard such wonderful things about your abilities in the kitchen. I must say what food I've had here has surpassed any I've had elsewhere in America."

The man's chest puffed out at this. He touched his index finger to his pencil-thin mustache. "But of course it has." His French accent reminded Phoebe that someone had mentioned his being in America only a short time.

She quickly switched to French. "Would you prefer we speak in your own language?"

His face lit up, and he beamed her a smile of pure delight. "It would be such a relief, *mademoiselle*."

"I know how difficult it can be, *monsieur*. I, too, am away from my home on the Rhine."

The man nodded with great enthusiasm. "You are French?"

"German." She saw the man stiffen.

"I was but a boy in Paris when your Bismarck marched his troops down our streets in a victory parade."

"It would seem our leaders have done many troubling things," she admitted, "but my heart is ever a part of France. You surely would not hold my birthplace against me." She smiled in a way that had won her many a heart.

The man considered her statement, then nodded. "I am so happy to hear my beloved tongue that I could weep. You speak it quite beautifully, so how could I hold anything against you?"

Phoebe knew it would be best to turn the conversation back to focus on the chef. "It must be so hard for you to be here in America. Especially isolated here in the West."

"I have been here for six months and desire nothing more than to return to France, but alas, I signed a contract and will endeavor to honor it."

Phoebe saw that he was relaxing and took advantage of it with unmerited praise. "You are such a good man. There are few as honorable as you."

The man nodded and gave a shrug. "You are so very kind to say so. A rare flower in a garden of weeds."

Phoebe smiled. She knew now she had made a conquest, and seeing to the menu would be no trouble at all.

"Come and sit here." The chef motioned and led her to a table in the farthest corner of the room. "Now tell me what you desire."

She unfolded a piece of paper. "As you see, Chef . . . goodness, but I do not know your name."

"You may call me Chef Michel." He leaned in to whisper. "But only you may call me by my given name. I allow no one else."

She gave a light laugh and touched her hand to her heart for effect. "You honor me, Chef Michel." She gave a little sigh to assure him of her contentment and then continued. "For our opening course, we would like citrus pickled oysters with English cucumbers and dill."

"You will want the oysters prepared in warm champagne, lime and lemon juice, *oui*?"

"Oui. Father would like that served with a fine Picpoul."

The man tilted his head to the left and gave a slight shrug. "But of course."

"The next course should be *potage à la tortue* paired with amontillado sherry. After that, *blini Demidoff*. I'm certain you will pair that with a fine champagne."

"Perhaps a Veuve Clicquot."

"Perfect." Phoebe looked to her list once again. "For the fourth course, grilled salmon."

"Oh, may I suggest *saumon avec sauce diplomate*. The sauce is a culinary delight of cream, brandy, lobster butter, and truffles. We have an excellent Riesling to accompany it."

"That sounds quite good. I will defer to you on that matter." Phoebe referenced her list. "After that, *selle d'agneau aux herbes* with *tomates farcies d'oeuf*." The lamb was one of her favorites, while the egg-stuffed tomato with herb mayonnaise was her father's. They had served this on many occasions back at home.

"After that course, we should like quail in puff-pastry shells with *foie gras* and truffle sauce. To be followed by an endive salad and Coteaux du Languedoc Saint-Christol Cuvée to drink."

She looked up and gave Chef Michel a coy smile. "And for dessert, *savarin au rhum avec des figues et des poires.*"

Chef Michel put both hands over his heart. The look of sheer ecstasy on his face told Phoebe that he wholeheartedly approved. She had to admit the rum sponge cake with figs and pears had been her own personal choice. Phoebe instructed him on the champagne she wanted and then told him to follow that up with the appropriate cheeses and fruits.

"And might I suggest ending the evening with coffee with Cognac Frapin—vintage 1888." He looked at her with a hopeful expression.

"Perfect. My father will be delighted, and the guests will have nothing to complain about." Phoebe looked over her list one final time, then pushed it across to the chef. "It's such a relief to know that a man of your capable skills will be in charge. I know with you arranging the menu, the party will be a complete success."

"Oui, mademoiselle. You leave it in my hands. We will have those barbaric American cowboys believing themselves whisked away to France."

Phoebe stood, and Chef Michel did as well. "*Merci*, Chef Michel. I am so pleased we could share this moment. I shall look forward all day to this marvelous feast."

"Should you desire anything at all that is not on the menu, you come to me." He lifted her hand and kissed it ever so lightly. "You have been a balm to my soul."

She left him then, smiling to herself at the way he had melted into complete agreement. It often took so little to get her way. A word here or a glance there and Phoebe found there was very little she couldn't accomplish.

Tonight's party was quite important to her father, and he counted on her to make things right while he tended to business elsewhere. Phoebe had hoped for more time, but her father insisted the dinner would have to be given that night, because Lord Putnam had already issued the invitations. Lord Putnam had also arranged the menu, but her father had quickly canceled that. He didn't trust Putnam to know what to serve. Instead, he put Phoebe in charge.

The city's wealthiest would be in attendance, along with some of the mining representatives. Her father told her that each of these men was important to the success of their trip. None of the details could be left to chance, which was why it was most critical to secure the tiniest of particulars regarding the meal. Beyond ensuring the setting and food, Phoebe was to be her charming self and act as hostess to the party—a role she had played on many occasions at home. A role her mother had once held.

The thought of her mother caused Phoebe's joy to diminish. At least a dozen questions whirled inside her head. Questions that wouldn't be answered easily. She needed most desperately to understand the past. The man her mother described was not entirely unknown to Phoebe, but she'd always presumed that her father's impatience and anger had been directed most generally toward those who deserved it. She presumed it was the same with the heads of all households. Perhaps she had been wrong.

She frowned as she wondered what Dieter might say if he were here. He had never held much interest in his sister, having things of far greater importance to keep him occupied. Not only that, but their father had never encouraged them to be close. Phoebe had tried once to speak to him about their mother, but Dieter had shut her up with a harsh reprimand that such talk would only serve to grieve their father.

What would Dieter think now?

"You seem tired, Miss Phoebe," Gerda said, putting the final touches on Phoebe's hair that evening.

"Ja, I must admit I am. I was unable to rest much this afternoon. My every thought has been about the party. Well, at least almost every one." She smiled at her reflection in the mirror. "You've done a beautiful job, Gerda." The maid had managed to pile curls upon curls atop her head in an artfully feminine display.

Phoebe got up from the dressing table while Gerda went to retrieve her two-piece gown. The evening dress was lavish and full in a delicate shade of powder blue with silver lace. The bodice was cut low with capped sleeves. Lace trimmed the neckline and sleeves, with tiny beaded designs added atop the delicate webs. Carefully placed beading splayed upward from the waist in a sunbeam effect on the pale-blue bodice. The bottom half, however, was the real star of this gown. Heavily embellished with beading and colorful embroidery, the lavish decoration made the gown quite heavy, and the small train that flared out behind only added to the weight. Phoebe had worn the gown in New York and several times back home, so she knew the challenge at hand. There was to be dancing, and in order to make it easier, she had chosen a simple flat shoe to ensure she wouldn't twist her ankle.

Gerda hooked the bodice to the skirt and then did up the back buttons while Phoebe arranged the bodice to drape properly. The mantel clock chimed the quarter hour, causing Phoebe to start.

"Goodness, the time has gotten away from me. Vater will expect me to join him in his suite, so we must hurry."

"Ja." Gerda came around to face Phoebe. "The buttons are

secured. Let me help you with your necklace." She reached over to the table and picked up a beautiful necklace of diamonds and sapphires. After Gerda secured the necklace, Phoebe added the matching earrings. The pieces had belonged to her mother, and it was one of the few sets of jewels Phoebe had inherited. Her others were all gifts from her father. He declared that the rest of her mother's jewels had been lost at sea when she died. But now, of course, that was clearly not true.

Phoebe pushed such thoughts aside, took up her gloves, and gave her hair one final check. She needed to be focused on the task at hand. "I must go." Phoebe drew a deep breath to steady her nerves. "You may feel free to enjoy the bath or perhaps go for a swim. I hear the waters at the natatorium are quite refreshing."

Gerda nodded. "Danke, gnädige Fräulein. I would like to try them."

Forgetting her resolve to speak in English, Phoebe replied absentmindedly in German. "One of these days, Gerda, I think I would like to as well." Thoughts of Ian Harper flashed through her mind as she wondered what he would think if he saw her now. Then she snapped back to the present. "But for the moment, I have a party to attend." Phoebe headed for the door to her room. "I hope to return by eleven."

"I will be waiting for you even earlier . . . just in case you tire."

Phoebe nodded. She knew her father would never accept such a silly excuse for leaving early. He loved to show her off like one of his prized horses. Phoebe had never given it much thought before now because she knew very well the games that were played in their society. Now, however, with the shadow of her mother's revelations hovering over her, Phoebe had no heart for such games. She needed answers to make sense of the past. Answers that would no doubt change her future.

She knocked lightly on her father's door and smiled when

the broad-shouldered Hubert opened it to admit her. Phoebe crossed the room to where her father sat sipping a drink, and she gave a slow turn. "So do you approve?"

Vater got to his feet and handed his drink to Hubert. He smiled ever so briefly. "You look lovely, as always. I've long thought that gown one of the most charming you own. You will have all of the men eating from your hand."

"I certainly hope not." She reached out to adjust her father's white bow tie. "You look quite dapper yourself."

"Perhaps I shall capture the attention of a rich widow, ja?"

The smile faded from Phoebe's face, causing her father to raise a brow. "You are worried that I might marry again?"

She wasn't at all sure what to say. Obviously he could not remarry. Not with her mother alive. "If you marry again, then I won't be able to hostess your parties."

"Well, that will come to an end anyway. You will marry soon and have a home of your own in which to hold parties."

Vater had been speaking more and more about her marrying. It wasn't a topic Phoebe found at all to her taste. Her father intended to arrange her marriage, as was most generally done among their class, but Phoebe hadn't cared for any of the men he was considering.

"But I have no desire to marry." She forced a smile. "And I know you would never force me to do something so undesirable."

He looked at her for a long moment, then shook his head. "Come, we will be late," her father said, offering her his arm. "There will be plenty of time to talk about this when I get back from the sapphire mine. I think you will be rather pleased at what I have come up with."

Phoebe said nothing more, hoping her father would just forget about the matter. As they walked through the hotel,

Phoebe found herself actually looking around as if she might espy her mother.

"Are you looking for someone?" her father asked.

She knew she would have to be more careful. "Always, Vater. You have taught me to be well apprised of my surroundings and to assess the people near me."

He looked down at her, never slowing his pace. "I'm glad to know you remember your training. Especially here, where danger might well lurk. People and places can be deceiving."

Phoebe looked away. "Ja. Indeed they can."

In the dining room a crowd had already gathered. Several dozen people milled around the open area of the dance floor while the orchestra played softly in the background. The women were beautifully gowned in an array of fashions that included some of the finest money could buy. Their jewels glittered in the soft light of the chandeliers. Meanwhile the men were resplendent in formal black coats and white ties.

Lord Putnam, her father's longtime friend and associate, came forward to make introductions. Phoebe smiled and received the well-wishes of the attendees. The women made effusive comments about her beauty and the richness of her gown, while the men conducted themselves in polite admiration.

"Graf Von Bergen, I would like to introduce you to that most talented lapidary I told you about. This is Mr. Ian Harper."

Phoebe's eyes widened as she recognized the man from the natatorium. He had traded his swimming costume for black tails and white bow tie. He smiled at her, then took hold of her father's hand. "It is an honor to meet you, Graf Von Bergen."

"The honor is mine. I have heard about your skills in faceting jewels. I think we might have cause to work together."

"So your associate mentioned. I should be happy to know more."

"This is my daughter, Fräulein Von Bergen." Vater looked to her. "This is Mr. Harper, whom we heard so much about."

"Miss Von Bergen." He bowed slightly.

"I am glad you could attend our party, Mr. Harper." She felt her heart skip a beat when he glanced up and gave her a wink. How bold that he should act in such a way! Phoebe turned to her father, hoping she wouldn't have to explain. Thankfully he was already speaking to someone else. She looked back to Ian Harper, who had straightened and watched her with a somewhat amused expression. Phoebe reined in her nervous reaction.

"The pleasure is all mine." His smile broadened. "I had rather hoped we'd see each other again." His blue eyes were dark and intense.

There were others to meet, and so Phoebe found herself quickly moved away from the handsome Mr. Harper. She couldn't help but glance around the room from time to time to see where he had gone. Generally he was caught up in conversation with two or three other gentlemen, but on occasion Phoebe found him being entertained by a beautiful woman or two. It surprised her to find herself wishing she might be among them.

"I don't believe we've met," a male voice sounded to her left. "Graf Von Bergen said that I should come and make your acquaintance."

Phoebe looked up and met the smile of yet another handsome stranger. She hadn't even realized her father had left her side, but she saw he was very much occupied in conversation.

"I am Ernst Eckhardt," the tall, blond-haired man announced. "And you are Fräulein Von Bergen."

"Ja." She immediately recognized the accent of her homeland. "You are German."

He smiled and whispered in German, "I am Prussian, but do not say as much. We are, after all, quite unified now, are we not?"

Phoebe laughed. "I suppose we are. What brings you here so far from home?"

"I had business in America and had heard about the Wild West. Cowboys and Indians. I wanted to see such sights for myself."

"I haven't seen any of the latter but did run across several of the cowboys. Dirty, smelly, and rather foulmouthed men. If one could call them men. They seemed hardly more than boys."

"Perhaps that is why they are called cowboys instead of cow-men." Ernst laughed and leaned closer. "What I want to know is whether they were wearing those big hats and shooting their six-guns."

Phoebe smiled. "I'm happy to say that while they were in possession of big hats, they seemed to be without any six-guns."

"So you were not able to see a shootout." He gave a *tsk*ing sound. He switched back to English. "Such a pity, for I have heard it can be most exciting."

"That is a type of excitement I can do without, I assure you." Phoebe heard dinner announced. "You must excuse me. I need to find my father."

"I would be happy to escort you to your place at the table," Eckhardt said, offering his arm.

Phoebe thought to refuse but then noted that her father was already at their table. "Very well. Danke."

The dinner went off as planned with each course more delicious than the last. Phoebe heard the overwhelming approval of the guests and saw her father's expression of great satisfaction. It was hard to imagine him acting in the heinous method her mother had described when he could be so very charming, as he was just now.

The orchestra had taken a slight break when the coffee and

brandy service had begun, but now they were back and striking up some glorious waltz music to encourage dancing.

"I do hope you would do me the honor of the first dance."

Phoebe looked up to find Ernst Eckhardt offering her his hand. She smiled. "I would be happy to dance with you." She adjusted her train, then allowed Eckhardt to sweep her into the circle of other dancers.

"Your party was quite successful, ja?"

"It would appear so." Phoebe caught sight of her father deep in conversation with several men. Apparently he was content with the situation, for he was laughing quite merrily.

"How long will you remain in America?"

Phoebe shook her head. "I have no way of knowing. Vater is on business, and I am only accompanying him for the pleasure of seeing the sights."

"Business in America must be taxing. There is so much distance to be covered from one place to another. It truly is a wild country out here in Montana. I myself will travel to San Francisco next."

"What a coincidence. We are planning to travel there as well, but not for any extended stay. We have booked passage on a ship that will take us first to Japan and then to Ceylon and India."

"So you are making a grand world tour. How wonderful!"

"I have enjoyed the trip thus far, I must admit." Phoebe smiled. "You are a superb dancer, sir. Perhaps the best partner I've had since arriving in America."

He chuckled. "I have trained in such arts since I was a young boy. My mutter insisted. She was always quite concerned with propriety."

The music ended, and Phoebe dropped her hold on Eckhardt. "Thank you for the dance."

"Perhaps we might share another yet tonight."

His tone sounded quite hopeful, and Phoebe didn't want to discourage him. "Perhaps. I would like that very much, but for now I must see to the other guests."

He led her from the dance floor, then paused, clicked his heels together, and bowed low. "Until later then."

Phoebe danced with numerous other men throughout the evening. Each seemed quite fascinated by her stories of life in Germany, especially as it pertained to her royal connections. Phoebe had come to find most Americans were quite fascinated by nobility. Perhaps because they had none of their own. In Europe every royal family was somehow connected, either through blood or marriage. It was like one great extended family with kings and queens, princes and princesses, and noblemen of every rank. And while Phoebe had never known anything else, she found that Americans were in awe of such things.

It was nearly ten when Phoebe finally had a chance to dance with Ian Harper. He had been occupied for most of the evening by her father and his cronies, but now he seemed to be completely devoted to her.

"I have watched you dance all evening, and I must say, I'm rather intimidated," he said, leading her onto the dance floor.

"But why should you be intimidated?"

He smiled. "I'm not much for dancing. I haven't had a lot of opportunity in my life."

"That is quite all right. If you'd rather not dance, I would be happy to just talk." She hoped she didn't sound too forward. There was something about this man that fascinated her. Since their first meeting she hadn't been able to put him from her mind, and with all that had happened since her arrival, Phoebe was grateful for the diversion.

"But if we stop dancing, you will be set upon by all of those other men who desire to dance." He took a slight misstep but quickly corrected his footing and kept Phoebe from looking awkward. "See? I told you."

Phoebe laughed, gazing into those wonderful blue eyes. "You are doing fine. So I gather that rather than spending your spare time dancing, you swim."

He gave a slight nod. "I love to swim, and the natatorium is a blessing to all who feel the same. Even when the hotel was closed for several years, the swimming continued. I tried to get over here as often as possible. But, as I recall, you do not swim."

"No, but it does sound like fun to at least wade in and enjoy the curative powers of the waters."

"Surely you aren't sick."

For a moment he held her gaze captive. Goodness, but he was handsome. Up until now she hadn't found American men all that appealing. They were much too rough around the edges, lacking the refinement that came with years of social placement. Even the poor in Europe knew their place, but here in America the classes crossed constantly. Those who were poor one day could find themselves among the socially elite the next. No one seemed to know their place, because those places could change at the drop of a hat. But Ian Harper was different. There was a soft gentleness to his expression. From his dark brows to his perfectly sized nose and rather pointed chin, he was most appealing.

"Are you sick?" he asked again with concern.

She started, realizing she had let her thoughts travel. "No. I'm quite healthy. In fact, I believe this Montana climate agrees with me."

"It's a wonderful place to live," he agreed. "I was born here."

"It's quite lovely."

"Have you had a chance to venture out and see much of the surrounding beauty?"

Phoebe couldn't take her gaze from him. There was something so enticing about the tiny laugh lines around his eyes—eyes that seemed to twinkle in delight as if he were privy to some wonderful amusement.

"I must say," she finally replied, "I haven't."

"We should remedy that. I would be happy to take you out riding. I cannot imagine anything more pleasant than to spend the day with a beautiful lady."

Phoebe felt herself flush. She lowered her face, uncertain as to what had come over her. She wasn't a shy wallflower unused to men's praise, but this man made her feel almost like a schoolgirl.

The music ended, and she dropped her hold rather quickly. She drew a deep breath and forced herself to look again to Ian Harper's face. "I believe I would very much enjoy riding out to see the area."

"Wonderful. I'll try to arrange something very soon. I'll send you word here at the hotel if that meets with your approval."

She nodded. "It does, Mr. Harper."

"Ian. You must call me Ian."

"Ian," she repeated. It was a very informal manner of address, but Phoebe thought it almost challenging. If not a little decadent. She smiled. "And you may call me Phoebe. Although perhaps not in my father's company."

He chuckled. "I understand. Phoebe is a rather unusual name. It's a Bible name."

"Yes, I suppose I do recall my mutter saying she chose that name from the Bible, but I'm not at all familiar with that. Phoebe is also a Titan goddess, but I'm certain that description doesn't fit me."

He chuckled. "I wouldn't know about Titan goddesses, but the Phoebe of the Bible was highly regarded as a woman of leadership and Christian charity. It's a beautiful name." His eyes looked directly into hers. "For a most beautiful lady."

Again Phoebe felt her emotions unravel a bit. The effect this man had on her was almost alarming. She'd never felt so aflutter.

"Thank you," she managed to say. To avoid embarrassing herself by showing her sudden case of nerves, Phoebe turned quickly and walked away to join her father.

8

*I*an returned home around eleven. He left the party after his dance with Phoebe, deciding that there was no better way to end the evening. Phoebe Von Bergen had captured his thoughts since that first encounter at the pool. He supposed it was because of his connection to Kenny and Elizabeth. But also because she was a strikingly beautiful woman who seemed displaced. There was something about her that spoke of sadness and tragedy, and now he knew why. However, one thought continued to run through his mind. Would realizing the truth cause further despair, or would it set her free?

"Jesus said the truth would set us free," Ian whispered, glancing upward at the night skies.

He supposed Phoebe's feelings were also a reflection of being away from her home and country. Ian couldn't imagine what it would be like to leave America for foreign soil. Here she knew only a handful of people, but back in Germany she no doubt had friends and even other family members with whom she could talk and spend her days. But being away from those people and her homeland paled in comparison to the growing intrigue between Phoebe and Elizabeth. And Graf Von Bergen.

"Lord," he whispered as he approached the back door of his home, "I need wisdom. If Elizabeth has come like I asked, then we'll have to iron out the details of what's to be done. This is a powder keg just waiting to be set off. I don't want her to suffer, and I certainly don't want Kenny to bear the brunt of a violent and overbearing father. Still, I can't help but feel it isn't right to get in the middle of this." He put his hand on the doorknob and drew a deep breath. "You gave Solomon wisdom. Please give me some as well."

He found his mother and Elizabeth in the living room, waiting for him with expressions that betrayed their worry. He knew that neither woman would expect or desire him to offer pleasantries. He hadn't looked forward to their discussion of what was to be done, but he knew it couldn't be postponed. He pushed a wing chair closer to where his mother and Elizabeth sat on the couch.

"I had a long talk with Phoebe," Elizabeth began. "She has read the letters and knows about her father's threats, not only to me, but to her."

"And what did she say?" Ian posed the question as he pulled off his bow tie.

"She agreed to say nothing to her father just yet."

"Would you mind if I were to make myself informal?"

"Please," Elizabeth said. "I wouldn't want you to be uncomfortable. After all, this is your home."

Ian nodded and cast off his tailed coat. "I heard that your husband intends to travel. I met and spoke with him. It seems he plans to visit some of the sapphire mines east of here." He paused, seeing the weariness in Elizabeth's eyes. For all these years she had carried the weight of the world on her shoulders, constantly in fear that the past might catch up with her.

"With him gone," Ian continued, "I thought it might buy you some time to talk to Pastor Clearwater."

"I have to admit we were just discussing that." Elizabeth looked to Georgia. "Ever since Kenny went to bed, we've done little else."

Ian's mother got up and walked to where her son had deposited the evening coat. Ian gave her a smile and loosened his collar. "Glad to be out of that coat. It was very warm and stiff. I can't say I enjoy formal evenings."

"Your father never cared much for them either." His mother had the offending coat in hand and was already moving across the room to drape it on the back of a chair. "I told Elizabeth about the things we discussed. She understands your misgivings about interfering in her marriage," his mother said from across the room.

"I'm glad." He looked at Elizabeth. "I don't want to see you in a position of abuse, but neither am I comfortable with helping you lie."

Elizabeth nodded and began to wring her hands. "If it were just me, I wouldn't care. I would show myself and let Frederick manage all of Phoebe's questions about the lies he told her and Dieter. But there's Kenny. I cannot allow him to be harmed. Frederick would be livid should he learn that I have his son with me. There would be absolutely no peace about it, and he would no doubt have the authorities involved."

"I understand, Elizabeth." Ian took a seat. "I clearly see the delicacy of the matter, but I don't know what to do about it. That's why I suggest you speak with the pastor. Perhaps you could arrange to meet your husband with witnesses and discuss the situation. Maybe the man has changed. Maybe he has regretted his actions of the past. Sometimes people do as they grow older. A change of heart and spirit is not impossible."

"Phoebe suggested the same thing, but I cannot gamble with Kenny's future that way. The boy is not yet ten, and you know yourself he has such a sweet nature. Frederick's anger and ugliness would destroy him."

Ian knew she was right when it came to the boy. Kenny was a generous and loving lad. He was tender toward wounded animals and kind to the elderly people at church. On more than one occasion he had spoken to Ian about the poor in Helena and what could be done to help them. There were deep thoughts in the heart of that child.

"But if your husband has had a change of heart, the boy would benefit by knowing his father."

Elizabeth shook her head. "I just don't believe him capable of change. Frederick despised God and perceived gentleness as weakness. He would have had to completely put aside all that he believed, and for Frederick there was never any reason to do so. My leaving didn't even matter." Tears formed in her eyes. "If he finds out about Kenny, he will take him from me. Even if he has to kill me."

Ian could hear the fear in her voice. He hated that she was so afraid—so distraught. "Let's not worry about it tonight. Your husband is leaving very early in the morning. I think you should get a good night's sleep. You and Kenny will both be safe here with us, and then we can work on this tomorrow."

"But Kenny will be awake tomorrow, and keeping him occupied will be difficult," Elizabeth protested. "I know I'm quite emotional about all of this. However, I'm truly strong enough to bear it. I will speak to Pastor Clearwater tomorrow as you suggested, but would you please just keep Kenny with you until I can figure out what is to be done? I can't have Phoebe knowing about him. Not just yet."

"Phoebe's already met him, if you'll recall."

"Yes, but he was with you. If she sees him again in your care, she won't think anything of it. If she finds him with me, however, she'll no doubt guess the truth." Elizabeth's expression was one of pleading, mixed with anguish. "Please just agree to this much."

Ian considered the matter for a moment. It surely wouldn't hurt anything to give Elizabeth time to sort through the various complications. It was summer and school was out, so Kenny could stay there at the Harper house and Ian could even pay him to work in the shop. Kenny would love that.

"All right, Elizabeth. Kenny can stay with me—with us." He looked at his mother, who was nodding. "I'll give him a job in the shop." He smiled and hoped his solution would put Elizabeth at ease. "He loves hanging out there anyway, so he might as well get paid."

"Thank you." She wiped at her tears with a well-worn handkerchief. "I know that God has an answer for all of this. I know it was never right to lie, but up until now it wasn't really a lie. Frederick knew I was alive. He just didn't know that I had given him another son."

"Omission of the truth can be just as deadly as a lie purposefully told." Ian tried not to sound harsh, but the past haunted him. "I . . . well . . . there are things in my past where the omission of the truth proved deadly."

"With your wife?"

The question was innocent enough, but Ian felt himself stiffen. "I don't know what my mother has told you, but yes."

"I've said very little, Ian." His mother joined Elizabeth on the couch. "I told Elizabeth it was your story to tell. She knows you were married many years ago and knows that there were difficulties."

"To say the least," Ian replied with a bittersweet smile. "My marriage was built on lies. Nora lied to her parents and ran off to marry me. She lied to me about them being happy to have us wed, and she lied about so much else. I suppose you can understand why deception is a particularly sore subject for me. Lies ruined my life and proved deadly."

Elizabeth nodded and put aside her handkerchief. "I do understand. You don't have to share the details of it with me. You are a very considerate young man. You have always treated me with kindness and respect. You've always been a big brother to Kenny, showing him how to do things and spending time with him. You have no idea what that means to me. I value your counsel, Ian. I know you are most uncomfortable with this, and I promise you I will seek out Pastor Clearwater and find a way to resolve this. Perhaps I could speak with a lawyer as well. Just in case."

"Just start with the pastor. Let's see what he has to say first. The rest can come in time."

⁕

Elizabeth crept into the room where her son slept. For a moment all she could do was pray. She sank onto the edge of the bed and closed her eyes.

Lord, help us. I don't know what to do. I want to do what is right in your eyes, but I am so afraid. Please give me answers and show me the way.

She opened her eyes to find her son looking at her. "Mama, is something bad going to happen?"

Elizabeth reached out and touched his cheek. "Now, why would you ask something like that?"

"You seemed really sad tonight and worried. It feels like something is going to happen. Something bad."

She forced a smile. "I'm sorry that I've made you uneasy. There are some things going on that worry me." Elizabeth decided to be as honest as she could for the moment. "Kenny, there are people from long ago who might want to hurt me and you. Bad people. That's why I sent you to stay with Ian."

"But I can protect you," he said, sitting up in bed. "I won't let anybody hurt you."

"I know you mean that, Kenny. But you need to understand that this situation is rather complicated. For now, I need you to trust me. Can you do that?"

"Sure. But what else can I do?" He looked so concerned, and Elizabeth wanted only to shelter him from the painful truth.

"Kenny, the one thing you can do for me is stay here a few days with Ian and Grandma Harper. That is the most important. I need to talk to some people about what to do, but first I must know that you are safe."

"But I want you to be safe too," Kenny protested.

Elizabeth nodded. "I will be. I promise you that. Right now, there is no danger. But, Kenny, it's really important that you don't let anyone know who you are. I know that's hard to understand. But because there are people who might want to hurt us, I need for you to pretend for just a few days that . . . that . . . you don't have a mother. Just pretend you live with Ian and Grandma Harper, and if anyone asks you about your mother, you can just tell them that she's not with you and they can draw their own conclusions. If they press you for details or ask if I've died, tell them you don't wish to discuss it."

Kenny jumped into her arms. "But I don't want you to die!"

She wrapped him in a tight hold. "I'm not going to die, but if we're to get through this, I need time to work things out. And because I need time, I also need for you to remain safe and unknown. Stay with Ian and let people think you're a part of his family. Grandma Harper and I will tell people at the hotel the same thing. They all seem to care about us, Kenny, so I think they'll remain silent until I know what to do." She pulled back and brushed his blond hair out of his eyes. "Kenny, it's really important. Can you do that for me?"

He pulled away but never took his gaze from her face. "You told me to never lie. That lying was a sin."

His words pierced her heart. "Yes, lying is a sin. I don't want you to lie. I just don't want you to give out any information—all right? If someone comes and asks you who your mother and father are—just don't answer them. Tell them you don't want to talk about it."

Kenny nodded, seeming to finally understand. "I'll stay quiet and let Ian do the talking."

"That would be perfect. And it's only for a short time. I plan to have it all figured out soon."

"And then we'll be safe again?"

Elizabeth nodded. "Yes. One way or another, we will be safe." She hugged him again, glad that he couldn't see the worry in her expression. Elizabeth had never been good at hiding her feelings, and she was certain that fear was clearly written on her face.

⁘

"Well, I'd say that went off quite well, save some problems with the wine." Frederick looked to his man Hubert and smiled. "I have made some very important connections, including ones with the governor and the mayor of Helena. There are some very wealthy men to be found in this town, and like most Americans, they are fascinated by European nobility and titles."

Hubert helped Frederick with his coat. "I am glad to hear that." He put the coat aside and returned to assist Frederick with his tie.

"I've even had a chance to rethink my initial thoughts on Mr. Thompson. The man may yet prove useful to me."

"Ja." Hubert pulled the tie and began to unfasten the collar and top buttons of his employer's shirt.

"We'll be leaving early tomorrow. I'll need you to make certain my clothes are packed. We'll be in the wilds, as I understand it. Quite primitive in accommodations and such. As I've said before, we'll need only the basics. Hopefully I'll be able to secure the number of sapphires I need and bring them back with me. After that we'll see about having them cut. I made the acquaintance of a skilled man who can facet the stones, but it remains to be seen whether or not we can agree upon a price and time schedule."

"Your packing has already been completed, gnädiger Herr. I saw to it earlier this evening."

"I knew I could count on you." Frederick stood stock-still as Hubert removed his suspenders. "I do hope we can shorten the trip, but I have committed to at least two weeks. They intend to show me the workings of the mine and introduce me to the officials in charge. We are supposed to be able to inspect the rough stones as well. But I don't see how that should take up all that much time. I suppose it shall all depend on the people there."

"Ja."

The evening had been filled with information and possibilities. The conversations had often taken him in the direction of investments and possible ways to make quick and easy money, but those things would have to be explored upon his return.

Overall, however, Frederick was more than pleased with the way things had turned out, and now he felt like celebrating.

As he slipped into the velvet robe Hubert held, he smiled with great satisfaction. "Go find Gerda. I want to instruct her about seeing after Phoebe."

Hubert again nodded. "I should imagine she and Fräulein Von Bergen have already prepared for bed."

"I'm sure you are right, but I need to speak with her, nevertheless." He frowned at the man. Over the years he had allowed Hubert great leeway in their relationship. "It isn't like you to question me. I hope you aren't developing bad habits. Now do as you're told."

"Ja." The valet took his leave and exited the bedroom.

Frederick heard him open and close the suite door. The man was generally compliant in all ways, but Frederick knew he disapproved of Gerda's place on this trip. She hadn't been a part of their household in Germany, and Hubert had his nose out of joint at her inclusion on the trip. However, she suited Frederick quite well. She was more than capable of seeing to Phoebe's needs, as well as his own.

Making his way into the sitting area of the suite, Frederick thought on the upcoming trip. Everything depended on his success at the sapphire mines. He went to pour himself a drink as Hubert and Gerda entered the room.

"Hubert, I believe we are done for the evening." He spoke in authoritative German. "You will need to see to your own packing and then get to bed. We'll need to be ready to depart the hotel at six."

"I will see to it that all is readied." He hesitated only a moment, then headed for the door to his bedchamber.

Frederick waited until the door was closed before turning to Gerda. "And what have you to report to me regarding Phoebe?"

Gerda smiled. "She has been most content. She takes long walks, and sometimes I accompany her. Other times she wants to be alone. She often reads for many hours, and we took the trolley to town, as you know."

"Good. Good. I'm glad to hear that she's found ways to amuse herself. Do you think she'll remain content while I'm gone? I wouldn't want her to become lonely."

"Given the attention she's received from the men here, I doubt she could ever be lonely."

He frowned. "Has anyone acted inappropriately toward her?"

"No. Not at all. Your daughter knows quite well how to put men in their place. She could freeze the heart of any offender with a simple glance."

Frederick chuckled. "I have seen her do so on many occasions." He tossed back his drink, then put the glass aside. "She will be under the care of a husband soon enough, and then such things will no longer be my concern."

"Have you heard from the duke, then?"

"I sent a telegram to let him know how to reach me. We are finalizing the financial agreement. He is going to post an announcement regarding the engagement and make all of the legal arrangements. I sent him a message to suggest that his sister take on the preparations for the civil wedding, and also that the church wedding date be set for the fifteenth of December."

"Do you think she will agree?"

"The duke's sister? I suppose she'll do whatever he asks of her."

Gerda shook her head. "*Nein.* I meant your daughter. Will she agree?"

"She will do as she's told. Phoebe has always been most

obedient, unlike her mother." He frowned and shook his head. "Never mind about that. I have no desire to focus further on Phoebe or the events of the evening. I have only a desire for you, my dear." He reached out and pulled her tight against him. "Come, let us celebrate my successes."

9

hoebe Von Bergen awoke the next morning with two things on her mind. One was her strange attraction to Ian Harper—she'd dreamed about him all night long. At least it seemed that way. The other was the need to speak with her mother. Before her father returned she intended to know everything possible about her mother's ten-year absence.

Stretching, Phoebe pushed back the covers and got to her feet. Light filtered in around the edges of the drapes, teasing Phoebe with the promise of a beautiful day. She crossed to the window and pulled back the drapes just as Gerda entered the room.

"I heard you moving about," the maid told her. She came and assisted Phoebe in tying back the beautiful silk-velvet panels. When that was accomplished Gerda pulled something out of her pocket and extended it. "Your father left this money for you before leaving this morning." She handed Phoebe an envelope. A yawn escaped Gerda.

"You look so tired. Didn't you sleep well last night?" Phoebe looked inside the envelope. There was a generous amount of money for her to spend as she desired. Her father was always most generous with her. But even as that thought came to mind, she couldn't ward off the comments her mother had made about his violence.

"I slept well enough." Gerda went to the wardrobe. "What would you like to wear today?"

Phoebe put the money aside. "I plan to spend a very quiet day reading and resting. I believe I'll dress quite simply. The white sprigged gown will suit me just fine." The lightweight cotton and muslin was very comfortable, and the skirt of the gown was quite full, where so many of her newer fashions weren't.

She let Gerda help her dress and then style her hair in an upswept but simple fashion. Satisfied, Phoebe went to where various pairs of shoes awaited her choice. She picked a pair of well-worn ivory boots. Phoebe sat while Gerda came with the hook and began to secure the buttons. She yawned again but attempted to keep it from her mistress.

Phoebe couldn't help but worry about her maid. "I plan to do nothing more exciting than have breakfast in the dining room and then read. Why don't you take the rest of the day off? Get some rest, then maybe go swimming. They say the waters will cure most any ill."

The dark-haired woman smiled at this suggestion. "Danke. I am quite tired. I believe it would do me much good."

Phoebe smiled. Gerda had been most considerate on this trip, and it seemed only fair to reward her. "While Vater's gone I don't think I need to worry about formal dressing and such. We both might as well enjoy the time. In fact, this evening I'll order my meal brought here, and that way neither of us need concern ourselves with my evening attire."

"You are a kindhearted woman, meine gnädige Fräulein. Your father is no doubt very proud of the young woman you've become."

The maid's words should have pleased Phoebe, but instead they only served to remind her of her mother. Was Mutter proud of the woman she'd become?

"Well, I know what it is to be weary."

"Your kindness serves you well. You will make a wonderful wife."

Phoebe frowned. Had her father said something to Gerda about his plans? She wanted to ask but, on the other hand, had no desire to delay her departure.

"If you'll excuse me, I'm going to make my way to the dining room. I want very much to thank Chef Michel for the exquisite meal he prepared last night. The guests were quite impressed." Phoebe headed for the door, taking with her a wide-brimmed straw hat. "After that I intend to walk about the grounds."

The halls were void of people, much to Phoebe's surprise. Perhaps many of the guests had left for other venues. She spotted a couple of the hotel maids and again thought of her mother. What had possessed a woman of means and social standing to leave her husband and children to take on manual labor in America? Her mother's stories must be true. She had, after all, quite openly shared the letters she'd written, as well as the one Phoebe's father had sent. But even so, Phoebe could still not quite accept that her father was the brute her mother claimed him to be. How could she have lived with him all these years and not been a victim of his rage?

Of course, there were those times when she had heard him rail at Dieter, and other times when he'd been most grieved with peers. But, after all, weren't all men given to those type of rages?

The dining room was completely empty by the time Phoebe entered. She hoped it wasn't too late for breakfast. She had slept quite late.

"Table for one, Miss Von Bergen?" a waiter asked.

Phoebe nodded and followed him to a table by one of the windows. From this vantage point she could look out on some of the beautifully manicured lawns. The waiter helped her with her chair, then handed her a menu.

"I'll have two poached eggs and toast," she said, handing him back the paper. "And tea please."

The man gave a slight bow and started to leave, but Phoebe called him back. "Would Chef Michel be in the kitchen?"

"I haven't yet seen him," the waiter replied.

"Well, when he does come, would you ask him to come see me?"

The man nodded and headed out of the dining room. In less than a minute he returned with a tray containing a teapot, sugar, and cream, as well as a plate with lemon slices. He placed the various pieces on the table, then poured tea into Phoebe's cup. "Would you like anything else?"

Phoebe shook her head. "This is fine." He nodded and placed the teapot on the table before exiting once again.

She glanced around the quiet dining room. It was the largest of the three and the place where she had taken all of her meals, except for last night. The tables were set with damask tablecloths, napkins, crystal, and silver, giving the room a refined appearance. The floors were highly polished, as were the tables and chairs. Only the strangely patterned curtains at the windows seemed out of place. Someone had mentioned they were from Mexico, and while they were colorful, Phoebe thought them garish.

She turned her attention to the scene outside the window and sipped her tea. The place seemed deserted. She had heard from some of the guests the night before that the hotel had been a terrible failure from the beginning. When Mr. Broadwater had built it, he'd been certain it would attract the crowned heads of

Europe. Sadly, however, the journey to get there was so arduous that few seemed inclined to endure it just to reach a large indoor swimming pool and isolated cottage hotel. Mr. Broadwater had died in the early nineties, and then his nephew had taken over the resort, only to close it a few years later. Now someone was once again attempting to breathe new life into it.

The waiter brought her breakfast, checked to make certain her tea was still hot, and then departed. He said nothing about Chef Michel, and Phoebe decided that perhaps the man had taken the morning off in light of having worked quite late on the party. It didn't matter. She would catch him at another time. But even as she settled on this thought, Chef Michel appeared. He looked most distraught.

"May I ask if your father is with you?" He spoke in rapid French.

Phoebe shook her head. "No, he has gone from the hotel and won't return for at least two weeks." She smiled. "Did you need to speak to him?"

"No." Chef Michel shook his head. "I have no desire to encounter that man ever again." He pursed his lips as if to force back other words he might have said.

"Whatever happened between the two of you?" Phoebe asked. She motioned to one of the chairs. "Please sit and tell me everything."

The man looked most uncomfortable. "No. Forgive me for my comment."

"Chef Michel, I asked for you in order to thank you for the wonderful food you created for us. The guests were quite impressed and did not stop talking about it throughout the evening. Won't you please sit for just a moment and talk about it with me?"

He squared his shoulders. "For you, mademoiselle. But only

you." He pulled out one of the beautiful wood chairs and sank onto it. He seemed weighed down—almost in despair.

"Now, tell me what happened to cause you such unhappiness. Did someone complain about something?"

"Your father was the one who complained. He was most unhappy with one of the wine choices and sought me out to voice his dissatisfaction. I defended the choice and told him it was exactly as you had requested. He told me I was being insolent. I protested, telling him that I had followed your instructions and had done a remarkable job, given the short notice. He was quite angry and he . . ." His words trailed off as he looked out the window. "He slapped me. Not once, but twice."

Phoebe gasped. "He didn't!"

"I assure you, mademoiselle, he did. When I spoke, he cursed at me and told me to be silent—that he would not be dealt with in such a rude manner by a servant. A servant! He called me a servant! Of course I protested, and he struck me once more."

Thoughts of her mother's description of Vater's violent nature flooded Phoebe's mind. Along with this came other thoughts. Memories of times her father's temper had gotten the best of him. Too many memories. How could she have ignored them? Phoebe frowned.

"Chef Michel, I am so sorry. I apologize for my father's behavior. He has been under a great deal of pressure."

"I turned in my resignation. I told the manager I could not honor our agreement under the present circumstances. Americans are rude enough, but I cannot bear such treatment from noblemen who were raised to be better."

"But you needn't resign. Father will be gone for two weeks, and when he returns we will be able to go on our way."

The chef shook his head and touched his hand to his neckerchief. "I must. I am a man of my word, but I cannot honor my contract and endure this place any longer. You helped me to see that. I long for my homeland. The people there are refined and understand proper behavior and manners. I have been too long in this country. I will return to France and perhaps open a place of my own. It is time that I relax and enjoy my life."

Phoebe heard the determination in his voice. "I am sorry that my father brought all of that to a head for you. Obviously his behavior was uncalled for."

The man smiled. "You are a gracious and beautiful young woman. I was honored to work with you."

"The guests were delighted by all of your creations. I didn't lie when I said they spoke about it all throughout the evening." She reached out and touched his hand. "Chef Michel, you did a magnificent job, and despite my father's comments and despicable behavior toward you, everything was perfect."

He got to his feet and gave her a slight bow and smiled. "But of course it was perfect. I do nothing less."

Phoebe was glad to see him back to his proud and confident self. She laughed and rose. "I very much hope we will see each other again. If not here, then perhaps in France."

She picked up her straw hat. "Thank you again." She exited the dining room without further ado, finding her thoughts jumbled and confused. How could her father have made such a scene? There was no need. If he didn't like her choice of wine, all he needed to do was replace it. She knew he would find it offensive to have an employee of the hotel challenge him, but to strike the man was completely uncalled for. It was one thing to handle personal servants in such a manner—or was it?

Outside, the brilliant Montana sun made Phoebe glad for her hat. She put it on and secured the ties just as the breeze picked up and threatened to pull it from her head. She held on to the brim with one hand and her skirts with the other as she made her way down the porch steps.

"I must think this out or go mad." She drew a deep breath and headed down one of the garden paths that would take her in the direction of her mother's cottage.

Mutter had challenged her to think back on events where her father had lost his temper. She had commented that Dieter would have experienced more than a few examples of their father's violent behavior. Phoebe had recalled many times when she'd heard her father berate her brother. The arguments were usually behind closed doors but were always very noisy.

"How have I lived this long and not acknowledged my vater's temper? Could it be that he was truly as violent as Mutter suggested, and I chose to look the other way?"

But even as she posed the question, Phoebe began to remember additional examples of her father's anger. She had once seen him raise his crop to one of the stableboys. He had struck the boy with such force that it had left a cut on his cheek.

"Servants must be taught respect and obedience." Her father had told her this on more than one occasion. He was quite clear on how much he expected, and many a worker had been let go because of substandard results. Phoebe bit her lower lip and paused in her walk. She didn't like the way things were shaping up. And, of course, there was the fact that her father had lied to her and to Dieter. Not only lied, but threatened her mother's life if she were to even try to reveal his deceit.

"And he said he'd rather see me dead than with my mutter." Would he have truly ended her life if Phoebe had found out about her mother being alive?

That alone was reason enough to be angry and hurt. Phoebe had been so devastated after her mother's disappearance. She had mourned the loss of her mother with such a broken heart that she desired death. Mutter had been most important in her life. She had been a friend, and Phoebe hadn't had very many of those.

She had always felt that her father understood. That his own heartbreak caused him to send her away. Now it seemed that perhaps the reason he'd sent her off to Switzerland was to conceal his true feelings and to hide her away.

"How could you have done that to me?"

She looked out across the lawn as tears blurred her vision. She felt so betrayed. Nothing was as she had thought it to be. Nothing. Her pampered and spoiled existence was nothing more than a veil to hide the truth.

Her mother's cottage was only a few hundred yards away, and so Phoebe moved on. She needed to talk this out. She needed to know more about the man her father had been then, and try to figure out exactly who he was now. It was surely possible he could have changed. But Chef Michel's declaration came back to haunt her. If her father had changed, then how could he possibly be given over to striking a man he hardly knew? And all because the wine was not to his liking.

Phoebe knocked on her mother's door. When no one answered she felt at a loss as to what to do. She looked around for a few moments, then decided to walk on. She would walk around the lake and try to enjoy the beautiful day. After an hour or so, Phoebe tired of the outdoors and her despairing thoughts. She headed back to her mother's cottage. It remained empty. There was no sense in waiting around. Her mother was obviously not home, and who could say when she might return? Without further thought, Phoebe headed to the hotel. All she wanted was to rest and put thoughts of her parents aside. She had no way to reason through the issues without speaking to them, and neither was available.

She was halfway across the lobby when the hotel manager called her name. "Miss Von Bergen!"

Phoebe paused and waited as the man dashed out to where she stood. "I have a telegram for your father. I realize he departed this morning and thought perhaps you would like to take it. It might be important, and I wouldn't want to cause harm by delaying the delivery."

Phoebe took the envelope. She had no idea of anyone, save Dieter, knowing their whereabouts. Perhaps something was wrong at home, and Dieter had telegrammed to let Vater know.

"Thank you. I'll be certain to read it."

The man nodded and hurried back to the office. Phoebe opened the envelope and pulled out the telegram.

```
Your daughter's dowry is acceptable. Plans for the
betrothal are under way, as well as the wedding. The civil
union will take place on the thirteenth of December. The
church ceremony to follow on the fifteenth as agreed upon.
```

The name of the duke was one she recognized. The man was her father's age and had been married before. His wife and unborn child had passed away the year before, and the two sons she had given him had died years before that. The duke was in much need of a son and no doubt felt that Phoebe could give him that prize.

Phoebe stood in stunned silence just looking at the piece of paper and trying to make sense of it all. Her father had told her many times on the trip that he would soon arrange a marriage for her, but that he would seek a husband whom she could approve. The duke was not someone she wished to wed. He was old and not at all handsome. Not only that, but he smelled bad and had a horrible reputation of womanizing.

How could Vater go behind her back like this? He had promised to consult her. He had spoken on many occasions about the men who were available and met his approval. He had agreed they would meet each one and allow Phoebe time to get to know them.

Phoebe shuddered, carefully folded the telegram, and slipped it back in the envelope. This entire trip had turned into such madness that she was actually beginning to question her sanity. She looked around the hotel lobby and found, thankfully, that she was alone. She didn't want to have to interact with anyone. Not given this news.

With a pretense of confidence, Phoebe made her way up the beautifully polished oak stairs. She had no idea what she should do, but one thing was quite certain. Her father had betrayed her trust in more than one way. It only caused her to wonder what else he had lied about.

10

"But it's Friday, Ian. Couldn't we go to the hotel and go swimming? Or maybe fishing?"

Ian looked at Kenny's hopeful face. He had been cooped up in the shop all week, and the afternoon beckoned with promises of diversion. Elizabeth had been quite busy talking with the pastor and a lawyer. Her concerns were many, and while she had returned to the hotel in hopes of speaking with Phoebe, Kenny remained with the Harpers.

"I suppose we might find something to do," Ian said, putting aside an empty dop stick. He had to admit he was just as anxious to get outside. He had promised to take Phoebe Von Bergen riding, but the week hadn't allowed for him to do so. His mother had been helping Elizabeth as well as working in the bakery at the hotel, so keeping Kenny was his responsibility. Of course, he could take Kenny along. The boy's father was supposed to be gone for two weeks, so there was no risk of him seeing the child. The staff at the resort all knew Kenny was Elizabeth's son, but just to be on the safe side, Ian was certain they could avoid the staff too.

"You remember what your mama told you about keeping away from other people?" He untied his apron.

"I'm keeping my name and who I am a secret," Kenny replied. "I don't have to lie, but I'm just not supposed to talk about it."

Ian nodded and hung his apron on a nearby hook. "The people at the hotel know who you are, but we still need to avoid them so they won't accidentally say something that would cause your mother—or you—any problems."

An idea ran through his mind as Ian put away his tools. In spite of Elizabeth's desire to keep Kenny hidden, perhaps it would be good for Kenny and Phoebe to spend some time together. They would be able to get to know each other, and maybe that would help when the truth finally came out. Ian could get to know her better as well. Of course, there were dangers. Phoebe could pry and press to know who Kenny was, and that could cause problems. With a little maneuvering, however, Ian felt certain he could keep Phoebe from asking too many questions.

"We can send an invitation to our new friend Miss Phoebe and invite her to go riding with us. I'll borrow some horses from one of my friends. Do you think you'd like that?"

Kenny's face lit up. "Yes! I like Miss Phoebe. She is so nice, and you can teach her to swim."

Ian laughed. "Well, she would have to want to learn, and so far I've not heard her express that desire. Besides, it might be best if we avoid the pool for a time."

"But you said everybody needed to know how to swim." Kenny took off the apron Ian had cut down to size for him. He hung it on the hook beside Ian's. "I think Miss Phoebe wants to learn. I'll ask her when we see her. That way, when Mama figures everything out, we can go swimming again and teach Miss Phoebe."

"All right, but just remember, if Miss Phoebe asks questions about your mother, say nothing."

"I know." Kenny nodded and let go a sigh. "I'm supposed to say she's not with me, and that way it will sound like she died." The boy frowned. "But I don't have to lie," he reiterated once again.

"Right," Ian agreed. "No lies. That would not be pleasing to God." He felt a momentary sense of concern. Phoebe might very well ask questions about Kenny and his family, and Ian was determined to tell no falsehoods. Maybe this wasn't a good idea. But before he could suggest otherwise, Kenny was already out the door.

Ian decided the long walk to borrow the horses would do them both good. He hoped it would give Kenny some much-needed exercise, as well as an opportunity to talk all he wanted. Maybe if he chattered all the way to the resort, he'd be talked out by the time they got there. Of course, Ian had never known the boy to run out of things to say.

As they walked, Ian listened to Kenny talk about the various houses they passed. The boy had quite a love of architecture, and Ian had given him a book on various house styles the previous Christmas. It was hardly more than a collection of drawings pointing out the details for each specific style, but Kenny had very much enjoyed it.

Kenny pointed to one house. "I like the way the roof looks when it has a cross gable. And I like the way they put the verge-boards on the gables to decorate them. Don't you?"

Ian studied the house for a moment. "I do like that. It makes the house look like something out of a storybook. Don't you think?"

Kenny cocked his head to one side and looked again at the house. After a moment he nodded. "Especially the way they've painted it. Mama said that where she grew up, there were a lot of houses that had beautiful trim. She said it made the houses look so cheerful."

"I can well imagine."

"She said someday we're going to make a trip to England. That's where she grew up."

Ian nodded. "That would be fun and very educational."

They continued their walk, with Kenny talking about various houses. Ian marveled at the things the boy knew. Perhaps one day he would be an architect, even though he thought for the moment he wanted to be a lapidary. When they finally reached their destination, Ian paused.

"This place belongs to some friends of mine," he told Kenny. "They raise and rent out horses. They don't know you, but they know me, so I will just tell them you are a good friend of mine—because you are." He ruffled the boy's blond hair.

"And I won't say anything," Kenny replied in a most sober tone. "Not one word."

⁂

"We call these weathering piles," a man explained to Frederick Von Bergen. "The rock and clay are dug up and then piled here. In a matter of months it will deteriorate and the clay will become crumbly. After this the soil can be processed and the sapphires retrieved."

Frederick noted a man loading up dirt in a mule-drawn ore cart. "I notice that your equipment is still primitive here. I heard that over at the American mine they are modernizing with steam and pneumatic drills, as well as electrified hauling and lights. Why is it this mine continues in such a state?"

The man nodded. "We prefer it this way. The men we've hired understand it, and it makes us a better profit."

"And these men who work the mines—how much do you pay them?" Frederick pulled a handkerchief from his pocket and dabbed his neck. The day was quite warm.

"They are paid a standard wage of three dollars per day. Most are experienced in some form of mining. You must understand that across this state alone there are opportunities for the mining of gold, silver, copper, and much more. Almost every young Montana man has tried his hand at some form of mining."

"And how is it you keep the men from robbing you blind?" Frederick took off his hat and wiped his forehead. The breeze felt good against his balding head. "It would obviously be easy enough to slip stones into their pockets."

"That has always been of great concern. Charles Gadsden, our mining supervisor, whom you will meet tomorrow, has battled that issue successfully. He realizes that it is human nature to desire wealth, and the sapphires are clearly quite valuable. The men believe it a right, of sorts, to take the occasional stone. However, Gadsden oversees all of the sluice cleanup, which takes place four times a day. He also makes the men empty their pockets at the end of the day. It's all very carefully watched, and the men know what is expected."

"Speaking of men, I haven't seen many workers."

The man looked momentarily uncomfortable. "Right now we are not processing stone as much as we have in previous years."

"And why is that?" Frederick had already heard some talk about the local farmers filing suit against the mine and wanted to know more. He glanced at Lord Putnam, still rather angry that the man had told him nothing about the legal troubles. Putnam didn't seem to notice.

"In looking over the entire mining operation, you must realize that for every ton of rock processed, we retrieve only a few carats of sapphires. Therefore, once the dike rock is processed, we are left with a massive amount of tailings, or slums, as it is often called. These slums must be disposed of, and for a long time they were simply deposited at the east end of the mine. The waste water from the sluices washed down through this area and took much of the slums into the river. That in turn caused problems downstream as the irrigation ditches began to fill with the slums. The farmers are afraid it will ruin their ditches and harm their crops. Not only that, but the ranchers fear the effects on their livestock."

"And so they've filed suit against the mine?"

The man nodded. "I see you have heard at least in part what has happened. The Fergus County Court granted an injunction last year and put a stop to the dumping. However, our manager, Mr. Gadsden, realized that rather than fight in the courts, he would prove the situation to be no threat. In fact, he hoped to prove just the opposite. Mr. Gadsden arranged to purchase a nearby ranch—some five hundred sixty acres. It adjoins the mining land on the east. He had the fields planted earlier this spring in oats, alfalfa, and various vegetables. Next he created a shifting trap to remove larger tailing pieces. Then he ordered the remaining finer slums to be applied to the planted fields. You see, he and his wife have gardens in which the slums are spread, and the growth of their vegetables has been quite successful for several years. I'll be happy to show you the fields, and you will see for yourself that the crops being grown there are doing quite well. He also has livestock grazing in other areas, and they too are doing very well. He intends to have the court send witnesses to see for themselves that the slums are quite beneficial."

"But until then, you are not able to operate at any real capacity." Frederick hadn't known this until their arrival. The situation infuriated him, and he let Lord Putnam know his feelings in no uncertain terms.

"We are continuing to work with fewer men," the man explained. "Mr. Gadsden has solved the issue of the tailings, and it's just a matter of time until the courts see the truth for themselves. Meanwhile, we are doing what we can and believe we will soon be operating at full capacity."

"Yes, but that may be of no use to me. I need stones now. Perhaps I should speak to the Americans regarding their operations."

Lord Putnam stepped forward at this point. "I assured Graf Von Bergen that we would still be able to meet his needs. The owners in England assured me that Mr. Gadsden would cooperate."

"Of course." The man glanced over each shoulder before lowering his voice. "We are not quite so idle here as you might imagine."

Frederick smiled. "Good. I'm glad to hear it. I would hate for my trip to have been a waste of effort." He made a mental note to send a message to Mr. Thompson. He wasn't about to wait until he knew the full extent of the situation with the English. Wherever he procured them, he needed to know the stones could be had and that he would be able to have them at a very low price.

***

"Why, Ian, I must say I'm surprised to see you," Phoebe said as she descended the hotel stairs. "When I received your invitation to ride, I was just planning to take a walk down to the lake."

"Kenny's watering the horses at the lake as we speak." Ian turned his hat in his hands. "He's waiting there and is quite anxious that you should join us."

"It sounds wonderful. I appreciate that you waited for me

to change my clothes." Phoebe now wore an American-style riding costume complete with split skirt. She had already been told that sidesaddles were unavailable at the hotel, and while she had tried riding astride on a few other occasions, she had never had the proper outfit to make it much of a success.

"You look quite lovely," Ian commented.

"Thank you. I spied this outfit when I was in town with my maid. Knowing Vater would be busy, I had thought riding would be a wonderful way to occupy my time. The management informed me, however, that they don't have any sidesaddles. So I decided it would be best to Americanize my wardrobe."

Ian smiled. "American styles suit you quite well. Although I will say, there are women here in the West who don trousers for such outings. Personally I wouldn't recommend that style. It's far too . . . well . . . revealing." He momentarily looked away as if embarrassed.

"Well, if you're ready . . ." Ian offered her his arm, and Phoebe put her gloved hand lightly atop it. They made the leisurely stroll down to the lake, where Kenny awaited them with three saddled horses.

"Miss Phoebe!" He waved as they approached. "Look at our horses. Aren't they great?"

"They look quite fine. Thank you for inviting me to join you on this ride."

"You're welcome. It was Ian's idea, but I thought it was a real good one." He handed all but one of the sets of reins to Ian. "This red one is the one I'm riding," Kenny told her. "She's an old mare that's real gentle. That way I can ride by myself."

Phoebe smiled. "It's always nice to have a gentle mount."

"Yours is easy-natured as well," Ian told her as he assisted her into the saddle. "I had no idea of your capability. The stable hand assured me he has a most obedient nature."

Phoebe patted the neck of the beautiful dapple-gray. "He's lovely. I am quite an accomplished rider, but since I'm unfamiliar with the territory, a compliant horse seems wise." She glanced at the black Ian had chosen for himself. "Your mount is quite handsome."

"This gelding and I are good friends," Ian admitted. He handed Phoebe her reins, then assisted Kenny onto the back of his horse. Finally, he climbed atop his own mount and smiled. "He knows better than to act up."

Ian headed the horses away from the lake and down a small dirt road. Phoebe took in the scenery of rolling hills and distant mountains and smiled at the scent of honeysuckle in the air. Kenny chattered on about a dozen different things. The boy seemed quite intelligent and knew a great deal about the surroundings.

Phoebe tried to keep her mind on the things Ian told her about the area. Even so, she found herself constantly wondering about her mother. She hadn't returned to the cottage all week, and Phoebe feared something might have happened to her. She had wanted to ask the hotel manager of her whereabouts but decided it was too risky. Should he say something later to her father, then Phoebe would have to explain, and that might cause problems. And given her father's telegram, there would already be problems enough.

"So have you enjoyed your week of leisure?" Ian asked.

Phoebe glanced at him and nodded. "I have. I find this state agrees with me. I like the dry climate and the brilliance of the sun. However, I must admit I am getting a little bored. I have read all of the books I brought with me and have started those that the hotel offers. I've never been one for fancy needlework, and I have no artistic talents, so my choices are limited."

"We need to teach her how to fish," Ian told Kenny.

The boy nodded enthusiastically. "And swim."

"That's right. We still have that possibility," Ian offered.

Phoebe met his gaze and felt her heart skip a beat. He hadn't shaved, and the stubbly growth of facial hair gave him a daring and untamed look. Her father would call him a barbarian, but Phoebe thought him the handsomest man she'd ever met.

"I have to admit the water frightens me." She tore her gaze from Ian and looked at Kenny with a smile. "I suppose that's because I've not had much experience with it. We live close to the river, but my dealings with it have been few."

"Everybody should learn how to swim," Ian interjected. "You never know when it might come in handy, especially living by a river. Besides, it's just plain fun and is becoming the national pastime."

"Well, I suppose, given I am in the perfect place to learn, I shall have to oblige Kenny and come watch to see how it's done."

"Watch? No. We'll get you out there participating," Ian said, laughing. "There's nothing like experience to teach a person quickly."

They rode for another half hour before Ian headed them back to the small lake behind the hotel. They dismounted, and Kenny all but danced in circles waiting for Ian to untie the bag that held their treats. Ian tossed Kenny a blanket to spread on the ground.

"We don't want Miss Phoebe's pretty riding clothes to get grass-stained," he told the boy.

Phoebe felt her cheeks flush at the comment. So Ian thought her outfit pretty. The idea pleased her greatly.

"Where do you want to sit, Miss Phoebe?" Kenny asked, wrestling the blanket.

"I'm happy to sit wherever you think we should."

Kenny nodded. There weren't too many trees surrounding

the lake, but a large cottonwood was nearby, and it was under the spread of its leafy branches that he chose to place their blanket. Phoebe thought it quite perfect.

In fact, everything was perfect, and she found herself hoping the day would go on and on, even though the sun was moving ever to the west. Kenny made her laugh with his antics as he described his entanglement while trying to climb a tree. Phoebe found the boy most amusing. He seemed always happy—so positively delighted with the world and everything in it. When they finally settled onto the blanket with the food, Phoebe thought she too was happier than she'd been in some time. She credited the company and the fact that Ian had been able to take her mind off her worried thoughts.

"You seem to have enjoyed yourself," Ian commented. "Perhaps you would be interested in another outing with us."

"Of course." Phoebe tried not to sound too excited. It would be most embarrassing if the handsome and broad-shouldered Mr. Harper thought her overenthusiastic—even if that was the way she felt. "As I said, I've been quite bored. What did you have in mind?"

"Fourth of July is next week."

Phoebe nodded. "I realize that."

He chuckled. "I'm sorry. I forget that you are probably not all that familiar with why that date is special to us." He looked at Kenny. "Do you want to tell Miss Phoebe why we celebrate the Fourth of July?"

Kenny jumped up on his knees. "That's our independence day. We fought the British and won our freedom to be a new nation."

Phoebe nodded, suddenly remembering that she had heard about the significance of that day while in New York. "Of course. How silly of me to have forgotten."

"Well, in Helena," Ian continued, "there will be a big celebration. Parades and games, food and rodeos. I wondered if maybe you would like to accompany me, and Kenny, of course, and spend the day celebrating."

Kenny nodded. "You can celebrate even if you aren't American."

Phoebe laughed. "It sounds marvelous. I heard some cowboys speak of rodeos when I was on the train. I wondered at the time if I should have the chance to see one. I would love to join you."

They continued discussing their plans for that day, but Phoebe's mind was already on what she would wear and how marvelous it would be to spend the day in Ian's company.

After they'd enjoyed the snack packed for them by Ian's mother, Kenny decided to explore. While he sought adventure on the far side of the lake, Ian stretched out in the sun.

"I hope we haven't kept you from anything important," Ian said. "I realize this wasn't much of a supper, but I'm certain you can get a tray sent to your room if you're still hungry later on."

"I'm fine." Phoebe couldn't help but notice the deep blue of his eyes. She found that she wanted to know everything about him. "Tell me about your family. I know your mother works here and that you are a lapidary, but little else."

"My father is dead. My older brother too. We were all in the lapidary business. Father had a real talent for cutting stones of every kind, as did his father before him. He came from Holland to this country when he was a young man. He worked for a time in Chicago, but then he met my mother while she was visiting relatives. One thing led to another, and when he learned she was from Montana, he decided to move west."

Ian put his hands behind his head. "They married soon after, and Father set up business here in Helena. For a time we not only had the jewelry shop but sold other things as well. After my father and Edgar died, however, it was too much to run by myself—even with my mother's help. I made the decision to sell the store inventory and moved the lapidary shop and jewelry to a little house next door to my mother's house. I don't sell as much jewelry as we used to, but I'm happy with the business.

"Besides all of that, I have three sisters who married and moved to various locations. They now have a bevy of children, and my mother likes to travel from time to time to see her grandchildren." He smiled. "We live quite comfortably. Father was good to arrange things so Mother wouldn't want for anything."

"Then why does she work here?"

"She loves it. She would come here and work even if they didn't pay her. She said it's just too sad to sit around the empty house, even with me next door. When they reopened the resort and she heard they were looking for a head baker, she thought it would be amusing to apply. Once they tasted the food she was capable of creating, they were happy to hire her on. I didn't like the idea of her having to work in the middle of the night, however, so they arranged it so that Mother leaves her instructions for the next day's baked goods and others prepare it and begin the baking. Mother comes in the mornings and often stays much too late in the evening, but she is truly happiest when she's busy."

Phoebe thought it amazing that the woman worked because she wanted to, but then she supposed she could understand. At home Phoebe was often bored, despite the parties and social obligations. Perhaps *lonely* was a better way to describe it.

"What about your wife?" The question seemed to surprise Ian. He looked away rather quickly, and Phoebe immediately regretted asking.

"She died ten years ago in childbirth."

Phoebe frowned. "I am sorry. That must have been very hard for you."

He nodded. "It was."

For several minutes neither one said anything more. Phoebe could finally no longer bear the silence. "I'm sure Kenny has been a comfort."

As if on cue the boy came running. "Look what I found!" He all but collided into Ian, who had jumped to his feet. "It's a blue butterfly."

"It is indeed."

Phoebe rose, having a strong feeling that their party had come to an end. She admired the butterfly, then watched as Kenny released him to fly away.

She offered him a smile. "It's wonderful that you could catch him and not hurt him."

Kenny shrugged. "You just have to be gentle." He beamed her a smile. "That's what Grandma Harper taught me. She can catch just about anything—even snakes."

Phoebe shuddered. "Well, I'd prefer we not catch any of those. I've never liked snakes."

Kenny took hold of her hand. "Miss Phoebe, if any snakes come, I'll catch them and get them away from you. I don't want you to ever be afraid."

11

"I'm sorry I haven't been around," Elizabeth said as she ushered Phoebe into her cottage. "I've had some things that needed tending. Please sit." She made a quick glance around the room to make certain there were no telltale signs of Kenny.

Phoebe sat in the same chair she'd used the last time she visited. She was dressed in a simple skirt and white blouse. Her hair was pulled back but left to hang down her back. It made her seem younger somehow, more vulnerable. Her expression bore the unmistakable look of confusion and concern. Elizabeth wanted nothing more than to assure her daughter of her love and to wipe away the memories of the past.

"I have really struggled to understand what has happened," Phoebe admitted. "With Vater gone, I've had a lot of time to think. I know you're right when you say that he can be a very harsh and unforgiving man." She looked up to where Elizabeth still stood. "I've also come to realize that Vater seems inclined toward lying."

"I'm so sorry, Phoebe. Has something else happened?" She took a seat in the rocker and waited for Phoebe to speak.

"He lied to me about arranging a marriage. He told me he would come up with a list of possible suitors and allow me to pick a husband." She looked down at her folded hands. "But he lied. I just found out a few days ago that he's arranged for me to marry an old duke—a man his own age—a man I've never cared for." She raised her face and met Elizabeth's gaze. "He's not only set up the arrangement, he's fixed the wedding date."

"Oh, Phoebe. I am so sorry." Elizabeth determined she would do whatever she could to prevent her daughter from going into a loveless marriage.

"It really hurts me to know he's lied. Lied to me about you. Lied about this." Phoebe shook her head. "I've hardly been able to think about anything else."

"You don't have to go through with it. Your father cannot force you to go back with him and marry this man. You could stay here—with me."

"Surprisingly enough I have considered that very thing."

Phoebe fell silent, and Elizabeth found herself uncertain what to say. She didn't want to say or do anything to further her daughter's pain. After a while, Elizabeth decided to share her heart.

"Phoebe, I cannot tell you how much it means to me that you've come to speak with me. After seeing you and talking, I found that it filled a place in me that had long been empty. You are a very important part of my life, as is Dieter. Nothing has been completely right since losing the two of you.

"I want you to know that I am not here to speak ill of your father or of the choices he made. I do not desire to set you against him. I must admit that at one time I did want that, but not now. I have been praying a great deal about the past and have come to the conclusion that dwelling on it, and even making it the focus of our conversations here, would only serve to do more damage. What I hope for is that you and I might rekindle our love for each other. I want you to know that I love you most dearly and have never stopped."

To her surprise, Phoebe's eyes filled with tears. "After you had gone and I thought you dead, I used to lie in bed at night and imagine it wasn't so. I despaired of even living."

"Oh, my sweet daughter." Elizabeth felt a deep ache within at the thought of what her child had suffered.

"I told myself it was just a bad dream—that you were really just down the hall in your room and that in the morning I would see you at breakfast and I would tell you of my nightmare." Phoebe sniffed. "I hoped so many times that it was all a mistake. I couldn't bear having lost you." Her voice broke, and Phoebe rose from the chair and went to where Elizabeth sat. She sank to the floor at her mother's feet.

"I can't bear the thought of losing you again . . . *Mutti*." Phoebe laid her head on her mother's knee and cried in earnest.

Elizabeth didn't even attempt to hide her tears. She bent over her daughter and held her fast. She had never desired anything as much as she did this moment.

♒︎

Phoebe hadn't intended to fall apart. Such behavior wasn't acceptable for the daughter of a nobleman, but something deep inside broke like a dam. She knew she needed her mother more than anyone else, and to fight that, or give pretense of not wanting it, seemed foolish indeed.

For a long while Phoebe cried and held on to her mother. A decade of pain poured from her heart. Nothing that had gone before mattered as much as this moment. After a time, Mutter raised her head and began stroking her daughter's hair. The action reminded Phoebe of being a little girl once again. It soothed her like nothing else could, and her tears abated.

"My precious girl," her mother whispered, "everything will change now. We can build again on the solid foundation of what was, but no more will I dwell in the past. Not where you are concerned."

Phoebe lifted her face but held fast to her mother. "I am so confused as to what I should do. Vater will never understand how much this means to me. I don't want to hurt him, even though he's devastated me with these lies. I love him."

"I know you do, and I don't want you to stop. He has made a great many mistakes, but as human beings we are all inclined to sin."

"Sin? Is that what it truly amounts to?"

"I believe so. I've spent the last decade learning to depend on God, and in order to do that, I had to know Him better. The church I attended when you were a child didn't encourage that at all. It was sufficient to let those in charge know Him and share what they would with the congregation. It was far more important to be seen and to see others in attendance. But here, the thought is completely different."

Phoebe sat back and looked at her mother's red-rimmed eyes. "How is it different?" She didn't know why, but she found herself wanting very much to know the answer.

"We are like sheep. Remember the old farmer who lived near the village—the one who had the flock of sheep?"

Phoebe nodded. "I do. I always liked to visit when the new lambs were birthed."

"Sheep aren't the brightest of God's creation," her mother continued. "And we are a lot like them. We often don't stay where it's safe. We wander out to what appears to be better pastures only to find ourselves in great danger.

"In the Bible, God is revealed to be a shepherd who watches over us with tender love, just as that old man cared for his flock. When one of us goes astray, God finds us and gently herds us back to join the others. I found that rather comforting."

"It is a nice thought." She paused for a moment, remembering how adamantly her father despised such thinking. "Vater doesn't believe in God. He says the Bible is no different than Greek or Roman mythology—just a collection of stories to frighten mankind into some kind of order."

"I know. He never did believe and chided me for my opinions." Mutter frowned. "I know he has his philosophy, and each man must choose for himself. However, when I came to America—or rather when I came here to Helena—I found my eyes opened to so much more than mere religion and philosophy. I found a Savior."

Phoebe wished she could understand her mother's heart. She spoke the words in such a way that they seemed so comforting. She started to ask her to explain, but a knock sounded on the door to the cottage.

Both women jumped to their feet. Phoebe didn't know why, but the presence of someone else caused her to feel uncomfortable. What if Gerda had managed to follow her here?

Her mother hurried to the window. "It's my friend, Georgia."

"I should go." Phoebe looked around the room. "Is there another way I might leave?"

Elizabeth nodded. "Come this way." She led Phoebe into the kitchen to a back door. "Please tell me that you'll come again soon."

Phoebe nodded and hugged her mother close. "I will. I promise."

Crowded into the stands of cheering fans at the rodeo on the Fourth of July, Ian watched Phoebe laughing at the rodeo clowns as they hustled a fallen rider away from danger. She was completely enthralled by the activities. Kenny, too, was more than excited.

"This is the best rodeo ever," he told Ian. "I remember last year's, and this one is much better. The horses are wilder, and it's so exciting to see those cowboys ride them."

"Riding seems hardly the right word," Phoebe interjected. "It seems they are thrown precariously around and then deposited on the hard ground. I wince each time one of them gets thrown, knowing just how that feels."

Ian laughed. "It's a part of who these cowboys are. Rodeos are great places to show off their skills. Ranching isn't an easy life. It's hard work, and they have to have some amusement."

"You talk as one who knows." She looked at him with a raised brow and unspoken question.

She was so delicately beautiful—like a fine china doll he'd seen in one of the shop windows. Her German background kept her aloof and formal much of the time, but when her guard was down Phoebe was not only stunning but quite animated.

Ian smiled. "I am. I have an aunt and uncle who own a ranch. I spent summers there when I was a boy, and the work is very hard. Breaking a horse for riding is never easy. Thankfully, I've never had to do the job."

"I suppose I never considered the work that goes into such things," Phoebe admitted. "The horses were well broken by the time they came to me for riding."

"Can we have ice cream?" Kenny asked out of the blue. "I'm hot, and those people over there have ice cream and I want some too." He looked at Ian with great hope.

"I think that sounds good, as well," Phoebe announced. "I will make it my treat."

"You don't need to do that. After all, we invited you here today." Ian helped her to her feet and then down the grandstand steps. Once they were on solid ground, he let go of her. It wasn't for a lack of desire to keep holding on to her arm. He found he very much enjoyed her closeness. In fact, that was the problem. More and more, Phoebe Von Bergen was taking his thoughts captive, and feelings he'd forgotten were once again rising to the surface.

"I know where the ice cream is sold," Kenny said, reaching out to pull Ian in the right direction. "I hope they have strawberry."

Phoebe surprisingly kept pace with them. Ian had been glad she'd worn a very simple summer gown. He had seen her in some of her more expensive fashions and knew they'd never be comfortable for a day at the rodeo. Not only that, but he liked her like this, unadorned with jewels or fancy clothes. Dressed as she was, she seemed to fit right in with the other folks.

The crowd thickened with more people, and to Ian's surprise, a freight wagon careened around the corner just as they were about to cross the street. He barely had time to pull Kenny and Phoebe back from the curb. Dust swirled around them, causing Phoebe to cough, while expletives also filled the air from men less forgiving of the careless driver.

"That was a close one," Ian said, waiting to see that Phoebe was all right.

She nodded. "I never even saw him coming." She looked around. "Is Kenny all right?"

"I'm fine, Miss Phoebe." He popped up from behind Ian. "But now I really want that ice cream. I got dust in my mouth."

Phoebe laughed. Ian directed them away from the rodeo

grounds to a shady spot. "Why don't you two wait here? That might be safer. I'll get the ice cream and bring it back to you. What flavor would you like, Miss Phoebe?"

She smiled at him in such a sincere manner that Ian felt his chest tighten. It had been so long since he'd allowed himself to enjoy the company of a woman. He chided himself to be cautious and not lose his heart, but he worried at the same time that it was too late.

"I think I would like to try the strawberry."

"It's the best," Kenny declared.

"All right then, three strawberry." Ian set out to retrieve the cold dessert without further ado.

The line was long but moved rather quickly. Ian placed his order, then realized as the cones were handed over that he was going to have quite a time managing three. He carefully balanced one in each hand, then allowed the clerk to position the third between those two, his fingers splayed so as to manage the trio of cones.

He started back for the place where he'd left Phoebe and Kenny but soon realized they'd moved a little closer to where they could watch some young boys in a contest of catching piglets. With their backs turned to Ian, they didn't realize he could hear their conversation.

"So then Ian told me the pigs had grease on them, and that's why it's so much harder to catch them and hold on to them."

Ian smiled to himself at the memory. Kenny had thought it quite silly that the boys couldn't catch the pigs and keep their hold. He started to comment but stopped short when Phoebe posed a question.

"Why do you call your father by his given name?"

For a moment Ian thought his heart had stopped. He wasn't at all sure if he should just jump right in and distract Phoebe with the ice cream—which was already starting to drip down his hands.

"Ian's not my father," Kenny replied.

Phoebe turned just a bit and looked down at the boy. "But I thought he was. You're always with him."

Ian wasted no time. "Here we are—three ice creams, and you'd best hurry to eat them before they completely melt."

It was the perfect diversion, but the encounter nevertheless left Ian somewhat worried. They'd managed to keep Phoebe no wiser about her brother for almost two weeks, but Ian knew the time was coming rapidly to a halt. Her father would soon return, and then Elizabeth would have to make a decision about what to do. It wouldn't be an easy matter to resolve.

Phoebe was exhausted by the time Ian suggested they head home. He borrowed a buckboard and put Kenny in the back before helping Phoebe climb up to the seat. She marveled at how Ian seemed to just jump up with ease to claim the bench beside her. It appeared to be no effort at all, but it didn't surprise her. She had felt the ironlike muscles in his forearms.

"It was a wonderful day. I can't remember when I've had so much fun, and the fireworks this evening were a wonderful way to end the affair," she said as Ian drove her back to the resort. "I must say I like this American celebration of liberty." She looked back, thinking Kenny might interject his thoughts, but found the boy was already asleep.

"I guess liberty wore Kenny out completely," she mused.

Ian chuckled. "We take our independence very seriously."

"As you should." Phoebe had heard all sorts of speakers that day, and all had focused on the topic of freedom. One man, a preacher, had even mentioned that Jesus was the ultimate source of freedom. It had piqued Phoebe's curiosity, given the things her mother had already shared.

"I wonder if you could explain something for me."

"I'll try," Ian said, his gaze fixed on the road ahead.

"Well, that one man—the preacher we heard—said that Jesus was the ultimate source of freedom. I don't understand what he meant by that, but it's stayed with me all this time. I know you said he was the preacher at your church, so I thought you might explain it."

Ian nodded but still didn't look at her. In the scant moonlight he appeared deep in thought. Phoebe hoped she hadn't offended him. Maybe he wasn't the sort who liked to talk about such personal things.

"It's really pretty simple," he began. "This world is full of sin . . . wrongdoing. We make choices we know we shouldn't and do things we know aren't right, like lying, stealing, and killing. Those sins bind us until we are so tangled up we can't move. We just keep making the same wrong choices and decisions. Jesus offers a way to set us free from that by our accepting Him as Savior."

"Savior?" Phoebe had heard her mother use that word earlier. "You mean to save us from those sins—to set us free from our mistakes?"

"Yes." Ian turned and looked at her. "If you're all tied up, you can't very well set yourself free. You need someone else to come and do it for you. Jesus was willing to accept responsibility for our mistakes—He allowed them to put Him to death on a cross."

"But why? Why kill Him if He was such a good man?"

"Because as God's Son, Jesus was the only one who could save us from our sin. You see, God had always required His people to make a blood sacrifice in order to be forgiven of their wrongdoing. There were strict rules about the sacrifice—what animal it should be and that it needed to be without blemish. Jesus became the final blood sacrifice. He alone was good enough."

"That seems awful. How could anyone take the life of an innocent man? How could God allow such a thing?"

Ian shrugged. "I guess it was because He loved us enough to give up His Son. He must have seen it as a worthwhile trade. I, for one, am glad He did."

Phoebe thought about Ian's words in silence. It wasn't long before she realized they'd arrived back at the hotel. Ian stopped the wagon and then climbed down. He came around to Phoebe and held up his arms. She nervously allowed him to put his hands on her waist. With little effort he lowered her to the ground, and for a moment all Phoebe could do was look into his eyes.

This man made her feel something no one else had. Was this what falling in love was all about? She began to tremble, uncertain what to say.

"You're cold," Ian said. "Let's get you inside."

Phoebe didn't argue. The truth was, she didn't feel the cold at all. What she did feel was the strange effect this man had on her, and how it confused her in a way she had never known before.

12

S o you see, Graf Von Bergen, my friends at the American Sapphire Company are not bound by the injunction, nor any troubling legalities, at this time," Mr. Thompson told Frederick as they surveyed the American operations.

"Not only that, but despite what Lord Putnam may have told you, I know for a fact Charles Gadsden will not be persuaded to sell you any of his gems."

"Why do you say that?" Frederick had been discussing matters with the man since early in the evening.

Thompson shrugged. "Gadsden looks at that operation as his own. He has run it for some time and does things the way he sees fit. He is completely loyal to the company, however, and each and every gemstone is packaged and shipped directly to England without fail."

"Lord Putnam has associations with those in England. He assured me that the sale would take place."

"Perhaps he has more power than I realized. But either way, our stones will be of just as fine a quality, and there will be no difficulty in arranging their sale. We are more than happy to help you in your endeavor."

Frederick swirled the amber liquor in his glass. "If you can meet the quantity and quality for the price you suggested, then I am more than interested. However, this arrangement must remain strictly between the two of us."

Thompson leaned back and smoothed his mustache with his index finger. "Of course. We are most discreet."

Frederick knew the man was underhanded and no doubt would do what he could to make this arrangement work to his benefit, but the graf also had a few tricks up his sleeve. He would have the stones checked and verified by that lapidary in Helena before he agreed to pay for them.

"So will you venture out to the English mine again before your trip home?"

Von Bergen nodded. "I have committed to do so. I intend to discuss the sapphire purchase with Mr. Gadsden. If he is, as you have said, unwilling to sell me his sapphires, then I will do business with you."

"Even if he is willing," Thompson said with a casual shrug, "he'll never give you the price I am willing to give."

"We shall see," Frederick replied.

The next morning he made his way via horseback to the English mine. Lord Putnam was at his side, sullen and quite unhappy. They had discussed the problem of getting Gadsden to part with his sapphires, as well as the fact that given the injunction, the English mine hadn't been able to produce the volume it once had.

"You led me astray, Putnam. I don't appreciate such things."

"It wasn't my desire to do so, Graf Von Bergen. I had been assured in England that the syndicate would allow for you to purchase the stones. It is hardly my fault they changed their minds due to the problems here in America. I have no say over such matters."

"That's true, but you had plenty of forewarning that the injunction was in place and that production had been greatly diminished."

"But I wasn't told that," Putnam argued. "I assure you, given our arrangements, I would not do anything to cause a problem. You know how important this deal was to me."

Von Bergen realized the truth in what the man said. It was best he not alienate or cause further despair to Lord Putnam. The man would be needed in the future, and Frederick could find other more subtle ways to punish him.

"Well, let us say no more about it. We shall put the matter behind us and move forward with the American group."

They rode in silence for several miles before arriving at the English mining site. Frederick dismounted and dusted off his coat while Putnam called for someone to take their horses.

Mr. Gadsden appeared almost immediately and came to greet them. "Gentlemen, would you care to have some refreshments? My wife has made some tea, and there are biscuits as well."

"No thank you," Von Bergen replied. He glanced around the area. "So what about selling me the sapphires I require?"

"I see you're a man who likes to get right down to business."

Frederick looked the mustached man over from head to toe. "I'm a man with a great deal to accomplish in a short amount of time. Now will you sell or not?"

"I'm afraid I can't. There simply isn't enough product to sell to you while also furnishing our owners with stones. I know what you were promised, but of course, no one could foresee this legal problem carrying on for so long."

"I understand." Of course, that didn't mean he was happy. Frederick wasn't about to let the man ruin his day, however.

"We have been fortunate enough to make arrangements with the American Sapphire Company, so there is no harm done."

"Wonderful. Now perhaps you would like to see how we have resolved the problem of separating out the large amounts of pyrite."

Gadsden had become quite capable of coming up with solutions that didn't cost his syndicate much in the way of money. It was well-known that he was given full credit for the mine's success.

"I'm afraid not. As I mentioned, I am pressed for time."

After concluding his dealings with Gadsden, Frederick and Lord Putnam made their way back to the American mines. The American operations had been established on Yogo Creek, where the company had their dike located in the limestone cliffs. However, it was easy to see this operation was not without its problems. Where the English mine was positioned on open benchlands, this operation was stuck in the narrow creek bed of Yogo Gulch. There wasn't enough room for dumping out the soil to weather, so the Americans had spent almost thirty thousand dollars for a mill to process one hundred tons per day.

Frederick thought it wise that the company had invested such money. The process was surely sped up, allowing for a quicker return on the labor. Thompson was quite happy to show his guests where the Americans had spent large sums to upgrade and modernize the mining operations as much as possible.

"The English are fools to keep their operations in the dark ages," Thompson said, laughing. "But I never did think they understood much when it came to this land and the work involved."

Lord Putnam stiffened at Frederick's side but said nothing. Frederick pointed to where a couple of men worked with a pneumatic drill. "At the English mine they are still using sledges and chisels to drill blasting holes."

Thompson laughed heartily. "They are most primitive and backward."

"But they are producing at a profit," Lord Putnam said, unable to let the slur on his countrymen continue. "And they make a large profit, at that."

"I beg to differ. For now, they are unable to make much of a profit at all," Mr. Thompson rebutted. "Not only that, but the time will soon be upon them when no miner will hire on to work in such dangerous and laborious ways. Modernizing makes things not only safer but also easier on the workmen."

Putnam fell silent, and Frederick nearly laughed aloud. The man was such a milksop. He had no spine and no ability to stand up for what he believed. It had served Frederick well enough in maintaining control over Putnam, but he despised the man and his ilk for such deficiencies.

"Well, I tend to agree with you, Mr. Thompson. We live in the twentieth century, and it would serve us well to move forward with the mechanisms and tools that scientific minds have created for us. I believe we can work quite well together." He fixed Thompson with a stern expression. "Let us discuss the financial aspects of our arrangement so that I may return to Helena."

❧

Phoebe sat quietly in the gardens enjoying a copy of a ladies' magazine when a shadow fell across her. She looked up to find Mr. Eckhardt smiling down at her. He was dressed in a finely tailored suit of pale blue-gray.

"Herr Eckhardt." She smiled. "How nice to see you again."

"The pleasure is mine, Fräulein Von Bergen. I am sorry, however, to interrupt your reading."

She closed the magazine. "It's of no concern. I was merely

keeping busy. Vater is due back today, and I was watching for him."

"Might I join you for a few minutes?"

"Of course. Please have a seat." Phoebe motioned to the bench across from her, hoping he wouldn't be so bold as to sit beside her.

He sat opposite her and smiled. "May I say you are quite the picture of loveliness?"

"Thank you."

"I have thought so since our first encounter." He shrugged. "But, of course, I did not wish to offend by being familiar."

Phoebe laughed. "Are you no longer worried about offending?"

He chuckled. "I suppose I am, but at the same time I hate for the opportunity to pass me by. You see, I'm uncertain as to how long my present business will take. I could be leaving before the end of summer."

"Oh?"

Eckhardt nodded. "As I said, I didn't want opportunity to pass me by."

Phoebe laid her magazine on the bench and folded her hands. "And what opportunity would that be?"

"To know you better, of course."

She couldn't help smiling. "I'm not sure such an opportunity is all that important."

"Where a beautiful woman from my homeland is concerned, I think it very important." He smiled back, revealing brilliant white teeth. "So tell me about yourself."

Phoebe gave a slight shrug. "I haven't that much to tell. You already know I'm the daughter of Graf Von Bergen, and I am from the Baden region of our fatherland."

"And your father is here on business. I believe I overheard

someone say he was purchasing sapphires. But how does that involve you?"

"I wanted to see America." She stared out at the mountains on the horizon. "My mother was . . . is . . . well, her ancestry is American and English. I had never seen America before, and when Vater mentioned this trip, I begged to be allowed to accompany him."

"And I'm so glad you did; otherwise, we might never have met." He studied her for a moment. "So have you enjoyed your time here in America?"

"I have. The country is so diverse. We started out seeing the larger cities back east, and then we headed west. It seemed the towns grew smaller and smaller. When we leave here, we are bound for the larger cities on the West Coast, first Seattle and then San Francisco."

"Yes, I recall your mentioning that. Perhaps we might share the same train and ship."

"Perhaps." Phoebe knew that if things continued as they were with her father trying to force her to marry, she might never leave Helena at all.

"And what will you do in San Francisco?"

Phoebe realized that the man was no longer pressing to know about her, but rather her plans—their plans. It made her uneasy, but she certainly saw no harm in the discussion. "I don't suppose it matters," she told Eckhardt, "but we will continue to the Orient."

"Ah yes. The grand tour." He smiled. "I know you will be delighted with the various cultures. There are many fascinating things in our world."

Phoebe decided to turn the tables on Eckhardt. "And what about you, Herr Eckhardt? Why are you bound for San Francisco?"

He eased back against the bench. "My business takes me there. I wanted to see the damage done by last year's earthquake. You see, I design large buildings and want very much to learn if there might be a way to better make them safe for such things as earthquakes and other natural disasters."

"How admirable! I don't suppose I have ever considered such things. I thought someone mentioned you were here to buy land."

"That is true. I have a relative who would very much like to invest in America. I promised to look around here with thought to buying land. Perhaps you would like to ride out with me and view the area. There are some beautiful tracts available, or so I'm told."

Just then Phoebe spied two carriages making their way toward the hotel. She also could hear her father's boisterous voice. She steeled herself. Tonight she planned to confront him about the telegram. Perhaps since he would be tired from his trip, he would not be inclined to argue.

"Riding out with you sounds like a wonderful time, but I haven't any idea of my schedule." She inclined her head. "It would appear Vater has arrived."

Eckhardt jumped to his feet and offered her his hand. Phoebe picked up her magazine and then accepted his assistance. "I do apologize for my abrupt departure, but as I told you, I was only here awaiting my vater's return."

"But, of course. There is no need to apologize." He raised her gloved hand slightly and clicked his heels. "The pleasure of your company will stay with me for some days to come. I hope we might again have time to enjoy a conversation, and should you find time for that ride, simply leave word for me at the front desk."

Phoebe felt a sense of relief when Eckhardt let go of her hand.

She gave him one last smile. "I do hope you have a pleasant day, Herr Eckhardt."

"Thank you, Fräulein. Your company has definitely added that element."

She hurried away, unwilling to hear any more of his sweet talk. A list of all she intended to say to her father continued to run through her thoughts. She wanted very much to approach him about her mother but still wasn't sure that she should.

"Phoebe," her father said as he approached from the carriage. "You look quite lovely."

She offered him a smile. "Thank you, Vater. How was your trip? Did it prove successful?"

"Indeed it did. I will discuss it with you later this evening." He offered her his arm. "For now I long for a bath and change of clothes. I've already sent Hubert ahead to prepare it." He motioned to a bellboy. "Please see that my bags are brought up to the Von Bergen suite."

The boy nodded and headed off toward the carriage. Phoebe allowed her father to lead her inside the hotel and up the grand staircase. For all the things she had practiced saying to him, Phoebe now found the words jumbled in her thoughts. Perhaps it would be better to wait.

"I saw you speaking with Herr Eckhardt," her father said as they reached his room. "What did he want?"

Phoebe was surprised by the suspicion in her father's tone. "He was simply passing the day. He saw me waiting for you. Why do you ask?"

Her father frowned and opened his door. "Because you are my daughter."

He left Phoebe standing in the hall to stare after him. Hubert appeared at the door and looked at her a moment. "Did you wish to come in, Fräulein?"

Phoebe shook her head. "No, but please tell Vater I would like to have supper with him—preferably here in private."

Hubert nodded. "I will tell him immediately." With that he closed the door.

Phoebe thought it all rather strange, but instead of making a scene, she decided a short nap might strengthen her resolve.

It was nearly six before Phoebe heard from her father again. Hubert came to announce that dinner had been brought to the suite and her father was eager to eat. Phoebe was to come immediately.

She turned to Gerda. "You might as well go eat too." The maid nodded. Phoebe turned back to Hubert. "Let us not keep him waiting."

She followed the valet to her father's suite and found the meal spread out on the table. It looked quite good, but Phoebe's stomach was in turmoil.

Hubert helped her with her chair and then awaited further instruction. Phoebe was relieved when her father dismissed him, suggesting he go see to his own dinner.

They ate in silence for several minutes. Phoebe forced herself to nibble on a variety of things, but with each bite she felt more uncertain of how to introduce the subject of the telegram and her unwillingness to marry the duke her father had chosen. She didn't have long to consider the matter, however.

"I'm glad we can have this time to ourselves," her father said before taking a generous portion of beef. "I have something to discuss with you."

"I believe I know what that is." Phoebe pulled the telegram from her pocket and handed it over to her father.

He opened the envelope and read very quickly. "Why did you open this?"

"Because you were gone, and the hotel manager gave it to

me in case it needed an immediate reply." She met her father's stern expression. "I'm hoping you might explain."

Her father shrugged. "I told you I was arranging your marriage."

"You also told me you would allow me to choose."

To Phoebe's great frustration, her father put the telegram aside and once again began eating. If he thought she would simply acquiesce to his arrangement, then he was greatly mistaken.

"I want an explanation."

His head shot up and he fixed her with a scowl. "You're my daughter. I owe you no explanation."

"Yes, I am your daughter. But I am also a woman of age. And while I have spent a lifetime respecting your wishes, this is one I will not honor. I will not marry the duke. He is far too old, and his reputation is not one I wish for in a husband."

Her father looked at her for a moment and then returned his attention to the food. "You will do as I say and marry him."

His tone was dismissive, but Phoebe wasn't about to yield. "No. I won't."

Vater slammed his fist onto the table with such fury it caused the dishes to rattle. Phoebe tried not to show her surprise. "I'm sorry if that upsets your plans."

"You haven't upset my plans. You will do as I say or you will bear the consequences."

"Consequences?" She eyed her father and decided she had nothing to lose. "Like those my mutter suffered?" By his expression Phoebe knew the question had hit its mark.

"We will not speak of her."

"Why? Why for all these years have you refused to speak or allow me to speak of my own mutter? She was a vital part of our family at one time. I see nothing wrong in discussing her."

His eyes narrowed. "I told you, we will not speak of her."

"Very well." Phoebe rose. "I can see then that we have little reason to share the meal."

"Sit down."

She looked at her father a moment, then shook her head. "I will not be bullied by you, Vater. You might well run the rest of the world, but you do not have the right to treat me like one of your servants."

Again his fist slammed down on the table. "I do not know what has gotten into you, but I suggest you take your seat. You will leave when I say you may."

Phoebe headed for the door but was still a foot away when her father grabbed hold of her and turned her in one fluid motion. He slammed her up against the door.

"I told you to take your seat. You will not defy me. Not in this and not in marriage. If I have to, I will drag you to the civil ceremony by your hair."

He was only inches away, but Phoebe didn't care. With the cool reserve she generally saved for unwanted suitors, she fixed her father with a look that would have made weaker men cower.

"Take your hands off of me . . . Vater." Her words were demanding and without fear.

This seemed to startle the older man, and to her surprise he let her go and took a step back. "I can see I was wrong in leaving you to your own devices. Apparently the wild American frontier brings out the defiant child in you. I have no choice, therefore, but to arrange for you to be at my side constantly, or else under guard locked in your room."

Phoebe shook her head. "As I said, I will not be bullied by you. You may impose your will on everyone else—beat them into submission as you are known to do . . ."

Smack! She hadn't expected the hard slap across the face, and for a moment it took Phoebe's breath. Tears instantly stung her eyes as she imagined her mother having endured this kind of treatment.

For a moment they just stood staring at each other. Phoebe felt anger unlike any she had ever known. Years of sorrow for the loss of her mother blended with the confusion of learning she was alive. And coupled with her father's violent behavior, Phoebe knew her rage might very well cause her to lose control and strike the man herself.

She swallowed the lump in her throat and refused to let her tears fall. "If you ever lay a hand on me again, it will be the last time you see me."

Her father's expression changed momentarily to one of surprise. He quickly covered his shock and moved away from the door. "You have never given me reason to strike you until now. If you don't want me to hit you again, you will refrain from defying me. Now come and let us finish supper. We still have much to discuss."

As he walked back to the table, Phoebe turned and opened the door. She quickly exited the room and crossed to her own without bothering to close her father's door. As she turned to shut her own door, she could see him standing at the table staring after her. Without a word, Phoebe closed him out and locked the door behind her. She needed time to think and figure out a plan.

13

I like working for you, Ian," Kenny announced. He had
been busy sweeping up the workshop, but he paused
for this declaration with a smile.

Ian laughed. "Well, I'm glad you do. Working for the wrong
man isn't worth the money you get paid. Say, that reminds me,
I plan to ask Miss Phoebe to join us for another picnic, and I
wondered if you wanted to come along."

"I would! I like Miss Phoebe—a lot."

"I like her too." It was the first time Ian had admitted this
aloud, and he couldn't help grinning. "A lot."

Kenny nodded. "She's really pretty, and she's so nice. I think
you should marry her."

Ian hadn't been prepared for that. "I . . . ah . . . really, Kenny.
I hardly know her."

The boy shrugged. "Well, if you marry her, you'll get to
know her real good."

Laughing, Ian tousled the boy's hair. "Kenny, when you're
older you'll understand what I'm about to say, but a man ought
never to marry a woman unless he really knows who she is

and what's important to her. If you don't believe in the same things, especially when it comes to faith issues, you'll be in for a lifetime of hurt and sorrow."

Just then the front door opened, jingling the bell Ian had affixed overhead. He gave a quick glance into the front of the shop and stiffened as he spied Von Bergen and Lord Putnam. He took Kenny by the hand and led him to the back of the room. He knelt beside the boy.

"Kenny, remember what your mama said about staying out of sight and not letting anyone know who you are?"

The boy nodded. "Did a bad man come to the shop?" He craned his neck to look over Ian's shoulder.

"I don't know if the men out there are bad or good, but I do know it wouldn't help your ma for you to be seen by them. I need you to wait a couple of minutes until I am speaking with them; then I want you to run over to the house and stay in your room until I come for you. Can you do that, and keep out of trouble?"

"Sure. I'll read my book."

Ian nodded. "Good." He rose. "Now, don't forget, wait just a minute for me to ask them what they want."

Feeling it was the best he could do to keep Kenny out of sight, Ian made his way to the front of the shop. "Good afternoon, Graf Von Bergen. Lord Putnam."

"Good afternoon, Mr. Harper," Von Bergen said. "We've come on important business."

Ian nodded, and Von Bergen presented him with two small bags. "These contain uncut sapphires. I would first like your opinion as to their quality and then may commission you to facet them."

Ian opened the bag and poured out some of the stones into his hand. "What did you have in mind?"

"They are all to be round cut in consistent size. The woman I work for has commissioned me to find stones for a necklace she is having made. This is just a portion."

Ian looked the stones over for a moment. "I see. And how soon do you need them?"

"As soon as possible," Von Bergen replied. "I still have to make my way to Ceylon for some of the larger stones needed. As I understand it, your Yogos are rarely ever larger than three or four carats."

"That's true enough." Ian continued to study the sapphires. "How many stones are you looking to have faceted?"

"A total of five hundred."

Ian raised his brow, certain he'd heard wrong. "Five hundred?"

Von Bergen nodded. "She is a wealthy and eccentric old woman who dresses herself in sapphires. She's had some outrageous necklace designed that will fan out across her bosom. The jeweler has decided a minimum of five hundred stones will be needed."

"It would take many months to facet that many stones, and I would have to put all other work aside." Ian shook his head. "Which I cannot do. I have agreements with others that cannot be broken."

The older man frowned. "I thought from our discussion at the party you would be able to help me."

"Help you, yes. I can facet some of the stones. Probably these two bags. However, you would need to have additional help to handle the rest."

The two older men exchanged a look. Von Bergen was none too happy. "You assured me we could get these stones cut in a timely fashion."

"Perhaps you should have it done in Ceylon," Lord Putnam

suggested. "I understand they have entire factories set up for this kind of thing."

Von Bergen drew a deep breath and looked back at Ian. "Very well. What is your opinion of the quality?"

"They are very nice. The Yogos have few flaws and require no heat treatment to bring out the color."

"Very good. Well, despite your busy schedule, I would like for you to work with these immediately."

"You haven't yet heard my price." Ian carefully put the stones back into the bag.

"Very well. What is your price?"

"Ten dollars a stone."

The graf began sputtering in protest, but Ian held up his hand. "Once finished, these stones will be worth no less than fifty dollars a carat. I have no idea what you paid for them in the rough, but I'm quite certain the value will be raised times ten once finished. Perhaps more."

Lord Putnam reached out to Von Bergen and whispered something. The graf seemed to calm. Putnam said something else, and Von Bergen began nodding.

"Very well. I accept your price. There are two hundred stones in these bags. I will want them as soon as possible."

Ian nodded. "You will need to give me a deposit of half the money now and the other half payable upon receipt of the stones."

"One thousand dollars now," the older man said, pinning Ian with a look of disdain. "Very well. I will arrange for the money at the bank and have it brought to you in the morning. How long will you need to complete the job?"

Ian picked up the bags. "Let me see how quickly I can finish my other projects without jeopardizing the quality, and then I'll better know how long it will take. Now, if you'll wait a moment, I'll write up a receipt for these stones."

Elizabeth Bergen sat in the front pew of the church she'd attended ever since coming to Helena. She knew the time for a decision was at hand. She'd already let a considerable amount of time pass, and no doubt Ian was nearing the end of his patience. Although given his nature, she was certain he'd never say as much.

Pastor Clearwater came to sit beside her. "So have you given thought to what we discussed last time?"

"You want me to meet with Frederick. Here." She twisted her hands. "You want me to be honest with him about Kenny."

The older man gave her a sympathetic nod. "It would be for the best, Elizabeth. In the company of witnesses, your husband will be no threat to you."

"Once he knows about our son, he will do whatever is necessary to punish me and take the boy." She shook her head. "I cannot let that happen."

"Elizabeth, do you believe God is watching over you?" His face bore a fatherly concern. "Do you trust Him? Do you trust that He wants the very best for you?"

Elizabeth considered his words for a moment. Did she truly believe that? Didn't her actions and attitude suggest otherwise?

"The Bible is full of verses about trusting God," he said, not waiting for her response. He took hold of her hand and gave it a pat. "The Psalms especially are full of such verses. One of my favorites is Psalm fifty-six, eleven. 'In God have I put my *trust*: I will not be afraid what man can do unto me.' Elizabeth, you have a great many friends who will stand beside you, in addition to the watchful eye of your heavenly Father. Trust Him to make this right."

"I want to trust." Elizabeth felt the weariness of ten years' hiding the truth. "I want this to be settled once and for all. I suppose I really have no choice."

"Of course you have a choice. You can continue to run. No one is stopping you."

Elizabeth knew he was right. Phoebe knew the truth and would now be able to confront her father with his lies. Her only real fear was for Kenny's safety, but she did have one piece of knowledge that Frederick would not want anyone to know. Perhaps it would allow her some leverage. It was a risk, but it might be enough.

"Very well, Pastor. Would you set up the meeting?"

"I will. I will have a message sent to the hotel, and I won't detail the reasons but merely ask your husband to come because of urgent business. Do you want your daughter to be there as well?"

Elizabeth considered this for a moment. "No. It will be difficult enough with just you there as a witness. After that initial meeting, I will better know what to do and how to handle the situation."

Pastor Clearwater smiled. "You're doing the right thing, Elizabeth. This will allow you to finally put the past behind you."

She wanted to believe that, but no one knew Frederick Von Bergen as she did. He was a hateful, vindictive man who would be angry when he learned the truth. Maybe angry enough to commit murder.

⁂

Ian was all but ready to close the shop when the door jangled and he looked up to find Ernst Eckhardt entering. The tall, blond-headed man smiled.

"I hope I am not intruding."

Ian shook his head. "Not at all. I was just finishing up for the day."

"Are you busy with many orders?" the man asked in a light-hearted manner.

"I am now. I just took on a rather large project."

"Graf Von Bergen, ja? I heard he was buying a great many sapphires."

"I'm surprised you know about that. He tells me it's all to be kept secret. I can't say as I blame him. If someone learned he was carrying around valuable stones, they might be inclined to rob him."

"But his daughter wears jewelry worth thousands. If someone were to rob them, would that not be enticement enough?"

"Most of those stones aren't authentic, and anyone who knows gems would easily recognize that." Ian hadn't meant to offer up the information, but for all he knew, Eckhardt was up to no good.

"Not authentic?"

Ian shook his head. "No. Now, is there something I might help you with?"

Eckhardt chuckled. "Oh, ja. I almost forgot. I remember that you said you grew up around here. I am in America on business, and one of the things I promised to do was investigate land for purchase. I have a relative who is most interested in buying an extensive piece of land, perhaps here in Montana."

"I see. Well, Montana is quite large, and I am sure you could find such acreage." Ian untied his apron. "What type of land are you looking for? Ranchland? Farmland? Something else?"

"Ranchland." Eckhardt smiled. "I thought maybe you might have time to escort me to see some of the acreage available."

"I'm sorry, I don't have that kind of time. Especially now that

I have stones to facet for Graf Von Bergen. However, I do know of a man who handles land sales. I could direct you to him."

"That would be very kind of you." Eckhardt paused to admire a few finished stones Ian had on display. "Are these for sale?"

There was something about the man Ian couldn't help but like. "They are. The darker red ones are garnets. The lighter ones are rubies. The yellow and green are, surprisingly enough, sapphires. All of the stones were found here in Montana."

"I did not realize sapphires could be anything but blue." Eckhardt met Ian's gaze. "It is most fascinating."

"Sapphires can be most any color. The stone is what we call corundum. When it is red we generally refer to the gem as a ruby. And when blue, a sapphire, and that blue can come in a wide variety of shades. There is a dark, almost black sapphire that comes from Australia, cobalt from Ceylon, and the cornflower blue of the Yogos, to name a few. However, there are other colors. We have found sapphires ranging from clear to pink to violet, as well as everything in between.

"A veritable rainbow," Eckhardt offered.

"Exactly."

"It is all quite fascinating," Eckhardt admitted. "Perhaps sometime you might show me how it is you cut the stones."

Ian smiled. "Stop by some morning and I would be happy to show you."

Eckhardt nodded. "In the meantime, I think I should enjoy purchasing the yellow and green sapphires. I believe they would look quite lovely in a tie pin."

After concluding business with Mr. Eckhardt, Ian locked up and pulled the shades. He had only one thought in mind and that was Phoebe. He had tried not to think about her too much, but with her little brother underfoot throughout the day and then her father's visit to bring the stones, Ian found his thoughts full of her. He hadn't seen her in a while, and every time he heard her name mentioned, he felt a growing need to be near her. He'd suggested to Kenny earlier in the day that they might take another horseback ride and invite Phoebe to join them. Kenny had heartily approved the idea, so Ian decided they would put a plan in action.

But when Ian came through the back door of his house, he heard Elizabeth speaking to his mother and his own thoughts were put aside. The women glanced up as he entered the kitchen. Both looked quite solemn, and Kenny was not there.

"I've agreed to the meeting," Elizabeth told him. "Pastor Clearwater said he would send Frederick word to meet him at the church."

"Would you like for us to be there as well?" Ian thought it only right he offer, since he was the one who'd all but forced her into this arrangement.

"No. Pastor Clearwater will stay with me. I will meet with Frederick and see what his attitude is toward me and whether or not he has changed. I had hoped to discuss the matter with Phoebe, but she's been under the weather for some days. I sent one of the hotel maids to deliver a message to her, and Phoebe's maid told her that Phoebe was unwell and couldn't be disturbed."

Ian frowned. He didn't like to hear that Phoebe was sick. "So when is the meeting to be?"

"I don't yet know. Pastor Clearwater told me he'd get word to me. I'm to wait until then. He will arrange for a time that meets with Frederick's approval." She looked at Ian's mother. "I am so afraid that all of this will only serve to cause problems worse than the ones I now face."

"The truth will set you free," Ian said before his mother could speak.

Elizabeth looked back at him and nodded. "I hope you're right." She glanced upward. "Soon I'll have to explain it all to Kenny."

Ian nodded. "Yes. He needs to understand what's happened and why. He also needs to know that Phoebe is his sister. He's very fond of her, and it might very well help soften the shock of it all."

"I can't tell him who she is or who his father is until I am certain Frederick will do nothing to take him from me. This first meeting will tell me a great deal. After that, well . . . after that the rest can be decided."

"Then perhaps," Ian's mother offered, "you needn't say anything to the boy until after your first meeting." She looked to Ian. "Surely that would not be any more damaging or deceptive than to tell him now."

Ian saw the abject fear on Elizabeth's face and finally nodded. "I think she's right. You should probably wait until after your first meeting. That way you'll know better what you intend to do."

Elizabeth seemed to consider this for a moment. "Very well. I will wait. I've waited ten years; I can wait a few more days."

14

Vater had posted a guard outside her door. A guard.

Phoebe had never thought her father capable of such actions, but when she attempted to leave her room, the man refused to let her pass. For days now she'd been imprisoned there. Each morning she attempted to leave, only to be told no. She'd finally reached the end of her patience.

"Sorry, miss. Your father said you weren't to leave unless escorted by him."

"Tell my vater I demand to see him at once." Phoebe had barely spoken the words in a civil manner. She slammed her door shut and found Gerda looking at her in surprise.

"This is preposterous, Gerda. I dared to disagree with him about marrying an ancient duke who needs a son, and he makes me a prisoner."

"He is trying to give you a good life, ja?"

"No. He's trying to sell me to the highest bidder." Phoebe crossed the room and plopped in an unladylike fashion into a chair. "If he thinks he's won this match, he's greatly mistaken."

"What will you do?"

"I'm not sure yet."

Lunch was delivered to her room as it had been every day since her father had put the guard in place. Phoebe ate, and all the while she tried to figure out how to get word to her mother. Suppertime came, and her father still did not send for her or even come to see her. He was clearly punishing her with his absence. It was his way of showing her that her thoughts and feelings on the matter were of no import.

After a restless night, Phoebe was no closer to knowing what to do than she had been when she'd first learned of her plight. She dressed, all but ignoring Gerda's comments about the day.

"Is that man still outside my door?"

Gerda nodded. "Ja, he's still there."

A knock sounded on the door, and Gerda immediately crossed to see who it was, with Phoebe following on her heels. Hubert stood beside the guard. He spoke to Phoebe in German but seemed anxious, as if afraid the guard might understand him. "Your father has asked me to bring you to breakfast in his suite."

Phoebe thought to refuse, then reconsidered. "Very well."

She said nothing more, although she gave the guard a glaring look as she walked past him. Her father had definitely overstepped his bounds, but perhaps there was wisdom in remaining calm.

Her father sat at the table in his suite reading a newspaper. He glanced over the top of the paper as Phoebe took her place. Without any word between them, Vater folded the paper and handed it to Hubert.

"That will be all for now."

"Very good, sir." Hubert took the paper and exited the suite.

Phoebe fixed her father with a stern look but said nothing. She was beyond anger and afraid that if she said anything at all, she might well regret it.

"I suppose you will continue to sit there pouting until I allow for this matter to be discussed," her father said, picking up his napkin. "So say what it is you wish to say, and let us be done with this."

Phoebe continued to stare. Her father helped himself to eggs and sausages while she said nothing. He looked up at one point, shrugged, and then poured himself a cup of tea.

"Since you are determined to remain silent, I will presume that means you have come to accept my punishment."

"I haven't accepted anything." Phoebe folded her arms against her breast.

"You acted like a child, so I thought it only right to treat you like one."

"No, you are treating me like a criminal. Is it your intention to imprison me until our departure?"

Vater took a sip of the tea before leaning back in his chair. "That is up to you."

Phoebe knew she would have to choose her words carefully. If she acted in further defiance, she would be forced back into her room and there would be no hope of getting word to her mother.

"So what are the terms of regaining my freedom?"

Her father actually smiled. "That you would go back to being the obedient child I raised and understand that the choices I've made on your behalf are for your benefit."

"I see."

Vater shook his head. "But I don't think you do. You gave me no chance to explain about the duke."

Phoebe nodded. It was to her benefit to at least pretend to be willing to hear him out. "Very well. Explain."

"You see, the duke is wealthy and well positioned. He can give you whatever you want, and all he wants in return are sons and a beautiful woman to host his parties and take charge of his household. You will be invited to the finest parties, wear the best clothes, and travel wherever you might choose. If you are discreet, you might even take a lover. You will have everything a woman could want."

"Except for love," Phoebe murmured.

"Love is a modern notion. Until this century daughters and even sons understood the importance of the alliances their parents made on their behalf. Arranging marriages for his children is the privilege of a father. It must benefit both parties, and this arrangement will do exactly that."

"So you have sold me to the duke. What is it you stand to gain from the arrangement?"

He laughed and picked up a piece of buttered toast. "I will gain a great deal. My daughter will be a duchess. All of society will receive me, and such an alliance will open doors for me that were previously closed. Above all else, it will put me in further good stead with the kaiser. The duke is his dear friend, and it will please the kaiser to no end to see him happily settled with heirs."

Phoebe tried to calm her anger. She had to be wise about this. Her father was used to playing this game, and if she was to best him at it, she would have to think as he did.

"I suppose I hadn't thought of the benefits." She picked up a piece of toast and nibbled on it. Perhaps if her father saw her eating, he would believe her to have acquiesced.

"See, now you are being reasonable." He smiled. "I know that this might seem difficult to understand, but in time you will thank me. The duke is a generous man. You will enjoy more wealth than you've ever known. And he lives in a palace. Imagine being mistress over one hundred servants and a house filled with treasures. You will entertain queens and kings."

"How wonderful." Phoebe hoped the sarcasm she felt wasn't evident in her voice.

"Exactly." Her father smiled. "Not only that, but once you give the duke sons, you will be set for life. The duke, as you pointed out, is older and . . ." Her father gave a shrug. "He won't live forever."

"So he might die in the coming years, leaving me with our children."

"And his wealth. He would leave that to his son, and you would manage it in his stead until the child reached his majority. Better still, you could appoint me to aid you in that matter, leaving you free to do whatever you choose."

"Ah, I see." Phoebe wanted to scream but forced herself to address the matter in the same cold, calculating manner of her father. "It all makes perfect sense—now."

"Since you understand, I would like to make things right between us. I have tickets for the theater tonight and thought you might accompany me."

"If that is your wish." Phoebe reasoned that if she could get him to return her freedom, she would seek out her mother. Together they would be able to figure out a way for Phoebe to escape her father.

"It is my wish. I believe we will have an excellent time. We will have an early supper and then join a new friend of mine, Mr. Thompson. He and his wife will accompany us. Tomorrow I have very important plans to meet with him."

Phoebe nodded and pretended to be more interested in the choice of fruit than she really was. The last thing she wanted to do was spend the evening trying to convince everyone she was happy.

"Now, I insist you have some breakfast. Gerda tells me you've been quite miserable and aren't eating. I would hate for you to grow ill. Ours was nothing more than a misunderstanding. I was tired, and my trip had taken its toll. There were very few modern conveniences at the mine, as well as some disappointing complications. Everything worked out in the end, but it all was to blame for my temper." He extended the platter of sausages.

Phoebe took one and placed it on her plate. "I presumed as much."

Her father seemed pleased that she wasn't going to say anything on the subject. He turned his attention in earnest to the meal at hand, while Phoebe continued to ponder her options.

⌒⟆⟆⟆⟆⌒

Phoebe decided to stay in her room the rest of the morning. Perhaps if Vater saw that she wasn't all that desperate to leave her quarters, he would release the guard and believe all was well. It seemed to work. Phoebe noted more than once when Gerda left the room that no one was waiting outside. With plenty of time on her hands, Phoebe plotted exactly what she needed to do. Everything would hinge on Mutter.

That evening, Phoebe dressed with particular care. She donned a dark blue gown with jet-black trim. The midnight-blue attire suited her mood, and the style was of the latest fashion for the theater.

Earlier in the day Gerda had wisely accepted that Phoebe didn't wish to talk. She'd remained close at hand, however, silent. Phoebe had the feeling that Gerda was watching her for some response or reaction. Had Vater asked the maid for reports on her conduct? Phoebe wouldn't have put it past him. Then she recalled her father's statement that Gerda had told him Phoebe wasn't eating.

"Things are better with your vater, ja? You will have a good time tonight?"

Phoebe nodded but said nothing. She toyed with the clasp of her necklace instead. Once she had secured the pearl choker around her neck, Phoebe reached for her long gloves and pulled them on up over her elbows. After this she put a matching pearl bracelet on her left wrist.

"Do you wish to wear the earrings?" Gerda asked.

"No. Help me with this hat," Phoebe commanded, handing a black velvet cap with dark blue tulle and feathers that had been dyed to match the gown.

"You look quite beautiful. I think you will be the desire of every man at the theater."

"That is hardly my intent." Phoebe fussed with the tulle as Gerda secured a hatpin. She knew being sullen with Gerda was uncalled for, but the events of the day left Phoebe in a quandary. She wasn't about to marry the duke, but neither could she make such a declaration. It was too great a risk that Gerda would report such a comment.

"You will soon marry, and then every man will have to hide his desire for you."

Phoebe turned and looked at the woman. "Did my vater tell you that I was soon to marry?"

"Ja," Gerda said, nodding. "It is a good thing, ja?" She smiled. "The duke is a good catch. You will be the envy of all."

Phoebe said nothing. Her growing suspicions had been confirmed. It was clear that her father had confided in the woman, just as Gerda had shared information with him. A sense of dread settled over Phoebe. Gerda was her father's means of keeping tabs on her.

I wasn't the one who chose her to accompany me. Vater found her and made the arrangements. What a fool I've been!

Gerda no doubt reports to him on my every move—my every comment.

In order to test this, Phoebe decided to share some sort of information with Gerda and see how quickly it reached her father's ear.

"I do hope Herr Eckhardt is at the theater this evening." Phoebe offered the information quite casually. "I thought him to be most fascinating. He . . . ah . . . well, he invited me to go riding with him. We were to go tomorrow," she lied. "I don't suppose Vater would approve, but then again, he doesn't have to know." She smiled at Gerda. "I know Vater mentioned he would be busy with Mr. Thompson all day."

Gerda said nothing. She retrieved a black lace shawl for Phoebe and then curtsied. "I'll be waiting for your return tonight. Should I have a bath drawn?"

"No. I have no idea of when we'll be back. Given the water is easy enough to come by, we will manage it upon my return."

"Ja." Gerda nodded and began picking up Phoebe's discarded clothes.

Phoebe could tell that Gerda was uncomfortable. It only served to convince Phoebe that she was on the right track. She'd know for certain, however, if her father changed his plans for the following day.

"Why don't you let Vater know that I'm ready to go?"

Gerda nodded, perhaps a little too enthusiastically. She hurried for the door as if she feared Phoebe would change her mind. Once she'd gone, Phoebe began to think through a plan. She needed to get word to her mother without Gerda or anyone else being the wiser. But how?

The evening was just as tedious and boring as Phoebe had feared it might be. The play was acceptable, but her mood made it impossible to enjoy the frivolity. The night seemed to go on and on, but finally the carriage made its way back to the resort, and Phoebe breathed a sigh of relief.

"Mr. Thompson has been quite useful to me," Vater said as he helped Phoebe from the carriage. "I'm certain we can conclude our business quickly with his help."

"No doubt you are right," Phoebe said. "Perhaps your meeting with him tomorrow will allow you to know just how much time you'll need."

"Well . . . about that. Mr. Thompson had something come up. We've postponed our meeting, and that leaves me free to enjoy the day with you. I'm afraid I have neglected you."

Phoebe shivered, but not from the cold. "But you said it was of the utmost importance that you meet tomorrow."

"I know what I said, Phoebe." He looked at her with a smile. "But plans can be changed."

"I see." She allowed him to guide her toward the stairs.

"Perhaps tomorrow we could go into Helena and buy you something pretty." He let go his hold on her arm as Phoebe began to climb the steps. She looked down at her father, who still stood at the bottom. "We will need to order you a new wedding wardrobe—one which your husband will pay for. You can't dress as the daughter of a graf once you are married to a duke."

"I suppose you are right on that account. There is a shop in town where I was able to purchase an American riding outfit. The woman there has a large collection of drawings showing the latest Worth gowns. Better still, she had a few designs of Paul Poiret, and I am a huge admirer of his work. I'm sure we could have the seamstress take my measurements, choose materials and such, and order the clothes via telegraph. We could pick them up in Paris on our return home."

"That's a brilliant idea," her father agreed. "Let us have breakfast in the morning and plan out our day. But not too early. I promised to have a drink with someone yet tonight. I might be several hours in discussing business. Come to think of it, let us have brunch instead of breakfast—say at eleven?"

Phoebe smiled. "That would be quite perfect." She came back down one step, then leaned over to kiss her father's forehead. "Good night."

He smiled, seeming quite pleased. Phoebe hurried up the stairs. Her thoughts were all about how she might rise early and sneak away before her father had a chance to know. Gerda had evidently told him about Eckhardt. He never would have changed his plans for any other reason.

She entered her suite and found Gerda waiting faithfully. Phoebe detested the woman's presence now that she knew exactly what was going on. Even so, she knew she couldn't let on.

"Oh my. I am quite exhausted. You know, I believe I will do as my vater plans to do and sleep quite late. We're going to have brunch together in the morning around eleven, so don't bother to wake me before ten. In fact, why don't you use the morning hours to see to the laundry?"

"Ja. That would be good. It's nice and cool in the morning hours."

Phoebe let Gerda help her disrobe. "We're going to go shopping after that, so I don't suppose I shall be able to go riding with Herr Eckhardt. Pity, because he is such a handsome man. But what can I do?" She smiled and shrugged. "I shall let Vater send him a note in the morning."

"Ja," Gerda said, nodding.

Phoebe pulled on her robe and headed toward the bathroom. "I won't need you anymore tonight, Gerda." She closed the door between them before Gerda could reply.

Drawing a deep breath, Phoebe sat on the edge of the tub and tried to figure out how she would manage things in the morning. If she could slip away to her mother's cottage, Phoebe knew she would be able to plan her escape. Mutter would be the one person who would understand and offer her assistance. No one else could be trusted.

"Phoebe! I've been so worried about you. They told me you were sick. Are you better now?"

"I wasn't sick." Phoebe offered nothing more but glanced over her shoulder as if worried someone was watching. "May I come in?"

Elizabeth looked at her daughter in complete surprise. It was only a little past seven, and Elizabeth had only been up for a short time. "Of course. I was just doing my Bible reading."

She noted that Phoebe glanced over her shoulder not once but twice and then hurried into the cottage. "I need to talk to you."

"Why don't you come sit at my kitchen table? Are you hungry? You look exhausted. Are you sure you haven't been ill?"

"I am quite well. I didn't sleep last night, though."

"Come have some breakfast and tell me what's wrong."

"I'm not hungry, but I do need to talk."

Elizabeth led the way and motioned for her daughter to take a chair. "Some tea, then?"

"Yes. Tea would be fine."

It was clear that Phoebe was upset about something. Their relationship was in such a delicate state, Elizabeth didn't want to do anything to put up a wall between them.

"I have a problem," Phoebe began without Elizabeth saying a word.

"Tell me." Elizabeth picked up the teapot and brought it to the table before going to the cupboard for another cup and saucer.

For several moments Phoebe said nothing. She stared at the cup as Elizabeth poured the tea, and she continued to stare at it after Elizabeth had taken her seat. Uncertain what she should do, Elizabeth sat in silence and glanced down at her open Bible. Psalm sixty-nine had been her focus that morning, and midway down she found that the words of the psalmist matched her own prayer.

But as for me, my prayer is unto thee, O Lord, *in an acceptable time: O God, in the multitude of thy mercy hear me, in the truth of thy salvation. Deliver me out of the mire, and let me not sink: let me be delivered from them that hate me, and out of the deep waters. Let not the waterflood overflow me, neither let the deep swallow me up, and let not the pit shut her mouth upon me. Hear me, O* Lord; *for thy lovingkindness is good: turn unto me according to the multitude of thy tender mercies. And hide not thy face from thy servant; for I am in trouble: hear me speedily. Draw nigh unto my soul, and redeem it: deliver me because of mine enemies.*

"I wasn't sick. Vater locked me in my room with a guard at the door and wouldn't let me leave."

Elizabeth's head snapped up. "What?"

"He was livid because I told him I wouldn't marry the duke. I've never seen him so angry, but then again I've never truly defied him."

"I thought you were ill. I've been praying for your recovery." Elizabeth shook her head. "The man is unconscionable in his behavior."

"I've determined that I cannot stay with him. Nor can I return home. He would only force me to marry, and then he would continue to find ways to run my life." She looked at Elizabeth with an expression of pure disgust. "Do you know that my own vater actually told me that I might take lovers after I married the duke—so long as I was discreet?"

"I'm so sorry, Phoebe. I had hoped that maybe you were right—that maybe he had changed."

"Apparently not. Now my problem is to figure out what I can do. I need to make plans."

Elizabeth could see the determination in her daughter's eyes but could only give a little nod. How was she supposed to help Phoebe with this matter?

"You are the only one I could come to. I need your help, Mutter."

"Of course, you have it." Elizabeth glanced back down at the Bible. "But I am not the only one. God will help you in this. You have only to put your trust in Him."

Phoebe shook her head. "There isn't time for that. Vater will have what he came for in a short time, and then he'll be ready to leave. We were to travel to Seattle by train and then to San Francisco by ship. I must do whatever I can to escape him before we leave Helena."

Elizabeth took a long sip of her tea and whispered a prayer for wisdom. She didn't know if it would help Phoebe or not, but she decided to tell her daughter about the upcoming meeting she'd allowed the pastor to arrange.

"I need to tell you something before we continue." Elizabeth met Phoebe's confused gaze. "I have arranged a meeting with your father."

"You have?" Phoebe's expression changed to surprise. "But why? As you said, he already knows you're alive. He needn't know you are here. If he knows that, he'll do whatever he can to keep us separated. He might even suspect my plans to leave him."

Elizabeth could hear the fear in Phoebe's voice. She reached out and covered her daughter's hand with her own. "There's much I need to tell you, but I can't. At least not just yet, because it involves someone other than myself. I need to see your father and determine if he is the same man I left."

"He is." Phoebe shook her head. "He's angry and cruel. He slapped me. He's never done that before, but when I defied him regarding his arrangement for my marriage—he grew enraged and hit me."

Phoebe's words came like a punch to Elizabeth's midsection. It very nearly took her breath, and for a moment all she could do was nod. "I was afraid of that," she finally spoke.

"Vater is cruel and intends to impose his will upon me. He told me that he would see me married to the duke even if he had to drag me to the ceremony by my hair. And I believe he would do just that. My maid is working for him, feeding him information, so I cannot trust her. I even had to sneak out this morning in order to come see you, and I must return before long or I'll be found out."

"Yes, it would be best that we not give your father any reason to be suspicious." She squeezed Phoebe's hand. "If you go along with him, then he won't have reason to hurt you."

"But for how long?"

Elizabeth considered her question a moment. They would have to handle things very carefully. "Let me meet with your father face-to-face. I promise you I will make it so that he cannot impose his demands on us."

"How? How could you ever make him do anything he doesn't wish to do? He's spent the last ten years telling me you were dead. He has arranged a marriage behind my back to a man more than twice my age. Vater doesn't listen to anyone."

"He'll listen to me." Elizabeth drew a deep breath. "I have the ability to cause great damage to his reputation and social standing. I never thought to use it against him, but it would seem that perhaps the time has come."

After Phoebe had gone, Elizabeth went back to her Bible and pulled out a letter she'd finished writing only the night before. She looked over the contents, knowing that this letter might be the only thing that would keep her husband from moving toward legal recourse to take Kenny back to Germany.

She looked upward. "Lord, I pray you will make this work out in such a way that Kenny and I will be safe from Frederick's violent temper. Please help us, Lord."

15

*L*ater that morning, Vater frowned at the piece of paper Hubert had just handed him. Phoebe wondered if this was the summons to meet with her mother.

"Is there a problem?" she asked casually.

"I am uncertain." Her father wadded up the paper. "It would seem I'm being requested to meet with someone at one of the churches in Helena."

"Ah, no doubt another sapphire-related meeting."

Her father nodded. "Perhaps. It doesn't clearly say." He shrugged as if casting the matter aside. "I suppose you could come with me. We might still be able to shop." He considered this for a few minutes. "But I have no way of knowing how long this meeting might run."

"That's perfectly all right, Vater. We can always shop tomorrow or another day."

Phoebe knew without a doubt that this was the encounter of which her mother had spoken. A part of her almost wished her father had insisted she come along with him. She couldn't imagine what information her mother held that gave her the assurance Vater would behave.

"I'm to be there at one," Vater muttered. He pulled out his pocket watch. "That doesn't give me much time." He pushed back from the table and got to his feet. "Hubert, arrange a buggy for me. Be quick about it."

"Yes, sir." The valet went out of the suite in a hurry.

Phoebe rose from the table. She wandered to the window and pulled back the curtains. "It looks like rain."

Her father didn't seem to hear her. Had he guessed the identity of the person summoning him? Surely he had no reason to suspect it might be Mutter, but then why did he look so upset? Mutter said he had gambling problems. Had he already managed to get into trouble here in Montana? Trouble enough that he now worried that those holding his debt might be about to cause him problems?

"Days like this make me feel rather tired." She gave her father a smile. "I think I shall just spend the day reading and resting."

"That would be good. We will plan to have dinner together."

Phoebe nodded. "I hope your meeting goes well." She opened the suite door to find Hubert about to reach for the knob on the other side. He seemed momentarily surprised but quickly recovered.

"*Entschuldigen Sie, bitte.*"

She excused Hubert and made her way to her room. Gerda was nowhere to be seen, and Phoebe breathed a little sigh of relief. Having finished the book she'd borrowed from the hotel's library, she decided to return it and find another volume that might occupy her time and mind.

The lobby downstairs was aflutter with the arrival of new guests, giving Phoebe a chance to pass all but unseen to the library. The room wasn't all that large, or perhaps it was the dark wood paneling and shelves that made it seem smaller. Phoebe perused the titles and finally settled on a thick volume of American history. She knew very little about this country and thought perhaps the book would serve her well.

When she exited the library, Phoebe found the lobby still quite overrun with people. She made her way around the edge of the room and then headed outside to the porch. Despite the overcast skies, Phoebe felt this would be the perfect place to begin her reading. What she didn't plan on, however, was Ian Harper.

He approached as if he'd come with no other intention than to see her. There were others walking past. He gave them a nod, then spoke to Phoebe in a very formal tone. "Miss Von Bergen, how nice to find you here." One of the women glanced over at Phoebe, then continued her conversation with the man at her side.

"Mr. Harper." She held up the book. "I had just come to read."

He nodded and waited for the guests to move beyond hearing. "With it raining off and on, I think holing up here on the porch is a good solution. What are you reading?"

"It's a history of America." She smiled at his look of surprise. "I thought perhaps it would benefit me to know more about this country."

"Knowledge is never a waste of time."

She noted his casual dress. "And what are you about today?"

"I . . . ah . . . well, it's kind of a . . . ah, complicated matter, but Kenny wanted to swim."

"Oh, and is he there now?"

Ian laughed. "No. He wanted to see my mother first. She usually has cookies for him or some other baked treat. He's around back in the bakery."

"I would love to see him. Even watch you teach him to swim. My vater has just headed into town for a meeting."

"Yes, I know."

Phoebe frowned. "You know?"

"Well . . . I knew he was headed to town. I saw him pass by in one of the carriages."

She nodded, relaxing her suspicious thoughts. "That makes perfect sense."

"Yes. Kenny and I took the trolley, and we saw your father just a few minutes ago."

"Well, although I had a late brunch with Vater, I wouldn't mind a cookie or two myself." She looked toward the dining room. "Perhaps you might introduce me to your mother as well."

Ian laughed. "I'd like that." He offered her his arm. "We should probably go around to the back rather than through the dining room. If you don't mind."

Phoebe took hold of his arm. "Not at all."

"So besides reading," Ian began, "how have you been keeping yourself busy?"

"It's been mostly reading. However, I have had opportunity to take several nice long strolls. And from time to time I've been able to talk to some of the people who work here." She didn't bother to tell him that one of them was her mother. It was best for now that Phoebe say as little as possible.

"Perhaps you might join us in the pool. Kenny would love for you to begin your swimming lessons."

Phoebe shook her head. "That doesn't sound too appealing today." She frowned at the thought of her mother facing her father. Would the pastor really be able to act as a buffer and keep her mother from harm?

"You look rather upset. Just a moment ago you were all smiles. Is something wrong?"

"I . . . well . . . there's been quite a bit going on in my life. Things that I'm not overly happy with, and I haven't yet determined how I will resolve them."

"Would it help to talk?"

Phoebe hadn't had any intention of replying in the affirmative. It wouldn't do to share her fears and concerns with Ian. He was, after all, working for her father and might let slip some detail of their conversation.

"I suppose you might not be comfortable with that," Ian said before she could reply. "I'm sorry if I seemed overly forward."

"No. It's not that." She glanced at him and saw his look of confusion. "It's just . . . well, as you said earlier about your trip here today . . . it's complicated."

"Then let us focus on something less worrisome. Do you suppose you would like to go for another ride with Kenny and me? Kenny has talked about nothing else. He really enjoyed himself."

"I enjoyed our time together as well." Phoebe relaxed a bit. "He's such a sweet and smart boy."

"He is. Do you know that he has a strong inclination toward architectural studies? He reads about various styles and then points them out to me when we're walking about town."

"You two spend a lot of time together." Phoebe allowed him to help her down the porch steps. "Yet Kenny told me you aren't his father."

"No, I'm not." Now it appeared Ian was the one uncomfortable with the conversation.

"I'm sorry if I've overstepped my bounds." Phoebe fell silent, uncertain if she'd offended him.

"Well . . . it's . . . ah . . ."

"Complicated?"

He met her gaze and gave her a weak smile. "Yes."

"Miss Phoebe!" Kenny came running toward them with an older woman following behind.

Phoebe laughed at Kenny's enthusiasm. He might very well have run right into her, but Ian took hold of him before they collided. "Are you gonna come swim with us?"

"I might come watch, but I'm not ready to brave the water." Phoebe was utterly charmed by the boy's smile. His face radiated happiness, and for a moment Phoebe wondered if she'd ever known that kind of joy.

"Phoebe, this is my mother, Georgia Harper. Phoebe thought she'd like to have a sweet treat, and I told her you were probably supplying Kenny with cookies enough for all."

The woman's name sounded strangely familiar, but Phoebe couldn't quite remember why. "How do you do? I'm Phoebe Von Bergen."

Mrs. Harper smiled and nodded. "I've seen you about. You're much too pretty to go unnoticed."

"She's pretty like—"

"Hey, Kenny, you'd better get those cookies from Grandma Harper and get on over to the natatorium," Ian interrupted. He fixed the boy with a look that seemed stern. "We don't have a lot of time."

Kenny immediately lost his smile and turned to grab up the cookies Mrs. Harper held in a knotted cloth. Without another word to any of them, he ran off in a mad dash. Phoebe thought it all so very curious.

"I should get over there," Ian said, looking at Phoebe. "He can't swim well enough to be left alone. Feel free to come watch . . . if you like."

Phoebe watched him go with a strange sense of loss at his departure. She turned to Mrs. Harper and saw the woman looked almost worried.

"Is something wrong, Mrs. Harper?"

The woman perked up. "Not at all, my dear. I'm very glad to meet you. I've heard some very nice things about you."

"Oh?" Phoebe thought it rather odd and looked back over her shoulder in the direction Ian and Kenny had gone.

Mrs. Harper chuckled. "Well, Ian for sure had some pleasant things to say, but I was speaking more about Chef Michel. He thought you hung the moon and the stars."

For a moment Phoebe actually felt disappointed that the source of praise wasn't solely from Ian. But just as quickly she smiled and nodded. "He was a remarkable man. I was sorry to hear he'd quit. I can't help but feel somewhat responsible."

"The man was homesick. He had been ever since coming here. I wouldn't give it another thought." Mrs. Harper took hold of Phoebe's arm and gave a little tug. "Why don't you come back to the kitchen with me, and I'll fix you up a plate of goodies. We can't let your sweet tooth go without satisfaction."

◦⁀⁀⁀◦

Ian sat down beside Kenny. He could see the boy was still upset. "I'm sorry for being so abrupt with you."

"Is Phoebe a bad person?"

Ian shook his head. "Why would you ask that?"

"'Cause Mama said I couldn't tell anybody who I was because there were some bad people who might hurt me."

"Phoebe isn't a bad person. I was just worried that if you told her again she was pretty like your mama . . . well . . . she might want to meet your mama. And with all the things that are worrying your mother right now, I don't think that would be wise." He wasn't going to lie to the child, but neither could he explain that Phoebe was his sister.

"I'm afraid, Ian." Kenny looked up, and the fear was clearly registered in his eyes. "What if someone hurts Mama?"

"We're doing all we can to make sure that doesn't happen, Kenny. Remember that God is watching over you and your mother. He loves you and He wants you to trust Him."

Kenny nodded, but his expression looked less than convinced. Ian decided distraction was the best thing to get the boy's mind off his troubles. "Today I'm going to teach you how to dive."

"Really?" Kenny perked up. "Oh boy! I've wanted to dive for a long time."

"I know, and I think you're finally swimming well enough that we can give it a go. Come on, let's get changed." Ian began to pull off his boots. "Last one dressed has to give the other one two of his cookies."

Kenny all but flew across the room, tearing off his clothes as he went, which made Ian laugh. Hopefully cookies and diving would keep his mind off the fact that there were bad people who wanted to hurt him and his mother.

It was nearly a half hour later when Phoebe arrived. Ian had thought perhaps she wouldn't come at all. In fact, he'd almost wished it for fear of Kenny saying something that would reveal their connection.

"Miss Phoebe!" Kenny waved from where he was treading water. "I'm learnin' to dive."

"*Das ist gut.*" Phoebe stood well away from the pool's edge. "That's the way we say *that is good* in German."

"Das ist gut." Kenny tried the words on for size.

Phoebe smiled. "Well, are you going to show me what you've learned?"

"Just watch me." Kenny swam to the side and climbed out of the pool. "I'm really good. Ian says it's like I was born in the water."

He went to the place where the water was deep enough and then, without further ado, made a perfect dive into the pool. Ian couldn't help but throw a smile at Phoebe.

"A fish couldn't do better."

"He is quite the swimmer," Phoebe agreed.

Kenny swam to the side where Phoebe stood. "Did you see me?"

"I did," Phoebe said, bending down. "You did quite well. I'm very impressed."

Kenny seemed pleased with her praise. "Ian's a good teacher. You'll see when you let him show you how to swim. Then pretty soon you'll learn how to dive too."

Phoebe straightened. Her expression sobered as Kenny kicked off from the side and began to swim across the pool. Seeing her face, Ian wondered if she was worried about her mother and the meeting that was taking place. He'd thought earlier she might talk about it, maybe not in so many words, but in a broad manner. She hadn't, however, citing complications—something that Ian was only too familiar with.

Ian swam to where Phoebe stood. "It was kind of you to come. It means a lot to the boy."

"He's very sweet, and I didn't want to disappoint him." She looked at Ian with an expression he couldn't quite decipher. "I would have been here sooner, but your mother gave me a plate of food and I felt I needed to put it in my room before coming here. Then when I got back to my room, my maid needed my attention and . . . well, it was . . ." She fell silent.

"Complicated?"

She met his gaze, and Ian felt his heart nearly pound out of his chest. "Yes. Complicated."

He wanted nothing more than to jump out of the pool and take her in his arms. She looked so worried and frightened.

Knowing what he did about her father and mother, Ian couldn't blame her.

"I . . . uh . . . need to go," she said, backing up a couple of steps.

Ian could tell by the look in her eyes that she was just as affected by the moment as he was, and it made him want to say that he knew what she was thinking—what was worrying her. He wanted to declare that he would help her and see her through this difficult time, but of course . . . he couldn't.

"Say, I have an idea." Ian glanced quickly back at Kenny. "How would you like to go fishing?"

"Fishing?" Phoebe asked. "I've never been, so I can hardly say whether it would be something I'd like to do."

"Well, since your father is tied up, I thought it might be the perfect time."

"Fishing." Phoebe seemed to consider the matter a moment. She had no chance to reply, however. Kenny had heard the word as well and eagerly swam to join them.

"Can we go fishing?" he asked.

"I was just inviting Miss Phoebe to go with us." Ian smiled as Kenny launched himself from the pool. "I thought we could take her to our special place."

Kenny's face lit up. "Please, Miss Phoebe. Please come fishing with us. It's a real pretty place. You'll like it a lot. Maybe you can teach me some more of those German words."

She looked at the boy oddly for a moment and then turned back to Ian. He saw something flash across her expression. It was a look of questioning, but as quickly as it had come, it was gone.

Finally she nodded. "I think that would be fun. Let me go change my clothes."

16

$\mathcal{P}$hoebe had little desire to thread a worm on a hook, but once Ian had done the deed and cast the line in the water, she accepted the pole. When his fingers brushed across her own, Phoebe felt her face flush and her heart pick up speed. She ducked her head and looked away, but not before she saw a longing in Ian's eyes that matched her own.

"Ah . . . this isn't all . . . that difficult," he stammered and moved back a couple of steps. "If you feel a little tug on the line that probably means you have a fish on the other end."

"And then what?" Phoebe asked, hoping her nerves would calm. She looked with great doubt at where the line disappeared into the water.

"Then you pull the fish out," Kenny said without waiting for Ian to reply. "It's real easy."

"Indeed, you make it sound so."

Phoebe had never been to this secluded area along the meandering creek. It was beautiful and cool, and she thought it might be very pleasant to never leave. Being here with Ian and even Kenny gave her a peace of mind and joy that she seemed unable to find anywhere else. Of course, her growing attraction to Ian left her confused as to what she should do. Phoebe had never been in love before, and venturing into that territory was more frightening than she cared to admit.

"Be careful, Kenny," Ian called out, pulling her thoughts back to the task at hand.

Kenny moved up and down the bank, pulling his line through the water. It was almost like a dance. He seemed so happy and carefree, and Phoebe envied that. Had she ever known such sheer pleasure from something so casual?

"He never sits still."

Ian's comment drew Phoebe's attention. "I've noticed that." She smiled. "I admire his ability to enjoy life no matter where he is. I've never seen him unhappy."

Ian shrugged. "At his age there are few problems that seem as insurmountable as they do to us."

"Who is he, Ian?"

"Excuse me?" Ian looked more than a little surprised.

"He isn't your son, yet I've never seen him in the care of anyone else."

"Yes, well, he's the son of a friend of ours—my mother and I. He's been helping me at the shop since school's out. We've been good friends for a long time now."

"I got one!" Kenny yelled. "I got one!" He yanked his pole upward, and the line pulled up from the water with a good-sized fish attached at the end.

Phoebe couldn't help but be excited for him. "Das ist gut, Kenny. He looks quite big."

"He's gonna make a good supper. Mama will be so surprised when she gets back from her meeting."

This was the first comment he'd made about his mother in

some time. The only other thing Phoebe could recall was his telling her that she was pretty like his mother.

Ian helped Kenny take the fish from the hook and put it into a fish bucket they had in the water. "All right, now go catch a dozen more," Ian encouraged.

Phoebe felt her own line flutter and gazed down at the water in surprise. When she felt a decided tug on the line, she jumped up and called for Ian. "I think there's a fish on my line!"

Ian left Kenny and came to where Phoebe now stood. She quickly thrust the pole in his direction, but Ian shook his head. "No, you need to see this through. Pull up, and I'll get him with the net."

She felt completely ill at ease with the task but did as instructed with Kenny cheering her on. Finally Ian had the large fish in the net. He stepped toward her with the thrashing beast. "He's bigger than yours, Kenny," Ian called out.

"Das ist gut," the boy yelled back in reply. Phoebe and Ian laughed, which only served to egg Kenny on. "I'm gonna get an even bigger one. We'll have a contest." Kenny laughed and then caught sight of something that caused even more excitement. "Ian, your pole is moving."

Ian handed Phoebe the net's handle and quickly went to his pole. He easily retrieved the fish but, much to his disappointment, noted it was the smallest of the three. "I'll starve if they're all this size."

"You can certainly have mine," Phoebe announced. "I wouldn't know what to do with him anyway. In fact, I believe I'll just watch for a little while. This is far more work than I counted on."

Ian laughed and took his fish from the hook. "I'll just throw him back and let him grow a little more." He tossed the fish into the creek, then came back to take the net from Phoebe. "But this one, we keep."

Phoebe sat back and watched them continue to fish. She was delighted to see Kenny so happy. He jumped from one perch to another, all while managing the pole. He seemed quite at home, and his antics made Phoebe laugh.

After an hour or so, Ian determined that they had more than enough for supper. Phoebe thought back to Kenny's comment that his mother would be surprised.

When she gets back from her meeting.

The words echoed in Phoebe's head like a warning bell. She looked at Kenny, only this time she gave him a thorough study. He had always reminded her of someone—a childhood playmate perhaps—but only now did it hit her who that someone was. *Dieter.* When she was quite young, Dieter had looked just like Kenny.

Her stomach clenched. Her mother had said that she needed to tell Phoebe something, but someone else was involved. She had presumed at the time Mutter was speaking of Vater, but now it seemed all too clear.

"I'm going to go look for sapphires," Kenny told Ian.

"Aren't you hungry? We have some sandwiches and cookies, and I don't think we should make Miss Phoebe wait too long to eat."

"You can start without me," Kenny replied, surprising them both. "I want to find a sapphire for Mama." He wandered down the bank, studying the ground as he went.

Phoebe felt almost dizzy as she considered the truth of who Kenny was. She looked at Ian and knew he would realize something was wrong. She did her best to force a smile and act nonchalant, but his expression told her she'd failed.

She looked away. There was nothing to be done but ask the question.

"Are you all right?" Ian asked. He knelt down beside her. "You look pale."

Phoebe turned and met his eyes. She bit her lip and momentarily lost herself in Ian's gaze.

"Phoebe?" He reached out and touched her cheek. "What's wrong?"

"Kenny." She spoke the name and watched as Ian's expression changed. "He's my little brother . . . isn't he?"

⁂

Frederick Von Bergen despised being summoned to a meeting by anyone, even the kaiser himself. But even more he hated being called to a meeting by someone he didn't know. Throughout his life he had made it a priority to be the one commanding each situation in his life. Now someone else was taking that position, and he resented it—greatly. Still, given it could prove to be advantageous to his financial situation, he didn't feel he could ignore the matter.

"I am glad you could come," an amiable older man said with a smile. He ushered Frederick inside, then paused in the church foyer. "I hope it did not inconvenience you."

"It did, but your note sounded as if the matter were life and death."

The stranger nodded. "Won't you come with me?"

"I'm sorry, but I don't believe we've met."

The tall man turned and smiled. "Indeed, where are my manners? I'm Pastor Clearwater. This is the church where I minister, and you are Mr. Von Bergen."

"Graf Von Bergen."

The pastor smiled. "Of course."

"What do you want with me?" Frederick was reaching the limit of his patience. "You sent me a note ordering me to be here today, but I have no idea of what it's about."

"I'm sorry that you thought my invitation an order. I assure you that while it was most important that you come, your presence was requested—not ordered."

His reply did little to calm Von Bergen's anger. "I am a man of great importance, and my schedule is quite full. I hardly have time for visiting churches, and if this is a request for some sort of charitable contribution, then you should know I hold little value in religion."

The insufferable man had the audacity to laugh. "Neither do I. Religion is a weapon used by the devil."

Frederick frowned. He was usually quite good at figuring men out, but this preacher had him quite perplexed.

"Now, if you'll just follow me." Pastor Clearwater began walking down the aisle of the small sanctuary. "There is someone here who wishes to see you. We thought this setting more fitting to sustain calm and clarity of thought."

It was only as he moved to follow the preacher that Frederick noticed there was a woman sitting in the front pew of the sanctuary. A straw hat covered her head, giving no indication of her age. Frederick hoped she was merely here to pray and had nothing to do with whatever it was the pastor had on his mind. He had no desire to meet some simpering woman. Unless, of course, she happened to be rich.

When they reached the front of the church, Pastor Clearwater stopped and turned once again to face Frederick. As he did this, the woman stood and turned as well.

Frederick frowned, his gaze fixed on the pastor. "What is this all about?"

"*Guten Tag*, Frederick."

The voice, a mix of British-accented German, was one he'd not heard in many years, but he recognized it all the same. Frederick hesitated to look at the woman. His heart raced, and he felt as if an icy hand had taken hold, physically forcing him to turn to her.

"Elizabeth." He barely breathed the name at the sight of the wife he'd not seen in ten years.

17

lizabeth fixed her husband with a look that she prayed was devoid of emotion. In his eyes she could see the anger—anger she knew only too well. The tight set of his mouth and reddening face left her little doubt that he was about to explode in rage. If she dared to show any reaction, Elizabeth knew it would only make things worse.

"How dare you demand my coming here?" Each word was stated in guarded precision.

"Why don't we sit," the pastor suggested.

"No. I won't be here long enough," Frederick replied. "I have no business with this woman. She is of a wanton nature. Did she tell you that she deserted her family? That she slipped off in the night, most likely to meet a lover, and left her husband and young children behind?"

Elizabeth felt her knees tremble and knew if she didn't sit, she might well collapse. This meeting was much too taxing. She sank to the pew. "You know that is a lie, Frederick."

"A lie?" He stared down at her in obvious contempt. "You deny that you left without a word?"

"No." She squared her shoulders and returned his gaze. She had to be strong for Kenny's sake. For Phoebe's too. "I had no choice. However, I also had no lover and have never done anything to compromise myself or my values."

"Please have a seat, Mr. . . . Graf Von Bergen." The pastor motioned to a straight-backed chair that had been placed not far from where Elizabeth sat. He, meanwhile, took a seat beside Elizabeth on the pew. "We should address this matter in a civilized manner."

Frederick gave a harsh laugh. "I can see she has filled your mind with her lies."

The pastor looked at Elizabeth as if to question her willingness for him to continue. They had already discussed how this meeting might play out, and now Elizabeth nodded, giving Pastor Clearwater clear permission to proceed.

"Graf Von Bergen, the mistakes of the past cannot be undone. However, there is a great deal at stake for the future."

"She is a liar and a schemer. She will stop at nothing to destroy those who love her."

"You know that is untrue, Frederick. You are the destructive one. You know very well why I had to leave."

"Because you refused to obey your husband." He leered down at her. "Deny that."

Elizabeth swallowed the growing lump in her throat. "You made my life unbearable with your violent temper. You beat me as one might beat a savage dog."

Frederick's face reddened. "More lies." He looked to the pastor. "As a man of God, you should honor and respect the vows taken between a man and his wife."

"I assure you I do." Pastor Clearwater seemed completely at ease. "It was I who encouraged Elizabeth to have this meeting.

We both wanted to address this situation in a manner pleasing to God."

"Bah! Don't hide behind your religiosity. I have no tolerance for such addle-minded nonsense. I do not believe in a deity, nor will I. This woman chose her path and destroyed her family. I will divorce her and see that she never bothers me again."

"Would you not first be willing to hear her reasons for taking such drastic actions?"

"He knows very well the reasons. He was given to violent fits of rage. Rage so blinding that he beat me whenever the notion took him. He was so abusive in his actions that he caused me to miscarry three babies." Elizabeth stared hard at her husband. "A fact he knows very well to be true."

Frederick's eyes narrowed. "You have no way of proving that."

"There were witnesses to your actions. We had a house full of witnesses." Elizabeth felt her strength returning just a bit. "I believe any one of those servants would be able to testify to your behavior. I know that my lady's maid would most certainly attest to the miscarriages and the beatings that preceded them. You'll recall she left shortly after I did, and we still manage to correspond from time to time."

"It's of no matter, Elizabeth. I simply do not care. You left me and our children."

"And you lied to them! You told them I was dead. You made our daughter suffer grievous pain, all because you were too angry to be honest."

"You know nothing about our daughter and what she endured."

"Oh, but I do." Elizabeth rose and faced her husband. "And she knows about your lies."

Frederick looked momentarily taken aback. "You . . . you have conspired with her?"

"I have seen her at the hotel. That is how I knew you were here. I work for the Broadwater Hotel, and when I learned of your presence I knew I would need to resolve our separation."

"It will be resolved," he countered. "I will divorce you on grounds of infidelity."

"I have not been unfaithful to our marriage," Elizabeth said. "Furthermore, I have shown your letter not only to Phoebe but to Pastor Clearwater."

"What letter?" The veins at his temples seemed to bulge. "I wrote you no letter."

"You did." She pulled the missive from her pocket. "After I wrote to Phoebe several times at the boarding school you forced her to attend, you sent this threatening letter to me. Or do you not remember that?"

Frederick stared at the letter for a moment. The look on his face betrayed the truth. "So what if I did? It changes nothing."

"Phoebe knows your violence was the reason I left." Elizabeth drew a deep breath. "I was with child, and I couldn't stand by and let you take his life as you had the others."

"What child? I knew nothing about another baby. You are making all of this up for the benefit of gaining sympathy. Sympathy which you do not deserve. I might very well have disciplined you in the past, but if you are honest, you will not deny that you defied me and brought such matters on yourself."

Elizabeth slowly shook her head. "I learned I was to have another baby, and the realization was both welcome and terrifying. I knew that in order to protect the child, I would have to separate from you. I planned to take Phoebe with me, knowing full well that you had already poisoned Dieter's mind against me. You know that I wanted Phoebe to join me. I sent a family friend to talk to you, but you threatened his life and mine, as well as any living family left to me.

"You were insufferable, Frederick. Your gambling robbed me of my family treasures and inheritance, and your temper very nearly took my life. I had no choice but to leave, and I wanted Phoebe to leave with me. I didn't want her to suffer your temper and acts of rage. I told her all of this."

"When? When did you have a chance to tell her anything?"

"When you first arrived at the hotel. I knew you were in residence and decided to keep my presence hidden. One day, when I learned you and Phoebe had both gone out, I went to speak with my manager. On my way I ran into Phoebe. Apparently she had returned early, and I didn't realize it. However, I cannot lie and say I was displeased. It was wonderful to finally let her know the truth.

"She was stunned to be sure. We had a chance to talk, and I let her read the letters I'd written her years earlier. The letters you had the school return to me unopened. I saved them for just such an occasion, and Phoebe could see for herself the truth of my love for her. I also had her read this letter—the one in which you told me you'd rather see her dead than with me. The one where you threatened to kill me."

Frederick finally seemed to understand the full truth of all that had happened right under his nose. "She has known that you were here all of this time?"

"Yes. I asked her not to say anything to you. I wanted time to figure out what I should do. I needed to protect myself and . . . my son."

"Son? What son? What are you talking about?" He looked to Pastor Clearwater. "She declares herself to have honored our vows, but now she tells me she has another child. Who is his father?"

"I told you, Frederick. The night I left you I had just learned that I was to have another baby. I knew in order to save his life I would have to leave."

"You had another child by me? *My* child, and you kept him from me?"

The fire in his eyes sent Elizabeth back in time to all those horrible rages she'd endured. For a moment all she wanted to do was run. Run away again and hide.

"It's all right, Elizabeth," Pastor Clearwater said, standing. He took hold of her arm. "You are safe. God is watching over you."

Frederick moved toward her, but the pastor positioned himself between them. "I will not allow you to harm this woman. I suggest you take a moment to calm down."

Frederick looked for a moment as if he would hit the taller man. "I want the truth. Where is my son?"

"He is . . . he is safe." Elizabeth pushed down her fears and stood her ground. "And he will remain so. I can see you haven't changed, and I will not subject another child to your rage."

"You will have no choice. I will seek out legal help and take him from you. I have wealth and the support of powerful men. I even have the governor's ear—the governor of this state. I will have little trouble taking our son."

The smug look on her husband's face sent a chill through Elizabeth. She would never allow for him to take Kenny. It was time she use the knowledge she had against Frederick. It was her only hope of regaining control. However, before she could speak, Frederick posed a question.

"Does Phoebe know about her brother?"

Elizabeth shook her head. "I didn't tell her for fear her loyalty to you might cause her to say something. I had to make certain that you learned about Kenny only when I was ready for you to."

"Kenny? That's the boy's name?"

"Kenneth. But I call him Kenny."

"After your father, I presume."

She nodded. "Yes, just as Dieter was named for yours. Phoebe has seen the boy but has no idea that he is her brother. She believes him to be the son of some hotel worker."

Frederick's expression darkened. "I will deal with her later. I will not allow for such deception and underhanded ways."

"You allow for them well enough when you are the instigator." Elizabeth crossed her arms against her breast as if she could somehow put a wall of protection between herself and her husband. "Phoebe knows nothing. And she did nothing to deceive you. Did you ask her if she'd seen her mother? Of course not. You told her I was dead."

"It doesn't matter. She withheld the truth, and that is just as bad."

"Well, sometimes withholding the truth is necessary to protect others. Just as Rahab did with the spies."

"What are you babbling about now? Who is this Rahab?"

Elizabeth smiled. "She was a woman in the Bible. When Joshua, the leader of the Israelites, sent spies into Jericho, she hid them from the officials. God blessed her for her actions, just as He has blessed me for mine."

"That blessing has come to an end. You were a fool to ask for this meeting. You had to realize I would never allow you to keep my son from me."

"You have no choice, Frederick." She looked at the pastor for a moment. "Pastor Clearwater, I need to speak alone with my husband. What I have to say is something he would not wish to be shared, and in order to make my point with him, I must keep this confidence . . . at least for the time."

Pastor Clearwater nodded and then looked at Frederick. "I

will not allow you to lay a hand on this woman. If you should, you may rest assured that I will have you arrested. We do not allow men to beat our women in America."

Frederick's eyes narrowed. "Perhaps you'd have a better country if you did."

The taller man shook his head. "Perhaps it's the men who would benefit from the beating." He turned to Elizabeth, assuring her again that he would be nearby in case she had any trouble. Then he walked away, with a firm look at Frederick, allowing Elizabeth to speak to him alone.

Frederick turned on her, his face reddening and his voice rising as he spluttered in German, "What is it you wish to tell me? Speak now and then I will show you the power I wield. Not only will I gain control of our son, but I will see you put in prison."

"I don't think so, Frederick," Elizabeth answered in German, moving back a pace. She hated his nearness, and despite the pastor's promise to assist her, she knew it would be easy for her husband to strike out. "You see, I know all about the Sapphire Duchess and your dealings with her."

His eyes widened, but he remained calm. "Of course you do. That was never something hidden from you."

"But your cheating her was. I learned about it early in our marriage. Quite by accident, but afterward I made it my duty to know."

He paled. "You know nothing."

"That's where you are wrong, Frederick. You kept all of your transactions recorded in a small leather-bound journal in your desk. I copied those entries. I know the dates and places you went, as well as the funds given you by the duchess and the money you cheated her out of. At least I know of all that took place prior to my escape."

He raised his fist. "How dare you! You accuse me? You are in no position to threaten me. I will see you dead."

"And if I die, those records will go immediately to the duchess." She paused and shook her head as he lowered his hand. "You see, Frederick, you taught me well about deception. You also taught me the importance of having power. Until now, I was never quite sure how I could ever make use of what I know, but now I am confident. I know the truth, and unless you want the duchess to know as well, you will leave this country without bothering me or our son further. You may have your divorce—I will happily accept that conclusion to our farce of a marriage—but you will not have anything to do with Kenny."

"You think you have this all figured out, don't you?" He laughed in his cruel way. "Threaten me as you will, but you are nothing to me, and I will stop at nothing to see you removed from my life. You will bring me your evidence, or I will simply have you watched and our child taken from you at the first possible moment."

Elizabeth knew he would make good his threats, but she couldn't back down now. "I have already spoken with a lawyer. If anything happens to me, he has instructions to send my evidence directly to the duchess. If you steal our son away, I will mail her the papers myself. You will be arrested and tried for your crimes, and I will happily bear testimony against you."

Frederick let out a growl. "You haven't won yet, Elizabeth. I will best you at this as I have bested every obstacle ever laid before me. This battle has only begun."

"Make careful choices, Frederick. I have very little mercy where you are concerned."

It was well after midnight, and Phoebe was surprised that her father had still not returned from meeting with her mother. No doubt the meeting was long over with, but for some reason her father hadn't returned to the hotel. Throughout the evening she had tried to put aside her worries and read. She'd taken her meal alone, and from time to time, like now, she walked the length of the room. Pacing back and forth seemed to help with her nervous energy, but it didn't keep her from replaying the events of the day. First the meeting early that morning with her mother and then her revelation that afternoon that Kenny was her brother.

Ian hadn't even tried to deny it. Instead he told her that Kenny knew nothing, and he'd appreciate it if she would wait to speak with her mother before sharing the truth with Kenny. Phoebe had been stunned, but as the shock wore off, she found herself wondering why it hadn't occurred to her much sooner. Even so, the truth pleased her. She adored Kenny and couldn't be happier to learn that he was her brother. She had always wanted to have a close relationship with Dieter, but Father had insisted that such things were only desired by women. Dieter had much too much to learn about being a graf. There was no time to play brother to a little sister.

Gerda entered the room with a yawn. "Your vater has still not returned. He must have been delayed in his affairs."

Phoebe turned and saw her maid was quite spent. "I think I'll go to bed. I can speak to him in the morning."

"Very good." Gerda yawned again. "Will you need anything more from me?"

"No." Phoebe waved her away. Gerda had already prepared everything, including turning down the covers. "I'm fine. Get some rest." The maid nodded and left Phoebe standing in the middle of the room.

Phoebe paced a bit more before she went to the window and looked out on the front lawn of the hotel. Her father had taken a carriage to town and would no doubt return the same way. Perhaps she would sit at the window and watch for him. But even if she did see him approach, Phoebe wasn't exactly sure what she would do. She wanted very much to confront her father regarding the truth, but at the same time she feared he might again unleash his temper upon her. Perhaps it was foolish to stay in the hotel.

"Maybe I should sneak out and stay with Mutter." She knew that somewhere in the conversation between her mother and father she would have been mentioned. If her mother mentioned that Phoebe knew about her, there was sure to be trouble.

"But I'm forewarned," she murmured. "I can best Vater if need be." But even as she spoke the words, Phoebe had doubts. He had been able to lock her in her room without any trouble, and he had slapped her. She bit her lip, not knowing whether to stay or go.

She wanted to confront him about the truth in private. If she remained here, she would be able to do exactly that, and no one else had to be the wiser. There was no sense in wasting any more time in worry. Morning would come soon enough, and she could speak to him over breakfast.

Climbing into bed, Phoebe found herself thinking again about what must have taken place. She wondered if her mother had told her father about Kenny. She wondered if Mutter had told him that Phoebe had no intention of marrying the old duke and instead planned to remain in America. When sleep finally came, Phoebe found her dreams torturous and full of still more unanswered questions.

"Get out of that bed!"

Phoebe woke to the harsh command of her father, followed by his throwing off her covers and dragging her to her feet. Without warning he backhanded her and sent her backward onto the bed once again.

She had no time to react or even speak before he had her back on her feet. He shook her violently. "You . . . you . . . are a . . . lying . . ." German words trailed into momentary silence. "Stupid woman."

The smell of liquor was strong on his breath, and given his muttered words, Phoebe was confident her father was drunk. No doubt her mother's presence had caused him a great deal of discomfort. He continued to shake her until Phoebe thought her neck might snap. She had to find a way to protect herself. She pushed at his chest, momentarily surprising him. He wasn't to be deterred, however, and grabbed her again.

"You knew . . . knew your mother was here. You knew it and kept it from me. You deserve . . . my . . . wrath." He swung his arm forward but missed her and momentarily threw himself off balance.

Phoebe took the opportunity to move away from him. "I didn't lie to you—you lied to me. You told me Mutter was dead. You let me suffer all those years believing she was lost to me forever."

Her father regained his footing and headed right at her. Phoebe knew that she was no match for the man. She spied Gerda in the doorway to her room. "Go get help, Gerda."

She barely got the words out before her father's fist connected with her face. Phoebe saw stars and fell back against the wall. She would have crumpled to the floor, but her father had ahold of her shoulders and pounded her back against the wall again and again.

"I will make you sorry you were ever born. You think you can defy me. You think . . . you think you can get away . . . from me. I'm your vater."

Phoebe tried to ward off her father's attack but was much too weak. She thought of Mutter telling her that God cared about her—that Phoebe had only to reach out to Him.

As blackness began to consume her mind, Phoebe found herself praying. *If you really do care about me, please help me.*

18

When Phoebe awoke, the first thing she knew was pain. Every part of her body screamed out in agony. Her eyes felt like lead weights, and she had to force them open. As her vision cleared, Phoebe saw Gerda approach with a knotted towel. Something was inside the bundle. As Gerda moved toward her, Phoebe flinched and pulled away, crying out in pain.

"Just don't move. I've brought some ice and it should help with the swelling. Your vater has gone to bed, and Hubert will let us know when he awakens."

At this, the memory of her father's rage came back. Phoebe didn't want to think of it, however. She knew now that her mother had been justified in running away. She only wished that she too had been able to go with her.

Phoebe settled back against the pillow, and Gerda touched the bundle to her face. Somehow her maid had been able to get ice despite the hour.

"You must lie still and rest. The ice will help, but . . . well . . . I don't know if you have any broken bones. Hubert said we mustn't send for the doctor."

"Of course . . ." Phoebe stopped talking. The effort hurt too much. Her lip felt swollen. She had been about to offer a sarcastic comment about how they couldn't do anything to bring shame or questioning to her father. However, between the pain and the knowledge that Gerda was his spy, Phoebe thought it senseless to speak her mind.

"Your vater surely didn't mean to cause such harm, after all." Gerda had the audacity to smile. "He was drunk and, well . . . when men are drunk they often behave poorly, ja?"

Phoebe could hardly believe the woman was defending him. How could any woman see another beaten like this and offer up an excuse for the offender? Obviously Gerda's loyalties were with Graf Von Bergen, even now.

The mantel clock chimed the hour. It was five in the morning. Gerda went to the draperies and pulled them back. The skies were just starting to lighten. Phoebe had no idea how long it had been since her father first yanked her out of bed to begin his assault. What she did know was that she wasn't going to lie around and allow him to do it again.

"Leave me," she ordered.

Gerda looked at her and shook her head. "But you need to—"

"I need to sleep." Phoebe closed her eyes. Her head throbbed, and her abdomen felt as though an elephant were sitting atop it.

"Are you certain you wouldn't want me to stay here and help you with the ice?"

Phoebe shook her head. "No. I just want to rest and forget all of this."

Gerda stared at her for several long moments and then nodded. "Very well. I will go rest too. We didn't have much sleep last night."

"No. We didn't." Phoebe had no strength for further conversation. Her only thought was to get Gerda to leave.

Finally, Gerda did just that. She went to the adjoining room door and stepped through. She paused a moment, and when Phoebe said nothing more, Gerda closed the door between them.

Phoebe waited for nearly fifteen minutes, hoping that as tired as Gerda was, she would fall asleep quickly. The last thing she needed was for Gerda to go running to Hubert or Vater and tell them that Phoebe was on the move.

Despite the intense pain, Phoebe pushed back the covers and rolled to her side. She pushed up off the mattress, biting her lower lip to keep from crying out. For a moment, Phoebe rested on the side of the bed and drew a deep breath. At least as deep as her injured body would allow.

Gradually she found the strength to rise. She pulled on her robe and glanced around the room. She didn't want to take the time to dress and instead gathered a few articles of clothing. Later she would send for the rest of her things, and if Vater refused to let her have them, then so be it. She still had most of the money he'd given her. Remembering this, she took up her purse and tucked it in with the clothes. She could only hope that no one would see or hear her. In the hallway all was quiet. Phoebe headed for the servants' stairs and slipped down the back way and out of the hotel.

Her escape seemed to take forever given her slower gait. Each step took a great deal of effort, but Phoebe found the movement actually helped relieve a bit of the stiffness. By the time she'd exited the building and reached the path that would take her to Mutter's cottage, Phoebe's eyes welled with tears. Everything had changed in coming to America. Her life would forever be altered. Hopefully for the better, but who could say?

She reached her mother's little house and knocked on the door. It took several moments, but finally Mutter came. She turned on the lights and opened the door. Her hair was still mussed from sleep, and her robe was yet untied.

When she got sight of Phoebe's face, the older woman burst into tears. "Oh, Phoebe! I feared that monster would do something like this." She put her arm around Phoebe and gently led her into the house. "I'm so sorry. I'm so sorry. I should have insisted you stay with me."

"I was asleep when he finally came back to the hotel." Phoebe felt as if her mouth were full of cotton.

"Don't try to talk. Believe me, I know how hard it can be." Mother led her to the bedroom. She took the bundle of clothes and Phoebe's purse and set them aside before helping Phoebe into the bed.

Phoebe made no protest. The bed was still warm from where her mother had slept. There was a faint scent of lavender on the pillow. The scent reminded Phoebe of when she was a little girl. Mutter had insisted all of their bedding be perfumed with lavender, believing it did much to soothe a person and aid their sleep.

"Now you rest, and later you can tell me more about what happened. Your father won't find you here, so you'll be safe."

Phoebe nodded and felt the exhaustion and misery of her ordeal overpower her. She closed her swollen eyes and let out a long sigh.

⁘

The first thing Elizabeth did was dress. She threw on her clothes in a quick, haphazard manner and barely took time to brush and pin her hair into some semblance of order. While Phoebe slept, Elizabeth went quickly to the hotel manager and explained the situation. She needed someone to go to town and get word to Georgia Harper. She wanted the older woman to know what had happened. There was no telling what Frederick might do once he rallied for the day. She wrote a hasty note, then handed it over to the man.

He glanced at the paper and nodded. "I'll send a boy right away."

"Thank you."

Elizabeth hurried to the ice house, arranged for one of the men to bring a block of ice to her cottage, and then returned to check on Phoebe. She was still sleeping, and Elizabeth couldn't help but take the opportunity to just gaze upon her.

It had been such a surprise to find her here, and yet the years seemed to just wash away with each conversation—each stolen moment together. Her daughter had been such a precious part of her life, and had she not been pregnant with Kenny, nothing would have taken her from Phoebe's side.

"I would have borne the abuse to stay with you," she whispered.

But now Phoebe was the one abused. Her bruised face brought back all of the pain and suffering Elizabeth had endured over the years. A tear escaped her as Elizabeth gently pushed back a strand of her daughter's blond hair.

"This was never yours to bear."

An hour later Elizabeth had just finished chipping ice into a bowl when she heard Phoebe stir. She found Phoebe sitting on the side of the bed, looking around as if trying to remember why she was there.

"How do you feel?"

"Terrible." She smiled and winced. "Especially my face. I suppose I look quite horrible."

"You have bruising and swelling, but you could never look horrible. Do you think you could eat something?"

"If it doesn't require much chewing. I don't think my jaw is broken, but it does hurt."

"Of course. I have some oatmeal. We can add cream and make it soupy. You should be able to very nearly drink it. I also have some ice for your face."

Phoebe nodded in a slow, cautious manner. "Can you help me dress?"

"Are you certain you wouldn't like to just remain in bed for the day? I can send someone to retrieve your things, and you can live here with me and . . ." Elizabeth fell silent.

"Kenny?" Phoebe asked.

Elizabeth nodded. "So you know."

"I figured it out yesterday. I don't know why I didn't see it sooner. He's so precious. I'm glad you left Vater in order to save him."

Elizabeth nodded. "I couldn't let your father take his life. I still mourn the unborn children he took from me, but I know I'll see them again one day."

"In heaven?"

"Yes." Elizabeth waited for Phoebe to say something.

Finally Phoebe rose. "I want to know more about that. You see, when Vater was beating me, I actually prayed. I don't know that I did it right, but I didn't know what else to do."

Elizabeth smiled and put her hand to Phoebe's cheek. "God doesn't require certain words. He hears the cries of those who would have Him save them."

"Well, I certainly needed saving. I think in that moment I knew that the things I've heard about God and His love for us bore further consideration. I remember going to church as a child and not really understanding what it was all about. Now I want to know what's required."

Elizabeth helped Phoebe from her robe and gown and explained as she helped her daughter dress. "God sent Jesus, His Son, to earth because He wanted to be reconciled with us. The Bible says that it's through His grace and mercy that we are saved."

"Must we do something special to get that grace?"

"No, sweetheart. It is a gift from God. We cannot earn it."

She helped Phoebe into her clothes while she continued. "A lot of people think it's enough to just live a good life and do good things, but we will never be perfect enough to be without sin, and we can never do enough good to earn salvation."

"I remember hearing a pastor speak at the Fourth of July celebration. He talked about sacrifice and why Jesus was the perfect one. Ian . . . Ian Harper explained it to me." She flushed a bit as if embarrassed.

"Ian is a wonderful young man. He and his mother have been good friends to me . . . to Kenny."

"I know. At least I do now. I thought at first he was Kenny's father because he showed such tenderness and kindness toward him."

"Ian is just that way with most folks." Elizabeth smiled and buttoned her daughter's waistband. "He's a very special man."

Phoebe nodded ever so slightly. "I know."

Just then a knock sounded on the cottage door. Elizabeth gave her daughter's arm a gentle pat, hoping it wouldn't cause pain to the bruises she'd seen before helping Phoebe into her blouse.

"That may well be him now. I sent a message to Georgia. I asked her to send Ian and Kenny."

"Don't you think it's dangerous to bring Kenny here?"

"It is a risk, but a necessary one. I need to explain to Kenny about all that has happened. And I couldn't very well leave you." She gave Phoebe a sad smile. "He doesn't realize that you are his sister, and he knows nothing about his father. You may listen from here, and when I am through telling him about your father, then you may join us."

Elizabeth left Phoebe and went to answer the door. Just as she had presumed, it was Ian with Kenny. Kenny threw himself into his mother's arms.

"I've missed you, Mama." He hugged her tight around the neck. "Can I come home now?"

"Not just yet. You know those bad people I told you about?"

He pulled away. "The ones that might hurt you?"

"Yes. Well, they hurt Phoebe, and she's come to stay with me."

Kenny frowned and took a step back. "Did the policemen take the bad men away?"

Elizabeth knelt beside him. "No. Kenny, you need to understand something, and I know it will be very hard. However, I need for you to be strong." Elizabeth glanced up to Ian. She could see in his expression that he was angry at the news that Von Bergen had hurt Phoebe.

"I can be strong, Mama. I'm almost ten years old." Kenny's sober expression left Elizabeth no doubt that he would do his best. He'd always been such a level-headed child.

"The bad man I told you about . . . well . . . he's your father." Kenny's eyes widened, and his mouth formed a silent O. Elizabeth hurried to explain. "Long ago, your father hurt me. He hurt me a great deal. Now Phoebe has a blackened eye and swollen lip—you'll see her in just a few minutes. I'm telling you this so you won't be so surprised. Your father hit her because she didn't tell him that I was here."

"Then how does he know?" Kenny asked.

"Because I had a meeting with him yesterday. Remember, I told you I had to go to a meeting, and then later I came back and had supper with you and Grandma Harper and Ian?"

Kenny nodded. "You went to talk to my father?"

"Yes." Elizabeth chose her words carefully. "You see, Kenny, he didn't know about you. I left—I ran away in the night because I was afraid he would hit me again. You were inside of me, not yet born, and I knew that if he hit me, you might never be born. I know this is hard for you to understand, but one day I will explain everything better. For now, you just need to know that your father is very angry and wants to take you away from me. That's why I need for you to stay a little longer with Ian and Grandma Harper."

"I won't let him take me away from you," Kenny said, again throwing his arms around Elizabeth's neck. "We can go away again."

She pulled him back so she could see his face. "We aren't going to worry about that just yet." She looked at Ian and then back to her son. "Kenny, Phoebe is going to live with us."

He smiled for the first time since she'd begun to tell him about his father. "I love Phoebe. She can be my sister now."

"Kenny"—Elizabeth paused to draw a deep breath—"Phoebe *is* your sister. That's why your father beat her. She knew about me and figured out about you, but she said nothing to your father because I asked her not to tell him. After our meeting he realized she knew about me, and that made him very mad—so mad that when he came back here to the hotel he hurt her."

Phoebe stepped slowly from the bedroom just then. Elizabeth heard Ian's sharp intake of air and rose to see if her daughter needed any help.

"I know I look a sight," Phoebe said, trying to smile. She winced and lowered her face. "I don't want you to worry, though. I'm really all right."

Kenny started for her, but Elizabeth took hold of him. "You

can't hug her like you did me. She might have broken ribs." She looked to Ian, who had just let out a heavy breath.

Ian crossed the room and offered Phoebe his arm. "You should probably sit down."

Phoebe didn't look up, but neither did she refuse his offer. Ian helped her into the rocking chair, and Kenny came to sit at her feet while Elizabeth looked on.

"We'll take good care of you, Phoebe. You're my sister, and I always wanted a sister or a brother."

"Well, you have a brother too," Phoebe replied. "But he lives in Germany, and he's a lot like our father."

"Then I don't want to know him."

Kenny's matter-of-fact statement made Elizabeth realize that perhaps she hadn't handled this matter as well as she could have.

"Kenny, I don't want you to hate your father or Dieter—your brother. Hate isn't what God would have us do. You need to pray for them. They don't believe in God, and because of that, they don't know how to love."

Phoebe put her hand out, and Kenny let her take hold of him. "Hate," she said, "only ends up hurting the person who's doing the hating. Mutti . . . Mama is right. We need to pray for them."

Ian smiled, but it didn't quite reach his eyes. Elizabeth knew he'd come to care for her daughter, and right now the anger he felt toward Frederick was battling with the truth he knew about God. Ian had to know God wouldn't have him resolve this matter in aggression and rage. That was Frederick's way— not God's.

"Do you want Phoebe to come stay with us?" Ian asked.

"I thought it might be best, and that's why I sent for you," Elizabeth replied. "I would hate for Frederick to do anything more to harm her."

Ian nodded, but Phoebe lifted her face. "I'm not leaving you to face him alone, Mutter. I will stay here with you, and I believe we need to face him together. After all, he's the one who separated us for all those years. I won't let him have that power again."

"But you're in no shape to endure his rage," Ian declared.

"I'm surely sore, and yes, my face is damaged, but I already feel stronger after rest and Mutter's care. I'm certain together we'll be better able to deal with Vater."

"You should take her to the pool," Elizabeth suggested. "The waters have done much to cure people of their ails. It would do her a wonder of good to soak for a long while in the warm waters. Frederick—if he reacts the way he did in the past—will sequester himself away for most of the day to sober up. By evening he will act as though nothing happened. I don't think you'll have to worry about running into him before then."

"I'll take her to the pool as soon as we leave you," Ian promised.

"Ian can start teaching you to swim," Kenny said. He withdrew his hand from hers and reached up to touch her bruised cheek. "I'm sorry you got hurt, Phoebe."

"It's going to be all right," Phoebe replied. "It was worth everything to get you as my brother and to have Mutter back in my life. I would do it all again."

"But you won't have to," Ian declared. "I'll see to that."

Elizabeth smiled at his words. Once when she had first met Ian, she had wished that Phoebe might meet a man as worthy and honorable. Wished that they would fall in love and marry. Now she saw that there was a great possibility her wish would come true.

"Can you walk to the natatorium?" Ian asked.

Phoebe nodded. "I think so. As I said, I'm doing better."

Elizabeth smiled. "I'll come along and help you change into one of the swimming suits."

❧

Phoebe didn't know when anything had felt so good. She sat on the steps in the shallow end of the pool and relished the warmth of the water. Kenny sat beside her holding her hand and reassuring her that he wouldn't let her float away.

"It would do more good if we got you completely immersed," Ian said as he waded through the water to reach them. "Do you trust me to see to it that no harm comes to you?"

His gaze met hers, and Phoebe felt her heart skip a beat. She nodded, knowing that Ian would do whatever was necessary to protect her. He held out his hand to her, and Phoebe let him take hold of her.

He pulled her from the steps toward him and then to the side of the pool. "We'll take it slow. You can hold on to the edge."

Phoebe did just that while Ian put his arm around her waist. His nearness left Phoebe almost breathless, but her sore muscles quickly reclaimed her attention. Kenny moved in from the other side and treaded water beside her. He looked so funny bobbing there that Phoebe couldn't help smiling. She looked at Ian, their faces only inches apart.

"You've done a good job teaching him."

"I told you he was part fish."

Phoebe watched his lips as he spoke. When she glanced back into his eyes, she could see the longing there—longing that matched her own. Ian leaned toward her just a bit, and she realized he was about to kiss her.

"Do you like it, Phoebe?" Kenny asked.

Phoebe trembled. "I like it very much." Her words were barely a whisper.

"I knew you would." Kenny pushed off from the wall and swam a semicircle around Phoebe and Ian. He rolled over on his back. "Since you're gonna stay, Ian will have lots of time to teach you to swim."

Phoebe realized Ian had pulled away from her just a bit. She was disappointed that there would be no kiss, but also relieved. She didn't fully understand all the emotions coursing through her, but she knew without a doubt that she had somehow managed to fall in love with Ian Harper. The thought delighted her and made her feel all the better. She'd never been in love before now, and given all she'd been told over the years, true love was a curative for many ills.

"This feels glorious. I wish I'd come here sooner." Phoebe let go of the pool's edge and smiled. "Now I'm completely in your hands."

Ian nodded with just a hint of a smile. "I think I like that idea."

19

*I*an attempted to work on Von Bergen's stones later that afternoon. He and Kenny had returned to the house after seeing Phoebe safely to her mother's cottage, but the image of her face and the things Von Bergen had done to her haunted him. He'd much rather throw the stones back in the man's face and then punch him square in the nose. In fact, he wanted very much to cause Von Bergen the same amount of pain as he'd inflicted upon Phoebe.

You know that wouldn't solve anything.

Ian sighed. His logical thinking had argued with his emotional heart ever since he'd learned what had happened. Even now, he couldn't even facet without the stone blurring into an image of Phoebe's injured face. She had been so misused.

The waters had done wonders, and Phoebe had declared herself much better. On their walk back to Elizabeth's, she had even seemed more surefooted and less stiff. Of course, her bruises wouldn't fade as quickly, but she was quite resilient, and Ian felt confident she would recover quickly. Then all he'd have to worry about was keeping her safe from it ever happening again.

But she isn't my responsibility.

Ian frowned. He cared about Phoebe. In the short time since meeting her, Ian found she was seldom far from his thoughts. At first he'd told himself that it was only because of knowing Elizabeth and Kenny. He worked hard to convince himself that while he was attracted to Phoebe and had come to care about her, he would never allow his heart to be entangled again. Especially in a situation where deception seemed to reign. But it hadn't been long before he realized he couldn't fight against his feelings.

She was beautiful. Of course, there were other beautiful women around him. There were several young ladies at church who had made it quite clear they wouldn't mind having Ian's attention. So any attempt to reason his feelings away based on infatuation with Phoebe's beauty was ridiculous. His feelings were based on Phoebe—the person deep within—not the external. In fact, after seeing her battered and bruised, Ian's feelings had only deepened. Her pain had become his own—especially the internal pain of suffering betrayal.

But what can I do? What should I do?

It was obvious his feelings for her were growing. He'd nearly kissed her in the pool and would have if Kenny hadn't been there. At the time he wasn't at all pleased for the interruption, but now he felt a sense of relief. The poor woman had a swollen lip and black eye. The last thing she needed was his advance.

But Ian knew his kiss would have been welcomed. It was clear that Phoebe felt the same way as he had. He'd seen it in her eyes. She'd wanted him to kiss her as much as he had wanted to give her that kiss.

"Do you think Phoebe will like living here in Montana?" Kenny asked. He'd been quietly reading a book while Ian tried to focus on working with the stones.

Ian set the dop stick aside and leaned back in the chair. "I think she will like it very much."

"But we don't have a big house. Phoebe used to live in a really big house—like a mansion. Remember, she told us about it with all those rooms and servants."

"I remember. But you should remember that a place isn't as important as the people in it. Phoebe will be happy, because she'll be with people who love her."

"Like you?"

Ian saw the boy's mischievous smile. There was no sense in denying his feelings. Kenny already knew them. Maybe it was time Ian admitted them as well.

"What do you think about me loving your sister?"

"I'm glad. You and me are like brothers, and now I have a sister too. I think it's good that we all love each other."

Ian laughed. The boy made it all sound so simple. "Well, I suppose given all the bad things that have happened, it's nice to have at least a few good things to balance it out."

"Do you want to marry Phoebe?"

"I have to admit I've been thinking about that very thing."

Kenny sobered and nodded. "Getting married is something you should think about a lot. You told me you needed to get to know a woman before you married her. Do you think you know Phoebe now?"

Ian paused. "I know her enough to know I'd like to spend the rest of my life with her." Speaking the words aloud finally gave Ian a sense of peace. He truly did want to spend his life with Phoebe. He wanted to show her the love he felt, protect her, and care for her. He wanted to have a family with her.

A smile replaced the sternness of Kenny's expression. "Well, that ought to be enough."

"Well, she needs to know me too." Ian's past experience

with love, and the pain caused by lies that strangled that love, made him more than a little cautious. He'd always told himself he would never again marry. Never again trust anyone. Now he felt differently. However, he also knew he would have to be open and honest with Phoebe about the past if they were to ever have a future together.

⁂

Phoebe remained hidden in her mother's cottage for nearly three days before deciding to venture out. With the help of the hotel cleaning staff, Mutter had arranged for Phoebe's things to be delivered to the cottage. They had also delivered a letter to Gerda and to Phoebe's father. In Gerda's case, Phoebe told her that her services were no longer needed. In Vater's, Phoebe stated that she would not be returning with him to Germany, nor going further on the trip with him. She made it clear that if he ever attempted to hurt her or her mother again, she would bring about legal actions.

There had been no reply sent by either. Not that Phoebe had truly expected one. She did, however, live in fear that her father would show up on the doorstep. Her mother feared this too and arranged with Georgia and Ian Harper to keep Kenny with them just a little longer. She also asked the hotel manager to arrange for some of the male staff members to keep an eye on her cottage. They needed time, Mutter had explained. Time to see exactly what Phoebe's father would do.

"If and when your father finds you again, he will most likely try to force your return," she had told Phoebe.

Phoebe, however, had assured her that nothing would take her away. Now that she knew what her father was capable of, she would be on her guard. Together they would face and defeat him.

Behind her mother's cottage was a little grotto where Phoebe could enjoy the sunshine without too much fear of being intruded upon. Even so, she didn't venture out unless her mother knew where she'd be and most of the time was also nearby. Today, however, Phoebe felt that her strength had been restored and decided to take a short walk near the cottage. Word had come from the hotel manager that Phoebe's father had taken one of the carriages and left for town. Phoebe saw this as the perfect opportunity to enjoy herself a bit.

The brilliance of the sun in the cloudless sky did much to lift Phoebe's spirits. She still had no idea what the future held, but she had a definite sense of relief. She hadn't realized just how oppressed her life had been. Father had a way of robbing everyone around him of their liberty and true happiness.

"I hope I'm not intruding."

Phoebe glanced to the right and saw Ernst Eckhardt approaching. She gave a hesitant smile. "Good morning, Mr. Eckhardt."

He studied her face for a moment. "It would seem you've met with some sort of accident."

Phoebe saw no reason to lie about the matter. "My vater was rather angry with me."

Eckhardt's brows drew together as he frowned. "I am sorry. Violence of such a type is never acceptable."

"Thank you." Phoebe continued to walk. "It won't happen again. I'm no longer staying with him." She let the matter-of-fact statement speak for itself. "And how are you, Herr Eckhardt? Were you able to purchase land for . . . it was for a relative, wasn't it?"

He fell into step beside her. "Yes, it was for a relative, but no, I haven't found the perfect place just yet. I do believe Montana has a great deal to offer, however."

"So do I. That's why I've decided to stay here."

"But with whom will you stay?"

"My mutter." Phoebe looked at the man who now walked at her side. "It's a long and complicated story, but my vater had once told me that my mutter was dead. As it turns out, she had left him because of his violence toward her. I learned she was here at the hotel and have now decided to remain with her."

"And how did your vater take the news? Was that why he hit you?"

"It was all related, but as for how he took the news of my leaving him—I don't know. Neither do I particularly care, although I am still afraid of what he might try. However, my mutter has shared her faith with me. Faith in God."

"Faith in God is a good thing." Eckhardt smiled. "My *tante* is a woman of faith. She and my mutter were sisters, and when my mutter died, my tante told me that if I put my trust in Jesus, I would one day see Mutter again."

Phoebe nodded and slowed her pace. "My vater doesn't believe in God, so he didn't encourage his *kinder* to believe. However, in speaking with my mutter and others, I've come to believe." She smiled. "In fact, I'm quite eager to know more about God. My mutter is taking me with her to church on Sunday and has shared her morning devotions with me. I must admit it's still all so new, but I can see that it is right and true."

For several minutes they continued walking without speaking. Phoebe couldn't help but feel that Eckhardt wanted to say something more. She hoped he wasn't going to speak to her of feelings and love. The last thing she wanted was to have him declare a romantic interest in her.

"Has your vater . . . concluded his business here in Montana?" Eckhardt finally asked.

Phoebe let go a sigh of relief. "I have no idea. I still hardly understand the reason we came here to begin with. I know Vater is on a trip to purchase stones for a woman back home, and that Montana has some very beautiful sapphires. However, I also know that the sapphires he is to purchase for the woman are to be from Ceylon. Otherwise I know nothing. Vater has never been one to be open about his business."

Eckhardt nodded. "I suppose that is only right. You are far too lovely to waste your time pondering his business affairs." He stopped, and Phoebe did likewise. "If you'll excuse me now, I'm afraid I must be about my business. I very much enjoyed our stroll." He clicked his heels together and gave her a bow. "Until another time."

"Yes. I hope that your business dealings are successful."

Phoebe watched him go. He was a very nice man, but he always left her feeling as though he was after something. She turned back toward her mother's cottage and found Mutter instructing seven or eight hotel maids just outside the door.

"I will come and inspect the work in one hour," she told the women. "At that time we will discuss what is next to be tackled." She looked up to see Phoebe and smiled. "I see my daughter has returned." The other women turned to acknowledge Phoebe.

The woman who had been responsible for cleaning Phoebe's suite frowned. It was the first time she'd seen Phoebe after her father's attack. The other women seemed just as concerned, but no one asked about the matter.

"Now, if you'll excuse us," Mutter told the ladies, "I need to speak with Phoebe."

The women nodded and bid them both good day before slipping away. Phoebe could see that they were uneasy. Perhaps they had dealt with her father's rage as well.

"I hope you had a nice walk," Mutter said, putting her arm around Phoebe's shoulders.

"I did. I ran into Ernst Eckhardt. Do you know him?"

Mutter shook her head. "I don't believe so."

Phoebe nodded. "He's staying here at the hotel and seemed quite surprised to find travelers from Germany. He's here to find land for a relative, as well as study the architecture in San Francisco."

"Is he in business with your father?" Her mother's tone suggested suspicion.

"No. Not that I know of. I know he was present at a party we hosted when we first arrived, but other than stating his interest in purchasing land and his plans for moving on to California, I've not known him to have other business."

They entered the house, where the unmistakable aroma of food wafted in the air. Phoebe smiled. "It smells wonderful in here."

"One of the girls brought us food from the kitchen. Our lunch." Mutter smiled. "Are you hungry?"

"I am." Phoebe smoothed down the sprigged muslin of her gown and smiled. "Walking in the fresh air always stirs my appetite."

She followed her mother to the kitchen table. She waited as Mutter removed the dish towels covering two plates of food. Phoebe noted the feast with surprise. "*Wiener schnitzel* and *spaetzle?*"

"And gravy," her mother declared and went to the counter to retrieve the gravy boat.

"I've never seen them serve food like this." Phoebe nodded as her mother offered to pour gravy over the veal.

Mutter took her seat and offered grace before they sampled the fare. Phoebe thought it as good as anything she'd had at home.

"They've managed to crisp the veal to perfection," her mother commented.

"Indeed. It's a wonderful surprise. However did you manage it?"

"I had mentioned to Georgia that seeing you and Frederick made me rather homesick for German food." She laughed and cut into her veal. "She mentioned it to the new chef, and here we are."

"The Harpers are so kind."

"They are." Mutter glanced up and met Phoebe's gaze. "I think you have a very definite fondness for one Harper in particular."

Phoebe swallowed and nodded. "I must say it has come as a surprise to me. I've never lost my heart before."

"And have you now?"

"I think so." Phoebe stopped eating and grew quite serious. "I'm not at all sure what to do about the way I feel."

"And how is it that you feel?"

"I think I'm in love."

Mutter beamed a smile, obviously approving of Phoebe's comment. "You couldn't find a better man. Although, I will say he does have a rather sad past. I don't know all of the details, but you do know he was married once before and his wife died in childbirth?"

Phoebe nodded. "I know little else. I suppose if we are to grow closer, Ian will need to tell me everything. At least everything relevant to our relationship."

"Have you told Ian how you feel?"

"Goodness, no." Phoebe began to eat again. She couldn't imagine sharing her heart with Ian. What if he didn't feel the same way? She knew he cared about her, but what if that was only because she was the daughter of Elizabeth Bergen and not because he was in love with Phoebe?

"Why not?" Mutter asked after a few moments of silence.

Phoebe paused her fork midway to her lips. "Because he might not feel the same way."

"But if you don't let him know, how will you ever find out? I think you should speak to him about how you have come to care—love him."

"What if I'm wrong? What if all I'm feeling is gratitude for his kindness?"

Mutter laughed. "Do you honestly think that's the foundation for your sentiment toward him?"

Phoebe put the fork down. "That's the problem. I'm quite perplexed by all of it. I've never felt this way about anyone else. Not with any of the suitors Vater has paraded in front of me over the years. When I was away at boarding school there were only girls around me. When I would come home from school, Vater kept me very secluded. I never went anywhere without him and Dieter at my side, so meeting anyone and forming an attachment wasn't possible."

"That doesn't surprise me." Mutter focused on her plate and pushed the food around as she considered the matter. "I still believe you should speak to Ian. I've watched him with you, and I believe he cares for you."

"I suppose talking to him would serve to let me know one way or another." Phoebe tried to imagine the intimacy of such a moment. What if he laughed? What if he told her she was just being childish?

She ate for a few minutes and let the memories of all that had passed between her and Ian go through her mind like a collection of photographs. "When we were at the pool he almost kissed me." She hadn't really meant to speak the words aloud, but once she did, Phoebe looked to her mother for comment.

Mutter smiled. "Why didn't he?"

"I don't know," Phoebe replied. She had thought about it

long after the event and came up with two conclusions. One, he realized what he was about to do and felt it would be wrong. Or two, he realized he didn't want to kiss her after all.

"Perhaps he didn't feel the time was right what with your lip being cut and your jaw swollen."

Phoebe sat back against the wooden chair. "I don't suppose I thought of that." She chuckled. "That seems quite a logical answer."

Mutter forked a piece of the meat and nodded. "I think you should have a talk with Ian. Maybe wait until you know your father is occupied elsewhere and then go see him at his shop. I know. You could go with me to the Harpers' this evening. I want to see Kenny, and I know he would want to see you. I'll go speak with Georgia and see if she's of a mind to have company, but I'm certain it will be fine."

Phoebe nodded. She felt her stomach do a flip. She wasn't very good at praying just yet, but she couldn't help but glance heavenward.

If you're listening, God, I could certainly use some wisdom.

20

Frederick Von Bergen cursed as the driver seemed to hit every bump and hole in the road on their return to the Broadwater Hotel. The day hadn't gone well at all, and now he was tired and angry—not to mention sore. When the driver hit yet another rough spot, Von Bergen let go a string of curses.

"Are you trying to kill me?"

"Sorry, sir," the driver replied, "this road is pretty bad. You should have let me take the long way back."

"I don't need your excuses. Just keep your eyes on the road and avoid those holes." Frederick settled back in the leather seat and shook his head. It seemed servants everywhere were mouthy these days.

There was still plenty of light in the sky when they arrived at the hotel just past eight. Von Bergen climbed down from the carriage and glared up at the hotel. Coming to Helena and the Broadwater had caused him serious distress. Not only was he risking a great deal by purchasing Yogo sapphires instead of Ceylon stones, but now he faced this situation with his wife and daughter. Not to mention a son he hadn't known anything about until a few days ago. No doubt the boy would have to be broken of every bad habit taught him by Elizabeth before he'd be of any use to Frederick, but he would see that the boy returned with him to Germany.

Hubert met him at the hotel room's door. He ushered his master into the suite and immediately began to help rid him of his hat and coat.

"Would you like to have dinner brought up, or have you already dined?" he asked in German.

Frederick all but ripped the buttons off his vest as he tried to undress. "I ate in town. What I want now is a hot bath and a glass of brandy."

"Very good, gnädiger Herr. I'll start the bath and then return to pour your drink."

Frederick pulled the vest off and then began to work on his tie. His anger at Elizabeth and Phoebe only mounted when Gerda knocked on the door and then peeked inside.

"I saw that you had returned."

"Ja. Come in. What news have you of my daughter and wife?"

"Not much," Gerda admitted. "I know that Miss Phoebe is staying with her mother here on the grounds, but the staff is very protective of your . . . wife. Apparently she has a little cottage and works here in charge of all the maids. Although I've not seen her."

Frederick shook his head. "And there's been no further messages or notes sent?"

"No, sir. Not since the letters we had right after Miss Phoebe left. The one to you and the one dismissing me."

Hubert returned and crossed to the liquor cabinet. Frederick went to the window and looked out on the grounds. "Well, there's bound to be someone who can be bought. I need information, and I need it as soon as possible."

"Ja, gnädiger Herr." Gerda met Frederick's gaze and offered him a sympathetic smile. "Can I help in any other way?"

Frederick nodded. "Ja." He didn't bother to elaborate but instead turned toward his valet. "Hubert, where is that brandy?"

Hubert turned without another word and handed him a snifter. "Should I lay out your nightclothes, or will you go out again yet this evening?"

"I have no need to go out, but neither do I need nightclothes. Just put my robe in the bathroom and then leave us."

Hubert cast a disapproving look at Gerda but knew better than to say anything. Frederick was in no mood to tolerate his servant's condemnation.

Once Hubert departed, Frederick looked at Gerda. "Come help me with my bath. I need to forget this day."

⁓⁕⁕⁓

Phoebe made her way next door to Ian's shop just as Georgia Harper had directed. She was instructed to let Kenny know their mother wanted to see him. She knew that her mother and Georgia were purposefully putting her and Ian together, but she really didn't mind.

"Hello?" she called out, coming through the back door.

"Phoebe?" Kenny came around the corner at a full run. "It is you!" He wrapped his arms around her waist and hugged her close. His tight grasp reminded her there was still some soreness in her muscles, but Phoebe didn't mind.

"*Wie geht es dir, mein Bruder?*"

He looked up and frowned. "What?"

She laughed. "How are you, my brother?"

"I'm fine, my sister." He laughed and pulled away. "I can't believe I really have a sister."

Phoebe laughed as well. "Well, you do. You have a mother too, and she wants to see you immediately. She's over in Grandma Harper's kitchen."

Kenny nodded and shot off toward the back door. Phoebe shook her head. He was such a happy-go-lucky child. Neither she nor Dieter had ever known the luxury of such joy.

She turned and found Ian watching her. His expression betrayed his feelings, and Phoebe felt a little lightheaded at the passion in his eyes. She wanted to talk to him about her feelings and knew that now was the perfect time to do so, but her tongue seemed to stick to the roof of her mouth.

Ian's eyes narrowed as he inspected her face. "Your bruises are fading nicely."

She put her hand to her cheek. "Ja—yes. I believe I'm very nearly healed. I'm not nearly so sore." She fell silent, uncertain what else to say.

"Would you like to see my shop?" Ian asked. His mood seemed to lighten. "Have you ever seen a lapidary at work?"

Phoebe shook her head. "No, not truly. I would love to see what you do."

He smiled. "Then come with me."

Phoebe followed him to the middle of the house, where Ian had several tables and pieces of equipment set up. "This is my workroom." He motioned to one particular table. "This is where I facet the stones."

She drew near and studied the various pieces of equipment. "It looks most confusing. I cannot imagine the attention that is needed."

He brought a small bag and opened it. "Hold out your hand."

She did so, and he shook out several stones into her hand. "These are roughs. They haven't been treated at all."

"They're still quite lovely," she said, admiring the blue stones.

"They are. Yogos are different than most sapphires. They don't require heat treatment to bring out their color. In fact, they have very few flaws, and although they are generally small in carat weight they result in beautiful pieces."

"And how is it that you take a stone like this and make it into a beautiful gem?"

He smiled. "I'll show you rather than tell." He took the stones she held and replaced them in the bag. Next he motioned her to follow.

Phoebe did as he said and stood beside Ian as he took a seat at the faceting table. He angled a reflector to give him optimum light from the table lamp. "When I set out to facet a stone, I first consider it for flaws. We look for feathers, which are tiny cracks and fissures. These can cause problems when the light passes through the stone. No one wants to find feathers in their stones because these can extend. I also look for clouds. Clouds make opaque-like patches in the stone, and this must be eliminated. Yogos rarely ever have clouds. I have worked with other sapphires and have found clouds and feathers, as well as silks, which are strings of tiny cavities that look like shimmery streaks."

"And these are all flaws in the stone?"

He nodded. "They affect the look of the gem as well as the way the light travels through the stone. It is my job to cut the stone in such a way that the light can pass more easily to enhance the brilliance of the gem. You see, it's the light that truly gives the stone its beauty."

He held up a stick. "This is a dop, and if you look here, you'll see one of the stones I've been working on today."

Phoebe bent closer, and Ian's hair brushed against her cheek. She could smell his cologne and feel the warmth of his skin. The moment made her all but forget what Ian was showing

245

her. Chiding herself, Phoebe did her best to focus on Ian's hand and the stick.

"We cement the stone on the end of the stick, and that way it stays secure while we work." He pointed out the jamb peg and told her about the various degrees each of the holes in the peg represented. Each was used to make a different angled cut.

"This is the grinding disc, which we call a lap. Over the years we've used a variety of laps, some of wood, some of metals. These are used with various powders and water to smooth away the stone's edge."

"How can a powder smooth away stone?" Phoebe asked, trying hard to stay focused on the equipment and stone rather than the man.

"The powders are varied. The harder the stone, the harder the grinding powder. Also, the faster the disc must rotate. Oh, and water is needed to reduce the heat of the friction." He reached over to release the cap from a bottle. Turning the bottle upside down, Ian placed it in a wire holder over the grinding disc. A very small trickle of water began to dampen the lap.

"It all sounds . . . complicated."

Ian turned to look at her, and Phoebe found her lips only inches from his. She straightened, somewhat unnerved by the situation. "Ah . . . how . . . ah . . . how do you turn the disc?"

Ian grinned and looked back at the table. "This little hand crank over here." He reached out with his left hand and tapped the handle. "There are newer machines with electricity being developed every day, but I haven't found one yet that I feel is just right. I kind of like gauging the speed by hand. Same with the dop. I like to feel the stone against the lap. There's a certain kind of pressure that should be applied, and after years and years of working with the stones, you just know by instinct what that should be."

He began to turn the disc, and Phoebe watched as Ian applied the stone to the lap. He said nothing and instead focused on manipulating the stone. For several minutes he worked with the piece and then finally stopped and held it up for Phoebe to inspect.

"There, I've finished the crown."

Phoebe looked at the beautiful stone of cornflower blue. "It's lovely."

Ian surprised her by jumping up. "Here, have a seat. Give it a try."

She shook her head. "Oh, no. I would just ruin everything."

"I'll give you one of the stones I was teaching Kenny with." He put aside the piece he'd been working on and went to another table to retrieve a second dop. "Kenny was working with this earlier, and I know he won't mind at all."

Phoebe stood staring at the machine. "But I wouldn't begin to know how."

"That's why I'll guide you. Now sit."

She finally did as he instructed. Her pulse raced from his nearness, and when Ian leaned over her, Phoebe thought her heart might very well pound itself right out of her chest.

"Now here, take hold of the dop. This end has the gem, and the other end will go into the peg." He guided her hand to position the stick in the right hole. "Now gently let the stone touch the lap."

Phoebe did this, but her mind was ever on his hand on hers. She listened as he told her what kind of pressure should be exerted.

"Now, with your left hand take hold of the crank."

She drew a deep breath and reached out. Ian closed his hand over hers. He now completely overshadowed her—his chest against her back. As he began to help her turn the crank, Phoebe felt the lap begin to grind against the stone. She said nothing, and neither did he. Instead, Ian would apply a bit more pressure to her hand to press the gem against the grinding stone or tighten against her left hand to turn the lap faster. Phoebe could scarcely breathe and wondered if Ian would even notice should she faint.

⁓⁂⁓

Ian felt the warmth of Phoebe's back against his chest. He felt the smoothness of her hands and breathed in the scent of her hair. It was no use fighting his feelings for her. He felt her breath quicken and wondered if she could feel the thundering pace of his heart. Something was happening between them— had already happened.

"I think I'm in love with you!" Phoebe blurted out, pulling her hands away from the dop stick and the crank.

The loss of her hands beneath his caused Ian to straighten rather abruptly. But he didn't stop there. He pulled Phoebe to her feet and turned her to face him. He looked deep into her eyes and saw the questioning look she gave him.

"I don't just think I love you," he whispered, "I know it."

Phoebe's eyes widened, and Ian lost himself in pools of sapphire. He drew her closer, determined to kiss her. His lips were nearly upon hers when the bell at the door jingled and a man called his name.

He felt Phoebe stiffen. She pushed to leave, but Ian held her fast. "Please don't go."

"Mr. Harper, it's Ernst Eckhardt. I saw the light. Are you still here?"

Phoebe seemed to regain her wits. "Go. I'll still be here."

Ian looked at her, hesitating as if this were just a dream and he might awaken at any moment. He didn't want to leave her.

"I'll be right there, Mr. Eckhardt," Ian finally called out. He never took his gaze from Phoebe's face. "Stay with me."

She nodded, and the look in her eyes made Ian wonder if she were agreeing to something more—something unspoken but definitely implied.

21

"Mr. Eckhardt, I was just about to close up shop," Ian said as they emerged from the back room. "What can I do for you?"

Phoebe met Eckhardt's smile. He nodded. "Fräulein Von Bergen, it is a pleasure to see you here as well. The truth is, I need the assistance of you both."

"Assistance?" Ian questioned. "Exactly what did you have in mind?"

Eckhardt glanced around toward the door. "Could we speak without fear of interruption?"

Ian nodded and left Phoebe's side to lock the door. Next he pulled down the window shades and then came back to Eckhardt. "There. Now what is it you need?"

"As Fräulein Von Bergen will tell you, I am from her homeland. What she doesn't know is that I am the nephew of an elderly woman whom many call the Sapphire Duchess."

Phoebe couldn't help but gasp. She looked at Eckhardt and shook her head. "But . . ." She couldn't find the words.

"It's all right. I assure you I am not your enemy. My aunt has long been suspicious of your vater's dealings and sent me to trail after him on his expedition to purchase stones for her necklace. I apologize that I couldn't say anything sooner, but I feared you might run to your vater with the news. Now, however, I feel certain you will be more inclined to help than to hinder me."

"Well, if you're here to ask me to stop faceting the stones for Von Bergen," Ian began, "I've already decided to do that. I plan to return his stones to him tomorrow."

"I would ask that you not do that," Eckhardt replied, surprising them both. "You see, I wish to catch Von Bergen with the stones completed. I know he still plans to continue on to Ceylon so that, should there be any question, he will have proof of his visit there. However, I also know that he has worked with the Montanans to purchase as many of their sapphires as they could spare."

Phoebe shook her head. "But why? That is what I've not understood. Why come here when the duchess specifically called for Ceylon sapphires?"

"Because they're cheaper," Eckhardt countered. "Although I must say the Yogos have very quickly been gaining in value. I believe they will soon exceed the quality and value of stones from elsewhere."

"I agree with you, Eckhardt. However, I don't want to see Phoebe or her mother put in further danger. As you can see, Phoebe has already borne the brunt of her father's displeasure."

"I do realize this. I knew all about Mrs. Von Bergen's supposed death. My tante told me it was commonly believed she was dead; however, there was evidence to suggest otherwise. It didn't take her all that much time to learn what had really happened. Neither of us knew she was here in Helena until just recently. It changes nothing in my task."

"And what exactly is that task?" Phoebe asked.

"To bring your vater to justice. We have no way of knowing exactly how much money he has stolen from my tante over the years, but we do know it to be a sizable amount. With this trip, we took care to keep every bit of money accounted for. I have shadowed you and your vater since you left Germany."

"I had no idea." Phoebe looked to Ian.

"So what do you need for us to do?" Ian asked.

"I need you to go ahead and complete the faceting of Von Bergen's stones. I need to know exactly what you are charging him, and when he takes possession of the stones, I need to account for the monies he pays you."

"But it's hardly fair for Ian to work only to have you take back the money," Phoebe said, shaking her head.

"Perhaps I didn't make myself understood," Eckhardt said with a smile. "Mr. Harper will keep whatever funds are given him. Just as those who sold the stones to your vater will keep the money paid to them. As I mentioned, this trip has long been in the works, and we knew full well there would be a great many expenses. However, my tante deemed it necessary and acceptable if the aim was to see your vater brought to justice."

Phoebe bit her lower lip at the thought of her father in prison. He would never allow such a thing to happen. Eckhardt and the Sapphire Duchess might believe they had the upper hand, but Phoebe knew how deceptive her father could be. He wasn't without his friends either. No doubt there were those of noble birth who would support and even defend her father.

"What is troubling you, Fräulein?"

Eckhardt studied her with a curious look, while Ian's expression bore concern. Phoebe shrugged. "I just know my vater. Other men have tried to cause trouble for him. I'm not all that familiar with his business dealings, but I do know he's managed to overcome any adversity to this point."

"I assure you, Miss Von Bergen, your vater will not be able to overcome this situation. My tante has the ear of the kaiser himself. I also have the cooperation of the legal authorities here in America. There are some very capable men working with me."

"I see." Phoebe let go a sigh. "I'm sure you will need them all. Vater is a dangerous man to fight against."

Eckhardt nodded. "I have only to look at your beautiful face to see that."

Phoebe touched her hand to her bruised cheek. "Indeed."

They listened to Eckhardt for another ten minutes as he explained what Ian's role would be. Ian in turn explained his timeline and when he could have the sapphires ready.

"When you are finished and plan to notify the graf that the stones are ready, send word to me first. I will come and make certain everything is arranged."

"And what do you need for me to do?" Phoebe asked when the men fell silent.

"I would very much like an introduction to your mutter," Eckhardt replied. "I have a feeling she might also be able to assist me."

Phoebe nodded. "I believe you're right. She's here with us— in the house next door. I can introduce you now if you like."

"Danke." He clicked his heels together. "That would work very well for me."

⌇⌇⌇

Elizabeth watched Eckhardt closely, hoping to see if she could discern any deceit in his statements. It would be just like Frederick to hire someone to cause such a diversion. Not only that, but now that Eckhardt had explained his position, he had pressed the question as to whether Elizabeth knew anything that might help him make a stronger case against her husband. What if Frederick had sent the man to rob her of her information?

"I do have knowledge of my husband's crimes against your . . . aunt." Elizabeth narrowed her eyes. "However, I am not at all comfortable with handing such information over to you. For all I know you could be his cohort."

Eckhardt nodded and reached into his coat. "And you are wise to question everyone related to this situation. I have a letter here from my tante. She wrote this letter for the purpose of presenting it to the legal authorities. However, I believe it might serve to convince you as well."

Elizabeth took the letter and unfolded it. She quickly perused the contents and nodded. It seemed perfectly in order, but her doubts were still strong, given her knowledge of Frederick's deceptive nature.

"I have already revealed to my husband that I know about his thievery. I needed to tell him this to give myself leverage in keeping him from taking our son—Phoebe's little brother. Frederick knew nothing about the boy, but when we met I told him about Kenny. He, of course, threatened me and promised to steal the boy away. Thus, I felt it important to explain to him that I was prepared to reveal to your aunt all that I knew."

"I see. Well, that needn't be a problem," Eckhart said after several thoughtful moments. "In fact, this entire situation should work to our benefit. With the graf preoccupied with your return to his life and the news that he has another son, he will hardly be worried about my dealings. However, I wonder if you do have written proof of what your husband has done in the past. Proof that would aid my case."

Elizabeth considered this for a moment. "I have some papers listing various transactions. I copied them before leaving Frederick. The information was taken from papers Frederick had in his desk. They show the dates and amounts of money given him by your aunt, his expenses in purchasing the gems, and then what he actually charged your aunt. The totals are vastly different, as you already presumed."

"Those records would do much to aid us in seeing Graf Von Bergen pay for his crimes."

Elizabeth nodded. "Then after I resolve this matter of custody and our marriage, you may have them. But not until. I cannot risk Frederick somehow getting ahold of them until after he agrees to my terms. The man is fully capable of altering the records and explaining away the discrepancies."

Eckhardt smiled and nodded. "I understand. Believe me, once I am able to catch him in the act, your husband will be taken by the authorities and deported. I will, of course, accompany him. It would be enough for you to mail the information to my tante."

This gave Elizabeth an immediate sense of peace. "Very well. I will help you in any way I can." A thought came to mind. "I could arrange another meeting with Frederick. Perhaps I could get him to admit to what he's doing here. You could have it witnessed."

"Perhaps. I will keep that in mind," Eckhardt replied. "For now, however, I will take my leave. I've kept you from your family far too long." He rose, clicked his heels, and bowed. "I thank you for your willingness to speak with me."

Elizabeth rose. "I wish you the very best in seeing my husband incarcerated. No one deserves it more than he does. However, I caution you to watch your back. Frederick wouldn't hesitate to have you beaten or even killed should he learn the truth of what you're doing."

"Do you have any problem killing women?" Frederick asked, eyeing the rough-looking man.

The man spit on the floor and then laughed. "I'd kill my own mother if the money was right. You pay me enough and I'll kill whoever you want."

"There are two women in particular. One has a young boy. I don't wish for any harm to come to the child. Do you understand me? If he suffers so much as a scratch, you'll answer to me."

The man's eyes narrowed. "I don't like threats, mister. I'm happy to do a job for pay, but I'm my own boss. If you can't work with that, then I'm not your man." He started to get up, but Von Bergen motioned him to remain seated.

"I don't intend to be your boss. I simply do not want to see harm come to my son."

The man smiled in a vile manner. "So you want me to kill your wife, is that it?"

"Yes. And my daughter. Neither are of any use to me anymore, and both deserve to die for the way they've deceived me. I want it done quickly and without any sign of who was responsible. I'll give you half the money now and the other half when the job is done."

To prove this, Frederick put the first half on the table. The man's eyes widened considerably at the large sum. His glance went momentarily to Hubert, who stood at the ready to defend his master, before he returned his gaze to Frederick.

"You got a deal, mister. I got me two brothers who'll be happy to help get the job done."

"I'm not paying any more than what I've already agreed to." Frederick leaned back in his chair and folded his arms. "So don't even think of asking."

"I wasn't gonna." The man reached for the cash, keeping an eye on Frederick the entire time. When he saw that Von Bergen didn't intend to stop him, he grabbed up the bills and stuffed them in his pocket.

Frederick watched him with stern caution. The man was scum, but that was the kind of man who would kill two women without asking questions or pointing fingers later.

"I need it done as soon as possible."

"Where will I find 'em?" The man lifted the nearly empty beer mug, eyed it with obvious displeasure, then looked at Frederick. "I could use another drink while you're explaining."

Frederick thought of telling the man he had more than enough money to buy his own beer, but he decided against it. Instead he motioned for the barkeeper to bring another beer.

"You'll find that the women live in a small cottage on the Broadwater Hotel grounds. I've drawn you a map." Frederick pulled the paper from his pocket. He'd paid dearly to get a groomsman to tell him where the women were living, but it had been worth it. At least it would be worth it if this scheme worked out.

"I want you to get in there, get them, and take them well away from here," Frederick said, handing over the map.

The man looked at the drawing for a moment, then nodded. "We'll grab 'em and ride out to one of the canyons. There's a lot of old abandoned mines. It'll be easy enough to dump the bodies there."

Frederick nodded and waited until the bartender brought the beer and took his money before continuing in a whisper. "Leave word for me here. I'll have my man check each day around two. When the job is done, just let the barkeeper know when you want to meet here again. He'll give my man the information, and I assure you, I will come."

The man nodded and drank the beer down in one long gulp. He got up from the table without another word. Frederick smiled, feeling quite satisfied with this turn of events. It felt good to have things arranged. Soon Elizabeth and Phoebe would no longer be a problem and the only thing left that he had to worry about was finding the boy and the papers that Elizabeth claimed to have.

It was the latter that particularly troubled Frederick. Elizabeth had told him she had given a lawyer the papers—the proof of his fraudulent dealings. He didn't know if she was really cunning enough to have done that, but she was smart enough to at least pretend she had. Still, he couldn't risk it being true and someone mailing those papers to the Sapphire Duchess. No, the only way to get the truth out of Elizabeth was if he had the boy.

"Wait," Frederick called out to the man who'd agreed to kill for pay. "I need something else. It involves the boy, and it might even make things easier for you in the long run."

A few minutes later with his business finally concluded, Frederick walked out of the bar and found Hubert waiting for him just outside the door. "Let's get out of here." Hubert nodded, looking quite happy to comply.

❧

"It's late, and you should just stay the night with us," Georgia Harper insisted. "You and Phoebe can have my room."

"No, let them have mine," Ian insisted. "The bed is bigger. I can take one of the third-floor bedrooms."

"There, you see," Georgia said with a smile. "It's all settled."

Phoebe felt rather strange at the thought of staying in the Harper house—in Ian's room and bed. Especially given that she and Ian had just declared their love for each other. She hadn't even had time to share that news with her mother.

"I should go check on Kenny," Mutter said. She got up and headed for the stairs.

"And I'll go make up Ian's bed for you and Phoebe. Meanwhile you two can just enjoy each other's company."

She gave Ian a wink. Phoebe felt her face grow hot. No doubt she was as red as a beet. Keeping her gaze lowered to the patterned living room carpet, she tried not to let her nerves get the best of her.

"I wonder if you might like to sit on the porch with me," Ian said, getting to his feet.

Phoebe nodded and stood. She followed him to the open front door. The sky was muted in the soft tones of twilight. Ian escorted her to a chair.

When he didn't move to claim a seat for himself, Phoebe looked up and found him watching her, his expression rather serious.

"Is something wrong?"

He shook his head and leaned back on the porch rail. "Not at all. I just figured we ought to talk about what happened earlier."

She nodded. "I suppose we should."

"I've wanted to tell you about my wife for some time now. I know I told you she died in childbirth."

"Yes."

Ian looked down at his boots. "We eloped. Nora—that was her name—assured me that our love was strong enough to endure anything. She didn't want a big church wedding. In fact, she really didn't want a wedding at all. She thought it far more romantic to elope. At least that's what she told me. So we left letters for our folks and took the train to Great Falls to be married there. Nora had always wanted to go to Seattle, so after we saw the justice of the peace, we boarded another train and headed for the coast. I had plenty of money. My father had always paid me and my brother well, and I'd been able to save most of it. In fact, I used part of my money to build the little house where I now have the shop. I had long planned to marry Nora and had already figured to build the house for us. It had just been completed when we eloped."

"Did Nora's folks live nearby?" Phoebe asked.

Ian nodded. "Her father was a bank manager. They'd moved to Helena from Bozeman in order for him to take the job. That was when Nora was seventeen and I was nineteen. We met at church and . . . well . . . it was love at first sight for the both of us." He laughed. "We were, as my mother used to say, silly in love."

Phoebe met his gaze and smiled. "I think that's wonderful."

"I thought so too." His tone was bittersweet and his smile more sad than joyful. "Nora was everything I thought a wife should be. Considerate, beautiful, and full of life. I knew we were young, but I had a good job and could provide her with a house and a living, so I threw caution to the wind and proposed. She accepted. After a short time she convinced me to elope. Nora assured me that her parents would be fine. She told me they really liked me and wanted us to marry and were in fact arranging an expensive wedding that Nora didn't think necessary or desirable. But that wasn't the case at all. When we got back, her parents were livid and tried to take Nora from me. They told me they'd have the marriage annulled. But then Nora announced that she was already expecting a baby."

"A honeymoon baby. How romantic."

He shook his head. "It wasn't that way at all. She lied about the baby, only I didn't know it until later. Her mother broke into tears, and her father stormed off. I didn't understand until later why they were so upset."

Phoebe heard the sorrow in his voice. "You don't have to tell me if it's too painful."

Ian shook his head. "No, I need for you to know. That way you'll understand why I hate lies so much and why there can never be any between us."

"I despise lies. You know very well why." Phoebe shook her head. "I won't lie to you, Ian."

He studied her for a moment. "And I won't lie to you." He drew a deep breath and let it out. "The reason her parents were so upset was that Nora had a weak heart. She'd had a bout of rheumatic fever just the year before they moved to Helena. The doctor told her parents that she should never exert herself—never marry and more importantly never have children. Her heart wasn't strong enough."

"And she never told you."

"No. And she should have. Her folks said I killed her, and I guess in some ways I did."

Phoebe could only imagine how hard it must have been to hear that news. Learning the truth about her mother had led to happiness, whereas Nora's lie only led to death.

"That's not true. She chose a life with you, even a short one, because she loved you."

"I don't know if she really did or if she just wanted to get away from her parents. They were quite overbearing. She lied to me about so much, and I don't see how love could exist in the heart of someone so steeped in falsehoods."

"I'm sorry, Ian." His expression was troubled. She wished she could ease his suffering, but she'd already told him he didn't need to tell her everything. What else could she say?

"Like I said earlier, she wasn't really pregnant, but her folks and I thought she was. That's when her father told me about her heart. I was really angry that Nora had kept the truth from me, but I didn't want her folks to know it. I promised them I would see that she had the best medical care. There was nothing else I could say.

"Nora thought it all a lot of fuss about nothing. When I confronted her about lying to me, she told me it wasn't a lie at all—that I'd never asked if she had a weak heart. She always had an excuse for her lies. If I'd known she wasn't expecting I would have . . . well . . . I would have seen to it that she didn't get that way." He cleared his throat. "I'm sorry to talk so openly, but I want you to understand."

"I do understand."

He looked at her and nodded. The fading light made it hard to see the details of his face, but Phoebe knew he was in misery at the memories.

"Nora lied about a lot of things. She bought things on credit but told me her folks had purchased the items for her—for us. Whenever I learned the truth, she'd sweet-talk me and explain how she just had to have whatever it was. Within a few weeks she was truly with child and confessed to me how she'd lied earlier to keep her parents from annulling our marriage. I was so hurt and angry, but the lies just continued.

"She lied about her doctor appointments, telling me the doctor had assured her she was doing fine and that her heart was stronger than they had originally thought. I guess I wanted so much to believe it I didn't question her." He shook his head. "But as time went by, it was clear she wasn't well. I finally had the doctor come to the house, and he told me he hadn't seen Nora in months. She had quit his care, telling him she was seeing another physician. She wasn't seeing anyone, and by then it was too late."

"How awful."

"The doctor told me she would never live long enough to

deliver the baby. The strain on her heart had been too great. He figured she'd be dead in a matter of a week—maybe two." Ian paused. "I was stunned. I never expected to hear that. I never thought it could be that bad. I arranged for her to be moved to the hospital, thinking that might keep her from dying. Of course, it didn't, and the move maybe even hurried her death. Within the week she was gone and so was our baby."

Phoebe felt a warm tear trickle down her cheek. She wanted only to go to him and hold him close, but she knew that wasn't an acceptable way to behave. For a long time, Ian said nothing more. Phoebe let the silence linger between them, praying that God would give Ian the comfort he needed. It was the first time she'd really prayed for someone else.

"I needed you to know the truth," Ian finally said. "I vowed I'd never marry again, because I didn't want to get hurt again. But now, I . . . I'm in love with you, and I want very much to marry again."

Phoebe felt her breath catch. Ian was proposing to her—at least in a sense. She remained silent, hoping he wouldn't notice she was trembling.

"Well, here you two are," Georgia declared as she pushed open the screen door. "I thought I heard voices. Looks like a nice evening."

"It is, Mother," Ian said. "Will you join us?"

Phoebe tried not to show her disappointment when Georgia Harper agreed and took the chair beside her. She supposed now Ian wouldn't continue with talk of marriage and love, and she was right. Instead, Georgia brought up the topic of the hotel and how poorly it was doing, and Ian said nothing more about his feelings or the past.

22

Phoebe and her mother returned to the Broadwater cottage just after breakfast. Ian had wanted them to stay, despite being hard-pressed to get anything done with Phoebe so near. He feared for their lives, but Elizabeth felt confident, given her threat of exposing Von Bergen's underhanded dealings, that her husband would cause no further problems. Ian only wished he could be sure.

Throughout the night he had tossed and turned, thinking about the problems at hand. He worried that his past with Nora had caused him to push Elizabeth and her children into a deadly situation. Had he been wrong to insist the truth be told? Surely not. God called for honesty. Ian considered all that Eckhardt had said about Von Bergen and the stones and had decided to dedicate himself to seeing the gems faceted as soon as possible. The sooner he completed the order, the sooner Von Bergen would leave. At least that was what he hoped.

Throughout the day and well into the evening Ian worked, faceting stone after stone. He lost track of time, and only his mother's appearance brought to mind the hour.

"You won't help either of your causes if you fall over dead." She stood with a tray, offering sandwiches and coffee.

Ian shook his head. "Either of my causes?" He took the plate and coffee, leaving his mother with the tray.

"Getting the stones completed so Eckhardt can have Phoebe's father arrested. And getting this all wrapped up so you can propose and marry Phoebe."

Ian laughed and set the plate aside. "I should have known there'd be no keeping my feelings from you. I suppose I've made quite a fool of myself." He drank the strong brew and hoped it might restore some energy.

"Not at all." She put her hand on his arm. "Elizabeth and I can see the love you hold for her, but I doubt anyone else would be suspicious. Besides, even if they were, you haven't acted the fool."

"I do plan to marry her."

She nodded. "And I'm delighted. You've been alone too long."

"I was afraid." He took a long drink.

"That other women would be like Nora?"

He let go a sigh. "Yes. Her deceptions were so hurtful. I thought I knew her character, and it really shook me up to realize I had been so deluded. I guess my pride was wounded. I hated losing her, but it hurt even more to realize I'd never really had her—I never really knew her. It caused me to doubt my own judgment."

His mother put her arm around him. "I am sorry for all that happened back then. Nora's lies hurt so many. I have often thought of her parents and how they moved away so quickly. I'm sure they needed to forget their pain, but I'm equally as sure that it accompanied them wherever they went. The pain of losing your brother is always with me." She let go her hold and turned Ian to face her. "I'm sorry too for the lies I told so casually. I know I was wrong, thinking they weren't anything important. I'm sorry the girls copied my behavior. I've long since told them it was wrong, but I also realize that my example caused them to believe it acceptable."

"We both made mistakes. I chose to ignore the truth, which is just as bad. Lies are just so clear and present in the world's thinking. No one considers it a problem to lie about things when it's more convenient or it saves face."

"Well, I want you to know that I appreciate your honesty, and I know too that you were right to insist Elizabeth be truthful and speak to her husband. It would have been simpler to avoid him altogether, but it would also be wrong. This way, she can get everything resolved and no longer have to live in fear."

"I hope so. I've been worried about that. I definitely felt responsible for what happened with Phoebe and her father. If I hadn't pushed for Elizabeth to speak to the pastor and arrange the meeting with Von Bergen, Phoebe wouldn't have been beaten."

"Von Bergen is to blame for that beating. Not you. Now, let us talk of something more pleasant. Have you proposed to Phoebe?"

Ian laughed. "Not exactly. We did declare our love, and I might have mentioned wanting to marry, but I didn't ask her. I thought I'd wait until I had the ring. I have a beautiful sapphire I've been saving back for something special." He laughed. "Although I never expected it to become a wedding ring."

He went to a desk at the far end of the room. "It's a Yogo, larger than most. Come, I'll show you." He pushed up the roll top and then opened a drawer. He took a small box from inside and opened it. His mother came to join him.

"I purchased this stone several years ago. I think I can get at least five carats out of the cut. I want to use it to make Phoebe's ring."

"It will mean all that much more to her—knowing that you've faceted the stone with her in mind." Georgia smiled. "Your father did that for me. I've always cherished my ring." She looked down at her hand and fingered the diamond-and-ruby-encrusted gold band. "It makes me feel as if a part of him is still with us."

"Father will always be with us," Ian said, putting his arm around her.

"Yes, he will," she admitted. "In his son and daughters, as well as the work he's done. He was always so proud of you and your brother. It meant so much to him that you followed in his footsteps, as he had with his father."

"I hope one day I'll teach my son. If I have a son. If not, maybe I'll teach my daughter."

His mother laughed. "I can't help but believe Phoebe might enjoy learning as well."

Ian nodded. "I have reason to believe you might be right."

⌘

Throughout the week Elizabeth stopped by with Phoebe to see Kenny and discuss the future. Ian was relieved to hear that Von Bergen had agreed to cooperate with her. Apparently the information she had was enough to keep the man in line. For that Ian was grateful. He and Phoebe had no real time alone, thanks to Kenny, but nevertheless, Ian used the time to get to know her better. Often he asked questions that seemed to interest Kenny as well, and this allowed Phoebe to spend the time regaling them both with stories of her youth.

After finally completing the sapphires for Von Bergen, Ian prayed that it would mean the man would pay him and leave without further trouble. Elizabeth had already talked to a lawyer about the legal procedures for ending the marriage. He didn't like the idea of divorce, but in Elizabeth's case Ian couldn't see how there could be any other solution.

The good thing was that with Von Bergen's cooperation the tension eased. Ian didn't trust the man, but Elizabeth seemed to finally feel safe enough that she allowed Kenny to rejoin her at the hotel. Ian promised to resume Kenny's swimming lessons as soon as possible, and now that all of the sapphires were cut, he could do exactly that.

"Are you still planning to go to the Broadwater?" his mother asked.

Ian had just finished locking up the shop and found his mother on her knees, weeding through some of her flowers that lined the walkway between the houses.

"I am. Did you change your mind and want to come with me?"

"No. I just thought I might send along some of the muffins I made this morning." She started to get to her feet, and Ian reached down to help her.

"I'm sure they'll enjoy the treat. You really should consider opening your own bakery, Mother. Your creations are better than any others I've had."

She laughed and shook her head. "No, a bakery would take up far too much of my time. In fact, once you and Phoebe marry, I figure to put in my notice at the hotel."

This took Ian by surprise. "Why?"

"Because I want plenty of time to get to know Phoebe, and then later to play with my grandbabies."

Ian rolled his eyes. "I haven't even proposed and already you have grandchildren."

"Well, I figure it's good to plan ahead." She smiled and linked her arm through his. "I was even thinking that maybe we should encourage Elizabeth and Kenny to come live with us again. At least live with me. I figure you and Phoebe might want to move over to the small house for privacy."

"But Elizabeth seems perfectly happy with her little cottage. Kenny too."

His mother nodded. "But there are rumors going about that the Broadwater will close after the summer season. Close for good. I don't want Elizabeth to be worried about a home."

"Well, she need never worry about that."

"Not only that, but I was also thinking that I could show Phoebe a few things. She's grown up with servants all of her life. I doubt she knows anything about baking or tending a household. I hope to teach her—if she wants to learn."

"I'm sure she will. Why don't you get those muffins together, and I'll go change my clothes." He leaned over and kissed her on the forehead. "I love you, you know?"

"Of course I know that." She laughed and gave his cheek a playful pinch. "Mothers always know."

Ian changed in record time and all but ran to catch the trolley out to the Broadwater Hotel. He hummed a tune and felt better than he had in years. The past was finally laid to rest, and now he could honestly look forward to a happy future. A future he'd never figured would be possible.

Lord, I know I've been guilty of hardening my heart. For years I pushed people away for fear of getting hurt again. Then you sent Elizabeth and Kenny into our lives and brought joy back into our house. For that I thank you. I know it probably saved Mother's life. I'm grateful too that you've given me the courage to love again. Phoebe is such a remarkable woman, and I know we can be happy together. I pray that you'll bless our union—that you will give us children to love and grow

270

old with. He smiled to himself and added, *You know Mother would never be happy if she didn't have some more grandchildren to spoil.*

⌗⌗⌗

Elizabeth finished her work at the hotel and made her way back to her cottage. She was tired but happy. Possibly happier than she'd ever been in her adult life. Her children were with her, save Dieter, and soon Frederick would return to Europe and never again trouble her. It would be wonderful to have matters settled between them.

In her little house, Elizabeth found a note left by Phoebe. She and Kenny had gone for a walk. It offered no other information, but Elizabeth wasn't concerned. She knew Phoebe had spent enough time on the grounds to know where she was going, and Kenny knew every rut and trail. She loved the way they had taken to each other. Learning about his father had troubled Kenny somewhat, but Phoebe had been able to speak to him as one sibling to another. Her viewpoint had given Kenny some of the answers he needed in order to understand.

He had asked Elizabeth, however, to let him at least meet his father. She told him she would consider the matter, and if the time presented itself and she was assured of his safety, she would arrange a meeting. Once Frederick agreed to all the legal matters, then and only then would Elizabeth feel safe in introducing the boy to his father.

She began to work on their evening meal, planning a nice chicken-and-vegetable pie. Georgia had taught her to make this when they'd first come to Helena. Georgia had commented at the time that making pie crust was very nearly as easy as breathing, and the rest was just a matter of boiling or retrieving leftovers. Elizabeth had taken quickly to the task. Since then Georgia had taught her a great many recipes and skills.

The chicken was on the stove boiling and Elizabeth was cutting potatoes when she heard the front door open. She smiled. "I'm in the kitchen."

She heard the door close and was just about to reach for an onion when a large man filled the doorway to the kitchen.

"Who are you?" A shudder went through her. "What do you want?"

The man laughed. "I'm here on business, Mrs. Von Bergen."

Elizabeth felt a chill run down her spine. People here at the hotel and at church knew her as Bergen, not Von Bergen. To have the man call her by that name left her little doubt that Frederick was behind this visitation.

She still held the paring knife in her hand and let it remain hidden in the folds of her apron. "I suppose my husband sent you."

"Well, ain't you the smart one?" He stood watching her for a moment. "Not smart enough, though."

Thoughts raced through her mind about Kenny and Phoebe. Were they safe, or had Frederick arranged for someone to interrupt their afternoon as well?

"Well, what does he want?"

The man laughed. "He wants you out of his life. Apparently you have caused a lot of trouble."

"You won't get away with this. Too many people know what's going on." Elizabeth did her best to sound firm. She didn't want the man to know how terrified she truly felt.

"Ain't nobody gonna know until long after we're gone from here. See, my brothers have taken care of your son and daughter. I think you'll cooperate with me, or else you'll never see them again." He stepped toward her, his arms reaching out to take her.

Elizabeth screamed, raised the knife, and slashed at the man's arm. He howled in pain, but it didn't keep him from knocking the knife from her hand. Without warning he had his hands around Elizabeth's throat.

"That was a stupid move on your part." His hands tightened. "But you won't be saying or doing anything more."

Phoebe laughed at Kenny's antics. The boy was a pure delight, and Phoebe liked to imagine that Dieter might have been just as happy and carefree had their father not ruined him with threats and beatings.

"I'm so happy that you're my sister—*schwester*," Kenny said, trying the German. He plopped down on the grassy bank beside the creek where Phoebe sat.

"I am too," she said, reaching over to ruffle his hair.

"I like learning German and hearing your stories about Germany and the river and the big house where you and Mama used to live. I wish I could see it."

Phoebe frowned. "I don't know if that will ever be possible, Kenny. Our vater is a harsh and difficult man. He won't be happy that he can't have you. Mutter won't risk anything that might put you in jeopardy."

Kenny gave a sober nod. "I know. Mama told me about him. I always wanted a father. I used to ask Mama about him, but she wouldn't say very much, and when I saw how sad it made her I stopped asking. She did tell me that when I was grown, she would explain."

"I'm sure she will, Kenny, and if she doesn't, I promise I will."

Kenny plucked a blade of grass and fingered it lightly. "Do you love Ian?"

Phoebe hadn't expected the question to follow so close on the heels of their previous topic. She met her brother's questioning gaze and smiled. "Ja. I do."

"He loves you." Kenny tossed the grass aside. "I thought he loved you for a real long time, but he wouldn't say so. But one day he asked me how I felt about him loving you."

"He did, did he?" Phoebe couldn't help laughing. "And what did you say?"

Kenny shrugged and grinned. "I don't remember the exact words, but I was happy about it. I'm pretty sure he's going to marry you."

Phoebe started to reply, but she heard something move in the brush and froze. There was still some concern about whether or not her father would try to take Kenny. She hadn't thought it dangerous to come here, since Ian told her few people knew of this place. Getting to her feet, Phoebe glanced around cautiously and let out a squeal when a rabbit skittered out from the bushes. The rabbit paused and looked at her as if he were just as surprised to find her there as she was to see him. Finally he hopped away, and Phoebe tried to calm her racing heart.

"What's wrong, Phoebe?" Kenny asked. He jumped up and smiled. "Did that rabbit scare you?"

She nodded, putting her hand to her throat. "I'm afraid so. I know I shouldn't worry. Mutter says that worry is a sin, but I guess I can't help it. I don't want to see anything happen to you."

"Well, just keep that thought in mind, missy, and we'll get along just fine," a man said as he emerged from the brush.

The man was big and needed a shave. He narrowed his eyes at her—eyes that reminded her of a tiger she'd once seen. Dangerous. Deadly. Phoebe shoved Kenny behind her. She took a stance, hoping the man might see her determination. He laughed at her effort and shook his head.

"You ain't gonna win this fight. My brother is right behind you."

✿

The trolley slowed and finally stopped as they approached the hotel. Ian jumped off the platform with the bundle of muffins in hand and made his way across the grounds. He intended not only to visit with Elizabeth and Phoebe but to find Ernst Eckhardt and let him know the stones were ready for Von Bergen.

Overhead the skies were dotted with white clouds. From the wispiness of them, Ian figured rain was probably on its way. They could use the moisture. For every little bit of rain, the chances of fires in the forests were lessened.

He turned down the path to Elizabeth's cottage only to see her and Ernst Eckhardt standing outside. Eckhardt had his arm around Elizabeth's shoulder, and it looked like she was crying. Ian picked up his pace.

"What's going on? Is something wrong?"

Eckhardt looked up and nodded. "There's been an attack. I just shot a man as he tried to kill Elizabeth. He's dead."

"What!" Ian looked around. "Where's Phoebe and Kenny?"

"They went for a walk," Eckhardt replied. "Unfortunately, we don't know where."

Elizabeth pulled away from Eckhardt. "You have to find them. That man—that man said his brothers had them." The look on her face was one of pure horror.

Ian thrust the muffins into her arms. "Where's the dead man?"

"Inside," Eckhardt answered.

"Elizabeth, go get help. Get the manager and have him send for the police. Eckhardt, you and I will go in the direction of the lake. If they aren't there, we'll head to the fishing hole where

Kenny likes to go. It's shaded and pretty, and Phoebe liked it too."

Eckhardt nodded. He turned to Elizabeth. "We'll find them. Try not to worry." He pulled a revolver from his coat pocket and looked to Ian. "Let's go."

Ian's mounting fear did nothing to aid in their search. When they found no one near the lake, Ian moved off toward Ten Mile Creek and the place where Kenny loved to fish. He prayed as they tore through the brush and trees. Prayed the same words over and over.

Lord, please let them be safe.

23

*P*hoebe knew she would have to fight if she and Kenny were to make it out alive. She surprised the big man by rushing at him. She threw herself against him, launching him backward. They both might have fallen but for a stand of trees directly behind the man. Nevertheless, the action bought her a moment's time.

Pushing off the man's chest, Phoebe whirled around in time to see a younger but equally scruffy-looking man take hold of Kenny. Kenny, however, had no desire to be held captive and bit the man's arm as it closed around him.

"Yeow! You little animal!"

"Run, Kenny!" Phoebe ordered, putting herself between him and his attacker. "Get help." Thankfully he did exactly as she told him and disappeared into the brush.

"Tie her up. I'll get the boy," the older man declared, thrusting her toward the younger man. He took off after Kenny, but by then the boy had several yards' head start.

Phoebe fought against the younger man, hoping she could throw him off balance as easily as she had his brother, but it wasn't to be. This man was smaller and moved more quickly than his larger brother. He pushed her to the ground and then put his foot on her back.

"Hold still or I'll hit you in the head with my gun and then you won't be a problem anymore."

Deciding it best to at least give the appearance of cooperation, Phoebe stopped fighting. "You won't get away with this," she said as he yanked her arms behind her.

"Sure we will. Nobody knows where you are."

"My mutter—mother does." Phoebe wasn't at all sure her mother would know where they'd gone, but she hoped the comment might cause him some concern.

"My brother is takin' care of your ma right now."

Phoebe cried out as he tied her hands together and pulled the rope tight. His comment left her with a sinking feeling. "How many of you are there?"

He pulled her to her feet. "Three of us. Dave's the one you just saw. Pete's the oldest, and he's the one that talked to your pa." The man, no more than a boy really, looked at her oddly for a moment, then shrugged. "I ain't never heard of a pa wanting to kill his girl child. Lot of men want to kill their wives, even their sons, but it seemed strange him wanting you dead. And you bein' so pretty and all."

"My vater—father is quite mad," Phoebe countered. "You can't hope to get away with this."

Just then Phoebe heard Ian calling her name. "I'm here, Ian! Help!" she yelled just before her captor put his dirty hand over her mouth. He held her in an iron grip against his foul-smelling body. "Be quiet," he said in a hush.

But Phoebe wasn't about to obey. Instead she raised her booted foot and kicked backward, thankful that she'd worn a simple, lightweight skirt. Her foot hit the man's shin square, causing him to let out another yell as he had when Kenny bit him.

It also caused him to let go of Phoebe, which gave her just the freedom she was hoping for. She took off running in the direction of the voices that continued to call for her.

⁂

Ian heard Phoebe's cry and then silence. He feared the worst but continued running through the brush and trees as fast as he could. Ernst Eckhardt was somewhere behind him, but Ian didn't have time to wait, and just as he rounded a grove of trees, Kenny came flying out.

The boy wrapped himself around Ian, but not before Ian saw why he was on the run. A large man barreled through the trees with his gun leveled at the boy's back. Ian did the only thing he could think of and twisted, throwing himself and Kenny to the ground. He tried to cushion the fall with his left hand but twisted it badly as they met the ground. The sound of shots being fired just over his head caused Ian to roll and cover Kenny with his body. Pain seared through his hand and wrist.

Behind him a loud thud hit the ground, and then Eckhardt called out, "It's all right. He's dead."

Ian rose ever so slightly to make certain Eckhardt was right. Not four feet away lay the body of the man who'd pursued Kenny. He lay flat on his back, eyes open and staring at the skies overhead. A bullet hole oozed blood from the middle of the man's forehead.

"That other man's got Phoebe," Kenny said, pushing at Ian. "You gotta save her."

Ian moved to get up and felt sharp pain shoot up his arm.

His wrist was either broken or badly sprained, but it wasn't going to stop him.

"Kenny, run as fast as you can back to the cottage, but don't go inside. If your mama isn't there outside, then go to the hotel and wait for the police. When the police arrive, you're going to need to tell them how to get here. Can you do that?"

Kenny nodded. His eyes were wide with fear as he glanced over at the dead man. "You won't let that other man hurt Phoebe, will you?"

Ian's anger began to overtake his fear. "Not if I have anything to say about it."

Kenny shot off down the path, and Ian turned to find that Eckhardt had already headed into the trees in the direction Kenny and the man had come. Ian hurried to follow after him.

A million thoughts raced through his mind, but the only one that mattered was that they reach Phoebe and save her from harm. Eckhardt was now just ahead and had stopped to listen.

"They've got to be close," he whispered.

Ian nodded and pointed to the area where Kenny liked to fish. Eckhardt's glance followed. There was no one in the clearing, but he felt certain they had to be in the general vicinity. Deciding to try bartering, Ian called out.

"We've killed your brothers, and now it's just you. You might as well come out."

"You'll just kill me too," a voice called out.

Eckhardt answered. "We won't kill you if you let Miss Von Bergen go and come out with your hands up."

A long silence settled over the woods, and only the rippling water from the creek could be heard. Even the birds were quiet. Finally, a rustling of brush sounded somewhere to Ian's right, and in another heartbeat Phoebe appeared with a man. He had her pulled close against him like a shield.

Ian could see the captor was hardly more than a boy. His face was drained of color, and he looked as if he were more afraid than Phoebe was.

"Look, we can pretty well guess that your brothers were the ones who got you involved in this," Eckhardt said, putting his gun away. "We don't want to hurt you or see anyone else hurt. So why don't you just let her go and we can talk."

The boy shook his head. "You'll kill me." He backed up just a pace, dragging Phoebe with him.

"We won't," Ian declared. "I give you my word. In fact, we can't kill you because we need your help."

This seemed to stir the boy's interest. "What help can I give you?"

Ian stepped forward despite the boy's look of fear. "You have to know about all of this. We need you to testify about who paid you to do this."

"It were her pa," the boy replied, looking around with a wild expression. He continued shaking his head. "Her own pa wanted her dead. Not me—not even my brothers."

"Son, just calm down. We know it was her father, but we need for you to tell that to the police. They're on their way, so you can't hope to escape. Now just let her go and talk to us about what you know."

Ian met Phoebe's gaze. He could see her fear and hated that she should ever have to face such a heinous act. Her father would rather see her and Elizabeth dead than simply admit defeat and let them go. Ian had never known such a monster as Graf Von Bergen.

Eckhardt stepped closer to Phoebe and her captor. "Let her go and help us put the blame on her vater, and we will do whatever we can to see the law goes easy on you."

"You're a foreigner—one of them," the boy replied, still agitated but a little calmer.

"He is that," Ian said. "But I'm not. We will do what we can to help you. You're only what, fifteen—sixteen?"

"I'm fifteen." The boy took his hand from Phoebe's mouth. "I never wanted to hurt anybody. Pete said I had to help him on account that I knew what he was planning to do. He and Dave told me I had to." The boy's voice broke, and at the same time Phoebe pushed away from him and ran to Ian.

He wrapped her in his arms, ignoring the pain that shot up his arm as he tightened his hold. "Are you all right?"

Phoebe nodded. "Is Kenny—Mutter . . ."

He put a finger to her lips. "They are fine."

Ian heard the boy sobbing and Eckhardt saying something, but he couldn't make out the words. Not that he really cared to. What mattered to him most was the woman in his arms. She was safe and hadn't been hurt.

"My hands are tied." Phoebe pulled away, and Ian let her go. She turned and presented her back to him. "Please undo them."

Ian wasn't at all sure he could manage the knot without using both hands. He attempted to pull at the rope using just his right hand, but he couldn't seem to budge the knot. His left hand was useless, and it was then he remembered his pocketknife.

"Hold on." He reached into his right pocket and pulled out the knife. With his thumb he managed to free the blade, then flicked it back to lock it in place. "Don't move," he warned Phoebe.

He sawed through the rope. It finally gave way and dropped to the ground, but Phoebe stood stock-still.

"Are you all right? Did I hurt you?"

"I'm fine. You said not to move."

Ian laughed and let out a heavy breath. "You can move now, but I'm glad to know you can follow directions when you have to."

She turned as Ian grimaced from the pain. "What happened?" She reached for his left hand, but Ian pulled away.

"I think it might be broken. I fell against it when I grabbed Kenny out of the way of that other man."

Phoebe nodded. "You saved our lives."

"It was really Eckhardt. He had the gun, and now two men are dead, all because of your father. I never should have made your mother meet with him, and I shouldn't have let you two return to the hotel."

Phoebe smiled. "Mutter has become fiercely independent, as if you didn't know. You couldn't have forced her to do or not do anything."

"I suppose you're just as stubborn."

She laughed in spite of all the gravity. "Ja, I can be. When I really need to be."

"And what would you ever need to be stubborn about?"

She never had a chance to reply. Eckhardt interrupted with the boy in hand. "John has agreed to help us."

※

The lightheartedness of her moment with Ian quickly passed as they drew nearer the cottage. Ian told her about the dead man who'd tried to strangle her mother. At the first sight of her mother, Phoebe's eyes welled with tears. She crossed the distance between them and fell sobbing into her mother's arms. The two women embraced and held each other tight for several minutes.

"Are you all right? Did they hurt you?" Mutter asked.

"I'm fine. I was so afraid they would hurt you or Kenny." Phoebe pulled back and looked into her mother's tear-filled eyes. "Where is he? Is he all right?"

"He's just fine. I had him stay up at the hotel. The police

are on their way, and when they arrive, the hotel manager will bring them and Kenny back here."

Phoebe nodded, barely registering anything past Kenny being all right. "I prayed," she murmured. She drew a deep breath and spoke up. "I prayed like never before, and I know God heard me."

Mutter smiled and nodded. "I know He did too." She reached up and smoothed back Phoebe's hair. In the struggle it had come unpinned and now fell loose around her shoulders. "God will always hear us, Phoebe. You need never worry that He won't, and even if the worst had happened to me—God would still have heard you."

"But it would have been harder to believe." Phoebe shook her head. "If we pray and God does nothing to help us, how can we know that He really hears us—that He cares?"

"Faith, Phoebe. You must have faith in Him."

"Faith is never easily had, Phoebe," Ian said, joining them. "If it was, they'd sell it on every street corner."

Mutter dropped her hold. "He's right, you know. Ian is quite a man of faith. I think he will be much better suited to teach you about such matters than I am."

"I don't know about that," Ian countered, "but right now we have a plan to go over, and I need the two of you to join us and help with the details."

Phoebe met his gaze and lost herself momentarily. When she had thought she might never see him again, the one thing on her mind was that she would never know his kiss. It was something she intended to rectify as soon as the opportunity presented itself.

24

Frederick Von Bergen sat at one of the hotel's outdoor tables, waiting for Ian Harper to bring him his sapphires. The day before there had been a flood of police, and rumor had it that two dead bodies had been found on the property. No one seemed to know anything more.

Frederick didn't need anyone to tell him anything more, however. He was certain the bodies found would belong to his wife and daughter. Something must have happened to keep the hired men from getting the women off the grounds before killing them, and while that complicated matters, it didn't take away from Von Bergen's satisfaction that things were finally going his way.

Harper had sent word just that morning that the stones were ready, and shortly after this came a message from the man he'd hired to kill his wife and daughter. If everything went his way, he'd soon be able to leave this horrible place with his son at his side.

The thought of having another son to train and use amused Frederick. He was getting a tidy dowry from the family of the young woman Dieter was to marry. Of course, the money was supposed to go to Dieter, but Von Bergen had already made it clear to his son that this wasn't going to be the case. Dieter would inherit the estate and all that went with it, and since Frederick would remain at the estate for years to come, they would use the dowry money to benefit the property. Of course, there was no need to explain to his son that he needed the money to pay off a debt that included their lands. Dieter would do as he was told and not question where his father planned to use the money.

It was a pity that Phoebe couldn't have been as pliable. He'd always spoiled her. That had been his biggest mistake. He wouldn't make it again. He hated the idea of telling the duke that Phoebe had died in America. The man had been positively delighted at the prospect of having a young and beautiful wife who could give him sons, and Frederick had been delighted at the connections and money he would have via Phoebe. All of that would change now.

He chided himself for being so quick to include Phoebe in the killing. She could have been brought into line by simply threatening to do the same to her as had been done to her mother. That way Frederick would have had her help with Kenneth and could have seen her married to the duke. Well, there was no use dwelling on it. Gerda would help with the boy.

Thinking of Gerda brought something else to mind. Perhaps another way he could make a tidy sum for himself. Now that his wife was truly dead, Frederick would be free to marry again. He wasn't all that old, and a rich young woman to warm his bed and fill his coffers might be just the trick. Should there be additional heirs, he would welcome them and manage them better than he had his daughter.

Of course, he still had yet to manage the boy. Kenneth was not yet ten, but no doubt his mutter's bad habits and lack of discipline had ruined the boy. It wouldn't be easy to break the boy of those traits.

"But break him, I will."

The graf gazed skyward with a smile. The clouds overhead suggested rain, but Von Bergen gave it no thought. Harper was due in less than ten minutes and would bring the sapphires. After that it would be a matter of meeting with his hired killer and then ascertaining the location of his son. He'd already instructed Hubert and Gerda that his plan was to leave in three days.

Von Bergen heard the trolley approaching and knew Harper would be on it. He took out the money he still owed and counted it for the third time. It was a pity to separate himself from such a vast sum. However, it was a small price compared to what he would manage to make once everything was said and done. He replaced the cash in his vest pocket and waited with a sense of satisfaction.

After about ten minutes, Von Bergen spied Harper making his way along the path from the hotel. Harper had apparently entered from the back of the hotel. Frederick had left word with the hotel manager and reception desk clerk as to where he'd be. He instructed them to send Harper and anyone else who asked for him to this somewhat secluded location. In fact, he had chosen this particular location for its privacy. Behind him was a rather lovely arrangement of blooming bushes and flowers along with a fine stand of trees. To his right was the hotel, and to the left was the natatorium. In front of him the hotel grounds extended a display of flowers, trees, and an occasional fountain, as well as tables where guests might enjoy outdoor dining when the weather was pleasant. The latter was something just now being experimented with for the warmer summer months. Frederick had to admit it suited him better than the stuffy dining rooms.

"I was happy to get your message, Mr. Harper," Frederick said as Ian approached. "Won't you have a seat? As you can see I have ordered us a light lunch." He motioned to the table, where cheese, fruit, and breads awaited their attention. Von Bergen was already drinking his third glass of wine.

"What will you have to drink, Harper?"

"Nothing. I won't be here that long."

The man was all business, but that suited Frederick just fine. It was when Harper reached into his coat that the graf noticed his injured hand. "What happened to you?"

Harper glanced at his left hand and then to Von Bergen. "I took a fall and broke my wrist and finger. Fortunately for you, I had already completed the stones." He placed the two bags on the table. "You will find them all there, but feel free to count them."

Laughing, Frederick withdrew the cash from his pocket. "No need for that. I trust you. I have heard from others that your reputation is impeccable. I would have liked to have you facet additional stones. I suppose that isn't possible now."

"No. I'm afraid not." Harper fixed him with a hard look. "I have other appointments, so if you don't mind, I'll take my money and leave you to your meal."

Von Bergen could see that Harper was more than a little anxious to be on his way. He handed the lapidary his money. "Feel free to count it."

Harper nodded and did just that. It irritated Frederick to no end. He had just given Harper the benefit of his trust by not counting the stones, but now the man actually took the time to assure himself he wasn't being cheated by Von Bergen.

Frederick said nothing, however. It wouldn't do to create a scene now that he had what he wanted.

When Harper finished counting the bills, he gave Von Bergen

a nod before tucking the money into his coat pocket. "I presume this concludes our business."

"I suppose it does." Von Bergen toyed with a piece of bread. "Unless, of course, you'd like to change your mind and join me for lunch?"

"No. I'm sorry. I have other things to tend to." With that Harper left, not even bidding Von Bergen good-bye. The man's rudeness was uncalled for, but typical of Americans.

Finding himself alone once again, Von Bergen checked his watch. His next meeting wouldn't be for nearly an hour. He was anxious to hear about his wife and daughter's demise. He tried to feel something other than satisfaction. After all, Phoebe and her mother had long been in his life. He should at least feel something of a loss at their passing. But he couldn't muster up the slightest thought of mourning. There was simply too much relief in knowing that the deed had been done and he was now free of anyone who could harm him.

There was the pesky issue of the information his wife had said she had, but Frederick had decided not to worry about it. After much consideration, he figured it would be a simple matter to deny whatever information showed up in the hands of the Sapphire Duchess. Frederick had already decided he would explain to the old woman that his wife had been alive all of these years, plotting and planning against him. He would tell the duchess, perhaps even with tears in his eyes, how Elizabeth had threatened to lie about him and ruin his good name unless he gave her a large sum of money. He thought he might even further the lie and tell the duchess how he had pleaded with Elizabeth to come back to him and their children, but that she had scorned him and refused.

Of course, he'd have to explain the boy, but Frederick saw that only as added proof of his wife's cruelty. He would take the boy with him when he presented the duchess with her gems. She had always seemed to enjoy children. Then before she had any chance to confront or accuse him, Von Bergen would share his sad story of his wife's stealing away in the night and of the son she had given birth to. Frederick smiled to himself. He would even bring up his wife's threats of lying to the duchess. He'd learned over the years that it was generally to his benefit to meet problems head on. It would be easy to win the duchess's sympathy by telling her of his wife's threats to lie about him and ruin his reputation. Perhaps he'd even go so far as to say that Elizabeth had threatened to send letters filled with lies to all of his colleagues, and even the kaiser himself. He would bemoan the tragedy as the price he paid for having loved a wayward woman.

"Are you Mr. Von Bergen?"

Frederick startled and looked up to find a boy standing only a few feet away. "What do you want?"

"Pete sent me to meet with you." The boy paused and frowned. "That is, if you're Mr. Von Bergen."

"I am, but I don't know who you are."

"I'm Pete's little brother John. Pete sent me to tell you that everything is settled. He took care of your wife and daughter. I'm here to get the rest of our money."

Frederick settled back in the chair and eyed the boy with contempt. "I don't work with underlings. You tell your brother that I won't pay another cent unless he comes to me personally."

The boy nodded. "He figured you'd try to back out on what you owed, so he got himself some insurance."

"Insurance?" Von Bergen laughed. "And what sort of insurance could your brother possibly have in this situation?"

"Your boy. Pete has your son."

The audacity of these criminals to take the boy and hold

him as assurance for payment sent Frederick into a rage. "How dare you! You listen to me, and listen well. I will not be threatened by the likes of you and your brother. You were hired to kill my wife and daughter—not to steal my son and hold him for ransom."

The boy shrugged. "All I know is that you owe my brother money and I'm supposed to get it."

Von Bergen slammed his hands down on the table. "And I told you I don't deal with underlings. You go tell your brother to bring my son to me, and then and only then will he get what's coming to him. If I don't see the boy safely produced and in my care within the next hour, I will call the police."

"I'm afraid you're hardly in a position to want the authorities brought here," a man declared from somewhere behind the graf.

Frederick turned to find Ernst Eckhardt and Ian Harper approaching. Von Bergen stiffened but said nothing. He had no idea what this man was talking about, nor why Ian Harper was back.

"I am having a private conversation if you don't mind," Von Bergen said, getting to his feet.

Eckhardt nodded. "A most interesting conversation, I must admit."

Tension tightened the cords in Von Bergen's neck. "Leave now. I've no interest in what you have to say."

"I believe you'll be more than a little interested in what I have to say," Eckhardt replied with a smile. "You see, I am the nephew of the Sapphire Duchess. My tante sent me to shadow you on this trip. I found it all quite interesting how you came to Montana rather than go straight to Ceylon to purchase the sapphires my aunt desired. And then I learned from those around that you were purchasing sapphires here in America."

Von Bergen eyed the man. "We can discuss this in private."

He turned to the boy. "Go to the hotel lobby and wait for me there."

"No, John is perfectly fine waiting here. You see, he's helping us."

Frederick frowned. "Helping you in what way?" He noticed several men approaching and shook his head. "Never mind. I refuse to conduct business with so many people around."

Ian glanced over his shoulder. "They're helping us too. We know all about your schemes, Von Bergen. We know that you wanted to purchase less expensive sapphires and pass them off to the duchess as being from Ceylon—that you've been doing it for years. And after comparing notes with Mr. Eckhardt, we also came to understand why the jewels worn by your daughter were paste and nothing more."

"Indeed," Eckhardt replied. "It would seem my tante has purchased stones from you that would perfectly match the settings worn by your daughter."

"So what?" Von Bergen said, trying hard to get control of his anger. "Those jewels were mine to sell. As for the other accusations, you are quite wrong. I have served the duchess faithfully for years. Your accusations were no doubt based on lies given you by my wife."

"I've only recently met your wife," Eckhardt replied. "And while she did offer me some interesting information, your underhanded deeds were suspected long before I came to America. In fact, my tante assures me she had been suspicious for years."

"This is all madness." Frederick patted his chest to reassure himself of the revolver he carried. "I'm afraid you have been quite misled."

"I think not," Eckhardt continued. "We also know that you intended to have John and his brothers kill your wife and daughter. First because John explained it to us, but now we just overheard you reiterate your request. I myself came to Mrs. Von Bergen's rescue and unfortunately had to kill John's eldest brother."

Frederick looked at the boy. "It's true," John murmured.

Frederick realized he'd been betrayed. He felt a tightness around his throat as if someone had placed a hangman's noose. He fought to rein in his thoughts.

"You're quite mad. All of you." The situation was most grave. Frederick felt like a caged animal and took a step back. "I've done nothing wrong. The sapphires I purchased here are for me—not the duchess." He smiled at Eckhardt. "Your tante is a very dear friend, and I would never dream of going against her wishes. And I have no knowledge of this boy and his brothers. I've never seen this boy before now."

"Don't embarrass yourself, Graf. As I've already said, my tante has been suspicious of you for years. That is the reason she sent me to follow you on this trip. Not only was she certain you were cheating her, but she knew about your wife being alive."

Ian Harper crossed his arms and nodded. "And while it's true that you are just now meeting John, you should know that the man you hired, along with John and their brother Dave, did attempt to kill Elizabeth and Phoebe, but they were not successful. The women are safe."

Everything was spinning out of control. All of his plans were crumbling before him. Frederick struggled for a way to extricate himself from this trouble, but nothing came easily to mind. He shook his head. "I assure you that I know nothing of such a plot, no matter what you say you overheard. This boy doesn't know me, and I don't know him or his siblings." He drew a deep breath and eyed the collection of men. "If you insist on accusing me, I will have to retain a lawyer, but I assure you I will see each of you pay for these accusations."

"You will definitely need a lawyer, Mr. Von Bergen," one of the newly arrived men declared. "You are under arrest for hiring the murder of your wife, Elizabeth Von Bergen, and daughter, Phoebe Von Bergen." The man revealed a badge to prove his authority. "You will have to come with us."

"This is madness. I will not be treated in such a manner. I am Graf Von Bergen, a man of great importance in my own homeland. The kaiser himself will come to my aid."

"That's extremely doubtful," Eckhardt said, crossing his arms. "No, you will be sent to an American prison and most likely will spend the rest of your life there."

Frederick wanted to punch Eckhardt in the mouth. The man stood there with his smug expression—believing he'd bested Frederick. No one could best Frederick Von Bergen. He'd been playing this game for far longer than any of these men had been alive.

Ian Harper stepped forward. "Elizabeth has given Mr. Eckhardt papers proving you cheated his aunt. Phoebe will testify to the fact that you were here to purchase sapphires for the duchess, and not only will she give testimony, but your good friend Lord Putnam has also agreed to share what he knows rather than be arrested as an accessory. You are done for, Von Bergen, and if it weren't for these officers and my broken hand, I would be inclined to tear you apart for what you did to Phoebe. Fortunately for you, as a man of God I have learned that acting on my anger isn't the right way to handle any matter. Therefore I will gladly watch you be apprehended by the police and jailed." He narrowed his eyes. "And even if you should somehow manage to get out of responsibility here for trying to have Phoebe and her mother killed, it pleases me to know that Eckhardt would have the complete cooperation of our government to see you returned to Germany to face your comeuppance there."

Frederick knew there was no hope of escape. Everyone had turned against him, and they would see him jailed—even hanged or shot. No, he wasn't going to let that happen. Before anyone could say another word, Von Bergen reached inside his coat and pulled out his revolver. Never in his life had he ever felt this overwhelming sensation of failure. His hand trembled under the additional weight of the gun.

"Get back." He waved the gun. "Get away from me now."

Ian shook his head. "You can only shoot one of us before the others take you down in a rush."

"He's right, Von Bergen," the officer declared. "We are all armed and prepared to do our duty." He raised his own gun.

Frederick felt his mouth turn to cotton. His stomach threatened to expel what little he'd eaten. He could see the truth of the matter. These men would see him pay for all that he had done. Even though his deeds weren't that bad. What was he guilty of? Taking money from an old lady who could well afford to lose it? Ridding himself of two women who sought only to cause him harm?

"This is madness, Von Bergen," Eckhardt declared. "Give it up."

Madness? Madness to save himself from the government that would kill him or jail him for the rest of his life? No, theirs was the madness. Frederick felt the gun begin to weigh his arm down. There was only one solution.

"No. No, I won't be taken. I won't be jailed. I'm Graf Von Bergen. No man forces me to do anything." He smiled as a sense of peace washed over him, and he raised the gun to position the barrel under his chin. "No one."

The explosion of Von Bergen's gun sent him backward. Ian watched in stunned disbelief, as did the others. Rather than be taken alive, Von Bergen had killed himself. The officers rushed forward and took charge of the situation while Ian and Eckhardt stepped back. Only John stayed where he was, his face drained of color.

"I never expected that," Eckhardt said, shaking his head. "I figured Von Bergen would fight to the end."

"I suppose he realized there was nothing he could do to escape—nothing but take his life." Ian too shook his head. "I've never in all my days seen anything like this. In fact, until a few days ago I'd never seen anyone killed. It's not something I ever hope to see again."

"I agree with you on that point." Eckhardt turned to the boy. "We will still work to see you are treated fairly. A boy in your position should be given a second chance—if you are of a mind to turn from the ways your brothers taught you."

John nodded. "I don't wanna do what they did—die like they did." He looked at Eckhardt, then Ian. "I ain't ever gonna touch another gun." He shuddered and looked to the ground, shaking his head.

A crowd of hotel staff and guests were beginning to gather. Ian could hear several of them asking what had happened. The hotel manager joined them, staring in disbelief at the lifeless body of Frederick Von Bergen.

One of the officers rejoined Eckhardt and Ian. "He's dead. I sent one of my men for a sheet in order to cover the body."

Ian looked at the others. "If you don't need anything else from me, I should go and let Mrs. Von Bergen know what's happened."

"You're free to go, Mr. Harper. We'll be in touch if we need anything more from you." He turned to Eckhardt. "I believe these are yours." He handed him the two gem bags.

Eckhardt took the bags and stared at them for a moment. "Troublesome little blue stones."

Ian took his leave and went to see his mother. She may have already heard about the commotion. She had known about the general plan. Elizabeth, Phoebe, and Kenny were even now safely hidden away in her house with a police guard. Ian wasn't at all sure how she'd take the news—how any of them would take it.

He entered the bakery section of the kitchen and found his mother slathering icing atop a cake. She smiled when she saw him, but grew serious when Ian didn't return the smile.

"What is it? What has happened?"

"Von Bergen—he's dead." Ian hadn't meant to be so blunt. "I'm sorry, I just couldn't think of an easier way to say it."

His mother's expression betrayed her shock, but she tried to remain stoic. "What happened?"

"We confronted him, and it was all too much. He drew a gun on us, and when he saw it was completely hopeless to escape justice, he . . . killed himself."

His mother no longer tried to appear strong. She gasped and put her hand to her mouth. Ian put his arm around her. "I wanted you to know from me. I'm sure there will soon be plenty of talk about it. There was quite a crowd gathered by the time I left to come see you."

"Oh, goodness. I never thought of him doing himself in. I had all sorts of horrible worries about him doing something to hurt you or the others, but he didn't seem the type to cause himself harm."

"I have to say it was a surprise to me as well, but now it's done and I need to get into town and let Elizabeth and Phoebe know what's happened."

"Yes. I will come with you." She began to take off her apron. "Give me just a moment."

She went to her bakery assistants. Ian overheard her explaining there had been a problem in the family and she needed to leave. Within a matter of minutes, she and Ian were heading for the trolley.

Ian wondered how Phoebe would take the news. She had been close to her father up until the last month or so. He knew she loved him, but he'd hurt her a great deal.

"Poor little Kenny," his mother said. "He's only just learned he had a father, and now he must lose him all over again."

"There's a difference between giving a child life and being a father. Kenny has never had an earthly father."

"No, I suppose you are right on that account. You're the closest thing to a father he's had. Or perhaps you're more of a big brother, but either way I am sure he'll need you to help him through this."

"And I will do what I can." Ian thought of how scared Kenny had been when his attacker had chased after him. All Ian had wanted to do then, as well as now, was reassure the boy that he was safe and no one would hurt him.

It seemed to take forever for the trolley to come, but once it did the trip to Helena was quick. Ian used the time to figure out what he would say once they arrived home. He hated having to tell Elizabeth and Phoebe what had happened. If he could have his way about it, they would never have had to experience such horrible things as they had known.

They got off the trolley and walked the remaining distance to the house. The clouds were growing dark overhead, matching Ian's mood, and he paused for a moment to draw a deep breath. No matter what he said or did, Ian couldn't escape the image of Von Bergen killing himself. He couldn't begin to understand being in a situation so bad that death was preferable.

"Are you all right?" his mother asked as they approached the house.

Ian shrugged. "I just keep reliving that horrible moment of Von Bergen pulling the trigger. I saw the hopelessness in his eyes—the emptiness."

"Try not to dwell on it, son. You know that it won't change anything. There are living people who need you more."

"This is probably one of the hardest things I've had to do."

His mother took hold of his hand and gave it a pat. "Just remember, you aren't alone. God has already made a way for this conversation to take place. He will console the hearts of those involved and give you the right words to say."

Ian nodded. "Of course you're right. Come on."

He led the way around to the back door, dismissed the police guards from his mother's house and the shop, and entered. Inside, the house smelled of apples and cinnamon. Apparently Elizabeth was busy baking.

"Elizabeth?" Mother called.

"Georgia," she said, returning to the kitchen from the hall. "I thought you were . . ." She fell silent at the sight of Ian. "What happened? Is it over with?"

Ian nodded. "Yes. Where are Kenny and Phoebe?"

"They're over in the shop. Tell me what happened." Elizabeth fixed him with a determined look. "Tell me now before they hear it."

Ian stepped away from his mother. "You might want to sit down." He motioned her to one of the chairs at the kitchen table.

Elizabeth did as he suggested. She folded her hands in her lap and then let go a sigh. "Is he dead?"

"Yes."

She nodded. "Is anyone else?"

"No. No one else was hurt. Your husband denied everything, of course, but when he saw that the evidence against him was too strong, he . . . well . . . he shot himself."

Elizabeth didn't seem at all surprised by the news. She lowered her gaze and sighed again. "I'm so glad he didn't hurt anyone else."

"The authorities arranged to have his body taken to an undertaker. Ernst Eckhardt said he would pay to have him buried. I'm sure Pastor Clearwater would say a few words over him."

"Frederick wouldn't want that. He didn't believe in God."

"I know, but we do. Pastor Clearwater's words will be for us," Ian said lightly, touching her shoulder.

Elizabeth looked up to reveal tears in her eyes. "I know it may sound silly, but I *am* sad that he is dead. He never had a chance to make peace with God. I can't imagine anything more tragic than losing one's soul."

"We all have a choice to make," Ian said. "Von Bergen made his, just as you made yours. It isn't what any of us wanted for him—or for you, but it is done and we must put it in God's hands."

She nodded, and Ian's mother came to hug her as Ian stepped away. "I'll go get Phoebe and Kenny."

"Wait," Elizabeth said, getting to her feet. "Send Kenny to me, but you go ahead and tell Phoebe. She'll be able to be by herself without worrying about how Kenny or I am taking the news. This will probably be harder on her than the rest of us—after all, she still loved him."

Ian nodded and exited the kitchen. He had wanted to see Phoebe ever since Von Bergen pulled the trigger. He wanted to assure himself that she was alive and well. That her father's anger and betrayal could no longer reach her. It was silly, he knew, because she was safely hidden, but it had bothered him nevertheless.

"Phoebe? Kenny?" He called to them as he entered the back of the shop.

Kenny came running. "I'm glad you're back." He hugged Ian around the waist. "Did the police take my . . . father to jail?" He pulled back to face Ian.

"Kenny, your mother wants to tell you all about it. You need to go to her."

"But—"

"Kenny, please go to Mutter. She probably needs you right now," Phoebe said. She stood just beyond them in the opening to the main part of the shop.

Kenny seemed to understand the gravity of the matter. He left without another word while Ian stood unable to look away from Phoebe. She was truly the most beautiful woman he'd ever known, yet there was a softness to her expression and a peace about her that hadn't been there when he first met her. God had a way of doing that for people.

"Tell me what happened."

Ian led her into the shop and to the chair that she'd sat in the night before. Ian had positioned it to the left of his worktable so she could watch him facet the stone that would be used in her wedding ring. She did not yet know about its intended purpose. She had, however, been able to turn the crank for him, since his left hand was useless for the time being.

"I never wanted to be one to give you bad news," Ian said, sitting at his table. "You've had a lot of bad over the years, and I want to be the one who gives you only good."

"No matter what," she said, reaching across him to take hold of his right hand, "I feel safe with you, Ian. Whatever you have to tell me . . . well . . . I know it will be all right. I would rather have the truth, painful though it might be, than a lie."

He knew she understood exactly how important that was

to him as well. Ian breathed a prayer and then told her of the situation they'd faced and all that had been said. She took the news fairly well, although Ian could see that it wasn't without its toll.

"It's hard to imagine Vater gone," Phoebe said, finally letting go of his hand. She leaned back against the chair. "I never wanted this for him."

"No one did. I think we all just wanted justice."

"Someone will have to telegraph Dieter. He'll be devastated." She shook her head. "But maybe not. I can't say that I even know Dieter's heart. He's so long been distant and unreachable. I know that was Vater's doing, but Dieter may be unable to change at this point."

"I've learned that if a man is willing to change, God can make it possible."

Phoebe nodded. "I suppose Vater never wanted to change." She bit her lip and shook her head.

"We can see how your mother wants to handle it. She might prefer sending Dieter the news herself."

"Poor Mutter. How did she handle it?"

"She did well, although she wasn't without tears. She grieves the loss of his soul more than anything." He shrugged. "Your mother is a good woman. I can't say I even thought about his soul."

Phoebe nodded. "I know. I was just thinking that myself."

"Actually, I've thought about little else but you." This brought a smile to her face. A sad smile that Ian knew was bittersweet.

"I was so worried something might happen to you, Ian. I never really thought about anything bad happening to Vater—just you. I could hardly bear the wait. I wanted to run to the trolley and make my way to the hotel just to make certain he hadn't hurt you." She paused, and tears dampened her lashes. "I know that sounds silly. I doubt there's much I could have done if my vater had attacked you."

"Maybe not, but I'm glad you care. You've become a very important part of my life."

"Of course I have," she said, her tone teasing. "You need me to work for you—turn the crank until your hand heals."

Ian shook his head. "No. I would never let you work for me."

Her expression changed, and she looked almost hurt. Ian only smiled. "You can't work *for* me, but I would love to have you work *with* me—as my wife."

"Ian Harper, if this is your awkward way of proposing to me, then I accept." She wiped at her tears.

"Well, it's not exactly the way I had it planned out in my mind, and my timing is definitely not the best, but I'm grateful to you for accepting. I'm not sure I could have come up with anything flowery or sentimental to say." He got to his feet and extended his good hand to her.

Phoebe put her hand in his and rose. "I don't need sentimental words," she said. "I don't need flowers or anything—just you. I feel as though my entire world has gone topsy-turvy with Vater dead and Mutter alive. One brother lost to me, another one gained." She shook her head. "I don't suppose any of this will make sense for a very long time."

"No, I don't suppose it will." Ian could see the sadness in her eyes. "You know, Phoebe, it's all right for you to mourn your father. No one will hold that against you. He did some bad things, no doubt about it, but I know you were once close to him."

"As close as he ever let anyone be."

"I just want you to know that I understand. I was so broken-hearted when Nora died, knowing she had betrayed my trust not just once or twice. At the same time I had lost what for me felt like the only love I would ever have." He dropped his hold on her hand. "But for a long time I wouldn't allow myself to mourn her, because my anger got me through the pain. Or so I thought. Instead, when the anger subsided and the reality of my loss settled in, the pain was even more acute. I wouldn't want to see you make that same mistake."

She nodded. "Thank you for your counsel. I promise I will take it to heart. I think initially, I'd just like to have some time to myself. You see, I was taught since I was a little girl to keep my feelings inside and to deal with them in private."

"But no one expects that of you now. I want you to share your feelings."

She reached up and touched his cheek. "Give me time, Ian. I promise you . . . I will. I want very much to share everything with you."

25

On the day they laid Phoebe's father to rest there was a definite change in the air. The warmth of summer seemed altered—not really chilly, but changed. People were already talking of signs pointing to an early winter, despite the fact that it was still August. Phoebe stood beside her mother and Kenny, listening to Pastor Clearwater speak. Ian and his mother stood beside them, lending support as they had from the beginning. The only other person to join them was Ernst Eckhardt.

The stigma of suicide caused people, especially good Christian people, to create a fuss about whether or not an unsaved soul who had taken his own life could be buried in hallowed ground. Pastor Clearwater said it was an archaic notion and that he for one would leave judgment of such things up to God. That, however, hadn't sat well with the church congregation, and the board had told him they would not accept having Frederick Von Bergen buried in their church cemetery. Pastor Clearwater had assured Phoebe's mother that he would go against the board of the church, the congregation, and all of Helena if necessary to see Frederick Von Bergen buried in the churchyard if that was her desire. Mutter knew it would only serve to cause division and strife, however. And given the fact that Vater would never have wanted a church service anyway, Mutter had accepted a different solution. He would be buried on a small piece of land provided by Ernst Eckhardt. The property, he had told them, would never be used for anything else, and due to its location, he doubted anything or anyone would ever disturb the site.

"The choices we make in life are often made in haste and without consideration of the future. At times our choice is to run away from our ordeal." The pastor looked at Phoebe's mother and smiled. Then he looked back at the closed casket. "And running away can take many forms. I didn't know this man well, but we can rest assured that God did, and rather than dwell on the negative aspects of what this man did or didn't do, what he believed or didn't believe, I'm here today in support of his wife and children.

"Let us not allow Satan a foothold in our hearts and minds. In the past there were places of pain and misery. There were times of unbearable grief and loss. You must choose for yourself where you will put your mind and heart. I would encourage you to look forward and forget that which is behind. Make a new start—let God do something new and wonderful in your lives." He smiled. "Let us pray."

Phoebe bowed her head and thought on the words the pastor had spoken. It had been hard to come to terms with all that had happened. Despite her father's heinous actions, Phoebe knew bitterness and anger would serve no good purpose. She couldn't see starting a new life with Ian until those haunting thoughts were laid to rest, and because of that, she intended to leave them here.

When the prayer was concluded, Phoebe waited with her mother and Georgia while Mr. Eckhardt, the pastor, Ian, and even Kenny worked together to lower the casket into the grave.

After this task was complete they shed their coats, then took up shovels and began to toss dirt in to fill the hole.

"I'm sure Frederick figured to have some grand funeral upon his death," Mutter said, looking at Phoebe. "I'm sure he figured to live until a ripe old age and die in his bed and be heralded as a grand nobleman."

"I would imagine so," Phoebe replied.

"It's funny the thoughts we have for our deaths," Ian's mother added. "Sometimes I think people worry more about that than living life. I for one don't intend to give it a second thought. When I die, I die, and those who are left will arrange for me. I hope it's a grand celebration where people remember me fondly and enjoy large quantities of delicious food."

Phoebe smiled. "The church folks would really be upset if that happened."

"Those ninnies." Mrs. Harper shook her head. "Sometimes I don't know what gets into folks. Ground is ground. A grave is a grave. Being next to a church isn't what makes a place holy. Goodness, there have been many churches standing in close proximity to the saloons."

"But none of that matters," Mutter said. "I'm rather glad Frederick is buried out here. I would hate to have to look at his grave every time I came to church. I'm afraid I would never be able to let go of the past, as Pastor Clearwater said we should, if I had to face that and the unhappy people of the church. No, this is a much better place for him to be. Even Dieter approved."

"I'm glad he responded to your telegram." Phoebe took hold of her mother's arm. "I'm sure the news was hard to hear, both of Vater's death and of your being alive. I hope one day he will come and visit us."

Mutter nodded. "I do too. I love all of my children, and it would be sad to have him be unwilling to be a part of my life."

"Perhaps you will visit him," Mrs. Harper encouraged.

"I believe one day I will," Mutter replied. "One day when Kenny is older, it would be good for him to see the estate and know about his father's land."

"I've already been teaching him German," Phoebe said in a rather conspiratorial manner. "He thinks it's great fun and hopes to surprise you, so do not mention that I told you."

Her mother smiled and nodded. "I shall be quite surprised."

When the grave was filled and covered with rocks to keep animals away, the funeral party headed back to town. Normally the church ladies would have inundated the house with food in order to lessen the workload of the mourners, but in this case they hadn't. Apparently such kindnesses were also questionable where suicide was involved. Instead, Ian's mother had prepared a meal for them prior to leaving for the burial, and after Ernst Eckhardt bid them good-bye at the train station, they made their way to the house.

No one seemed inclined to speak on much of anything and instead went about ferrying food to the dining room table. Even Ian and Kenny helped. Once everything was done, Ian led them in prayer, then urged everyone to dig in. To Phoebe it seemed a marvelous arrangement. She had never known a home to be filled with as much love as was the Harper household. She started to think back to times when she was a little girl—before her mother had gone away—but then chided herself to forget the past. What mattered now was the future.

crissge

"I still don't understand why you two aren't getting married until October," Mrs. Harper said after finishing her dessert. "After all, there's absolutely nothing standing in your way now."

Ian and Phoebe exchanged a smile. "Good things are worth waiting for. Besides, it's just a little over a month, and as much as I want to marry this beautiful young woman, I believe her reasons for waiting are sound. We will put all of this death and dying behind us, she will have a lovely gown made for our wedding, and all of you will put your heads together to create a very fussy wedding with flowers and ribbons and bows."

"And lots of people," Kenny declared. "'Cause everybody knows you and Grandma Harper."

Ian laughed. "He's absolutely right. We do know just about everybody."

"And, of course, Ian and Kenny are going to fix up the shop house so we can live there after our wedding," Phoebe added, giving Ian a smile that all but made him change his mind about waiting. She had no idea how she stirred his heart, and that only made her all the more precious to him.

ᴓᶻᶻᶻᶜᴗ

That evening Ian and Phoebe slipped outside to sit on the porch together, much to Kenny's disappointment. Even as they took a seat, they could hear Elizabeth.

"Kenny Bergen, you march yourself upstairs and take a bath. After that, I will let you stay up for another hour. Just think of it, you can spend that time drawing those houses you like to draw."

"But I want to have fun with Phoebe and Ian," the boy protested.

Phoebe giggled as Ian put his arm around her shoulder. "I doubt he'd enjoy our kind of fun quite so much," Ian murmured against her ear.

"I think I shall always cherish these times," Phoebe said with a sigh.

"I know I will. But I think I'm going to cherish every moment of every day with you." He loved the way she fit perfectly against him—loved the way she smelled—loved everything about Phoebe Von Bergen. She sighed, and it made him smile. She was just as happy in that moment as he was.

He couldn't help but remember it wasn't that long ago that Phoebe had been subjected to her father's rage. That memory made him frown. "You know," he began, "I've never asked you how you're doing . . . I mean in light of your father and how he treated you. Not to mention the men who tried to kill you."

Phoebe sat up and gave him a look of confusion. "What do you mean?"

"The beating you took. It seems to me that would leave you fearful—especially of men."

She shook her head. "My vater had never hit me until that first slap. Then the beating happened without warning. I honestly never believed him capable of hurting me." She looked away as if trying to figure out what to say. "I was always taught that showing emotion wasn't proper, and so I learned to bury things deep within."

Phoebe finally turned back to Ian. "I know it may sound strange, but I still can't believe those things of Vater. I know it in my head, but I guess I spent a great deal of time ignoring his bad behavior with others so that when it came to me, it seemed completely out of his character. At least the character I'd let myself see. As for those other men, I can honestly say that it happened so fast, it still doesn't seem real. I've always been a sensible and cautious person, because that was what was expected of me. Reason tells me that most men aren't violent; otherwise, I'd see more proof of that. I suppose I could be wrong, but I'm honestly not afraid of the future. Especially where you are concerned." She smiled and eased back into his arms.

TRACIE PETERSON

"I'm glad. I would never hurt you," he promised.

For a time neither one said anything. Ian was content to simply sit there and enjoy the evening and dream of the days to come. Phoebe filled a void that he'd carried for so many years. A void he hadn't really even acknowledged.

"So, do you think your mother will be able to convince mine to move into this house with her? I mean permanently and not just for a night or two."

Ian smiled and nodded. "My mother can be very persuasive. Besides, it doesn't look as if the hotel will remain open much longer. I think given the lack of guests they will definitely close early in September for the winter. Maybe for good. Not only that, but having your mother and Kenny living here will keep her from getting lonely."

"Well, it's not like we'll be far away."

"Maybe not, but I definitely intend to keep you to myself as much as possible."

Phoebe sighed again. "I think I would like that very much."

Ian pulled her closer. "I know we agreed to wait until after we said our vows to kiss, but I'm having second thoughts about that. Maybe it would be a good idea to just try it out now. You know, get a little practice in."

He received an elbow in his side as Phoebe moved away, laughing. "Your mother warned me about you."

"How traitorous." He shook his head. "Very well. I shall bide my time, but when our vows are said I intend to kiss you and kiss you often."

"And I shall let you." She stood and gave a shrug. "In fact, I shall probably initiate a good many of them."

The church was decorated in a rather fussy manner, just as Ian had predicted. Phoebe thought it all very beautiful and was deeply touched that their mothers would go to such effort to ensure a perfect setting. The women of the church begged to be allowed to host a reception after the wedding, and Mutter had agreed. It was their way of welcoming Phoebe into the church, as well as making up to Mutter for having refused Vater's burial in the churchyard.

"Are you ready to go, Phoebe?" Kenny asked, pulling at his collar. He was clearly uncomfortable in his new suit.

"I am." She turned to give one last look in the mirror. Her blond hair was done up in perfect order. Mutter had helped her to sweep it high atop her head with just a few small wisps of blond hair to curl around her face. The fashionable arrangement was crowned with a small tiara of sapphires and a long lacey veil. The Sapphire Duchess had insisted on having the tiara delivered as a wedding gift, although Phoebe had no idea where she would wear it in the future. For now it seemed quite fitting, since sapphires had brought her and Ian together.

"I'm nearly ready," Phoebe told her brother as she drew her veil forward to let it fall before her face. "Now we can go." Kenny held out his arm, doing his best to make a loop for Phoebe to slip her arm through. "You are quite handsome, and I am very honored that you are going to give me away."

"I'm not going to give you away, Phoebe. I'm just going to let Ian marry you. I waited too long to have a sister to give her away."

Phoebe wanted to laugh, but they were already approaching the sanctuary. Ahead of her awaited Ian and a life of what she prayed would be happiness. Ian smiled, looking quite dapper in his black suit and tie. His brown hair was combed back off his forehead, and the beard and mustache he'd grown was neatly trimmed. Phoebe liked the look and in fact had been the one to encourage Ian to grow it. She thought it made him look quite distinguished.

It was hard to take her gaze from his face, but Phoebe did so just long enough to meet her mother's eyes. She looked so very happy—happier than Phoebe had seen her in a long time. Mutter had gone through so much, sacrificed so much on her account. It made Phoebe appreciate her all the more.

Kenny brought her to the front of the church and stopped. Phoebe looked down at him and could see he appeared quite nervous. She slipped her hand into his and gave it a squeeze.

Pastor Clearwater cleared his throat and posed the question. "Who giveth this woman to be married?"

Kenny straightened. "Her mother and I do."

Phoebe smiled and gave him a nod of approval. He'd practiced his one and only line all week.

Kenny handed her over to Ian, then stepped back and stood beside his mother, seeming quite pleased with himself. Ian's mother stood beside him as his witness, while Mutter stood as Phoebe's. It was the only way they could think to do things, and although it was unconventional, no one seemed to mind.

Phoebe peered at Ian through the veil and felt her heart skip a beat. He would soon be her husband, and they would belong solely to each other. The thought of such intimacy caused her to tremble. Ian seemed to read her thoughts and gave her a wink. Phoebe flushed and looked back to the pastor, who even now had called them to prayer.

The vows were stated and agreed to, and then as Pastor Clearwater called for the ring, he paused. He held up the ring Ian had offered him and smiled.

"I learned only a few days ago that Ian crafted this ring himself. In fact, Phoebe also had a hand in faceting the stone." He lowered the ring. "You know bringing two people together in marriage is a precious occasion for me—one that I do not take lightly. Marriage requires that both the bride and groom be willing to work together, as well as give themselves over to the Master's touch.

"And given Ian's profession, I am reminded of how the Master sands down our rough edges and refines our beauty. He applies just the right pressure to enhance us, without breaking us. Without that sanding and cutting, however, the stone would never be able to reflect the light, and neither would we be able to reflect the light of God's Son. Without the Master to craft us, we would never attain our full purpose and beauty—just as this ring would never have been formed had Ian not brought it to perfection."

He prayed a blessing on them, handed the ring to Ian, and nodded. "You may place the ring upon your bride's finger and repeat after me. With this ring, I thee wed."

Ian took the ring and slipped it onto Phoebe's finger. "With this ring, I thee wed."

His voice was hardly more than a whisper. Phoebe heard the emotion in his words and knew he was just as moved as she was. What a wonder it was, this love between a man and woman.

"And with my body, I thee adore." Ian repeated the pastor's words, fixing his gaze on Phoebe's face.

"And with all my worldly goods, I thee endow," Pastor Clearwater spoke.

Ian nodded. "And with all my worldly goods, I thee endow." He gave her fingers a gentle squeeze.

"In the name of the Father, the Son, and the Holy Ghost." Pastor Clearwater smiled and gave Ian a nod.

Phoebe thought her knees might well give way. She was so overcome with emotion that she couldn't stop shaking, nor hold back her tears.

Ian smiled in understanding. "In the name of the Father, the Son, and the Holy Ghost," he murmured.

"Amen," Pastor Clearwater declared. "And now with the power vested in me, I declare you to be husband and wife. You may kiss your bride."

Ian gently lifted the veil and smoothed it back. His gaze never left hers, and Phoebe lost herself in the love so clearly revealed in his expression. As he took her into his arms, she fought a wave of dizziness and blinked several times to clear her vision.

Ian leaned closer. "Don't you dare faint on me—I've waited much too long to do this."

She barely had time to nod before he pressed his mouth to hers. His lips were warm and his kiss so very tender—just as she'd imagined. She had waited a lifetime for this moment—for this man—and both were exactly as she had hoped they'd be. Perfect.

Tracie Peterson is the award-winning author of over one hundred novels, both historical and contemporary. Her avid research resonates in her stories, as seen in her bestselling HEIRS OF MONTANA and ALASKAN QUEST series. Tracie and her family make their home in Montana. Visit Tracie's website at www .traciepeterson.com.

More From Tracie Peterson

Visit traciepeterson.com for a full list of her books.

Nanny Lillian Porter doesn't believe the dark rumors about her new employer. She feels called to help the Colton family. But when dangerous incidents begin to plague the farm, will she find the truth in time to prevent another tragedy?

Beyond the Silence (with Kimberley Woodhouse)

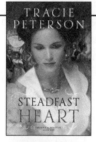

At twenty, Lenore's deepest desire is to find love. Her father is urging her to marry a man who could never capture her heart, but she's running out of time to find a man who can.

Steadfast Heart
BRIDES OF SEATTLE #1

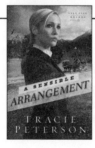

Marty and Jake agreed to a marriage of convenience only. But when love starts to soften their hearts, will they come to a different arrangement?

A Sensible Arrangement
LONE STAR BRIDES #1

BETHANYHOUSE

Stay up-to-date on your favorite books and authors with our free e-newsletters. Sign up today at bethanyhouse.com.

Find us on Facebook. facebook.com/bethanyhousepublishers

Free exclusive resources for your book group! bethanyhouse.com/anopenbook

You May Also Like . . .

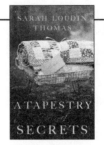

Perla Phillips has carried a secret for over sixty years. When she sees her granddaughter, Ella, struggling, Perla decides to share her story—then suffers a debilitating stroke. As Ella and her aunt look into her grandmother's past, they'll learn more than they expected about Perla, faith, and each other.

A Tapestry of Secrets by Sarah Loudin Thomas
sarahloudinthomas.com

Stella West has quit the art world and moved to Boston to solve the mysterious death of her sister, but she is in need of a well-connected ally. Fortunately, magazine owner Romulus White has been trying to hire her for years. Sparks fly when Stella and Romulus join forces, but will their investigation cost them everything?

From This Moment by Elizabeth Camden
elizabethcamden.com

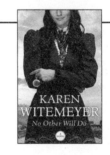

When the women's colony of Harper's Station is threatened, founder Emma Chandler is forced to admit she needs help from someone who can fight. The only man she trusts enough to ask is Malachi Shaw, whose life she once saved. As Mal returns the favor, danger mounts—and so does the attraction between them.

No Other Will Do by Karen Witemeyer
karenwitemeyer.com

BETHANYHOUSE